THE DEAD
OF WINTER

JACK NIGHT

Copyright © 2012 Jack Night

ISBN: 1479319201
ISBN-13: 978-1479319206

PROLOGUE

The blood that ran down and covered her legs grew cold under the touch of the winter wind. Her thighs would stick together then unstick with a soft sucking sound every time she tried to move.

She remained there underneath the canopy of leafless trees, weak from giving birth. On the small bed of leaves next to her the baby slept. Her baby. Her daughter.

As she gazed at the slumbering child all of the pains of labor and loss of blood finally began to catch up. Her eyes fluttered and closed then both mother and daughter were asleep.

When the crying woke her, the last chilled rays of winter light were disappearing along the horizon. The forest was growing dark and cold. There were voices moving in from the distance conversing in a language she still could not understand.

Her heart began to race as she frantically grabbed her child and tried to soothe it. The baby kept crying and the men's voices grew closer.

She tried to stand and run farther into the darkness of the woods but her legs wouldn't obey. Tears of frustration and terror welled up in her eyes as she tried to crawl, child clutched to her chest. Now the voices had found her.

Now they were on her.

"Don't hurt her! Please don't hurt my baby!"

As the infant was torn from her grasp she screamed and lashed out with every last bit of strength she had. It wasn't enough.

One of the men swung at her, his fist connecting with the side of her face. The wailing of her daughter grew faint as she slipped into blackness.

CHAPTER ONE

Emily Anderson stood at the back door of the house on Cauffield Street with her face pressed up against the screen. A little wisp of something sticking in the mesh brushed against her nose, tickling it. The screen smelled musty like a house shut up for too long but through it she gulped in great breaths of the dying days of fall. There was something magical about that smell. The scent of change in the air held more promise to a girl of eleven than her parents would ever know.

"Ems, honey, that thing's filthy. Get your face off of it."

Emily jumped and spun around at the sound of her mother's voice.

Rebecca Anderson was carrying a box into the dining room. Past her the front door stood propped open by a milk crate filled with old records.

Emily could see her father out in the street unloading their dining room chairs from the back of the U-Haul. She sighed and turned back to the screen, resting her nose against it. From behind, her mother's footsteps came echoing over the hardwood floors. Emily turned around again and waited, digging nervously at the bandage on her palm.

"Momma, can I go outside?"

Rebecca paused and looked at her daughter, then her gaze shifted to the expanse of lawn and the woods beyond.

"Pleeease, Momma. I want to see back in the trees."

Rebecca looked at her watch.

"Okay, you've got an hour. I mean it. No longer."

Emily jumped up and down with delight, then spun back to the door and undid the latch.

"Ems, stay where you can see the house. This isn't like Palmdale. Those woods go on for thirty miles or more and it's easy to get lost."

"Okay, Momma."

Rebecca smiled and Emily was out the door.

Thirty miles wasn't really a concept she could appreciate but the dark vastness struck her. These woods *weren't* like the ones in Palmdale. Those had been small, sparse, and full of scraggly pines. These woods stretched on in an unbroken line behind their house. They were dense and stacked with Black Oaks and Maples that were still shedding the last of their leaves before winter. Patches of red and orange still clung to the trees, but the ground was covered with a thick carpet of gold and brown. Even without their leaves the trees loomed dark and forbidding. The afternoon light dappled the bark with golden and amber hues that made the whole scene surreal somehow.

Emily strained her eyes but could only see a few feet past the sentinels that stood rooted along the edge. A breeze came up and blew her hair into her eyes. Through the strands of dark brown she could see as more shapes broke loose and pin-wheeled through the air. Spinning and fluttering reds, oranges, golds, and browns.

It was like looking through a kaleidoscope.

Emily walked down the steps of the back porch. The hole in her blue jeans snagged on the wicker rocker as she went past, then tugged loose.

Even the grass and dirt were different in Rockwell. Back in Palmdale the grass had been thick and strong and grew like a weed. Sometimes during the summer her Dad had to cut it twice a week. The dirt had been loose and sandy, too, not at all like the hard clay-looking soil here. In Rockwell the grass was still green but grew in long and slender blades that looked like if you stepped on them they might crush and die.

Emily remained aware of this as she stepped off the porch, trying to quickly shift her weight from foot to foot as she walked.

If anyone had ever thought that forests were the sole domain of little boys, they were wrong. The woods were something more than a land of makeshift forts and battlefields; they were like some great fairy kingdom. She could picture a different land beyond the trees, one in which a castle loomed, still thriving and hidden from the world around it. There would be knights and fair ladies there. Secrets, and magic.

As she neared the edge of the forest, the thick blanket of dead leaves rushed up to meet her. She no longer worried about the grass now as her feet made crunching sounds with each step.

Pausing for a moment at the edge, she stared up at the trees towering over her. Their thick bark gleamed like armor in the afternoon light.

Emily caught herself holding her breath as she plunged in.

As thick as the woods had looked from the outside, the illusion faded a little as you pressed on. Very little grew up out of the forest floor save for those massive trunks. The trees were spaced evenly enough to walk through as long as you didn't mind winding your path around the thicker places.

As she walked, Emily dragged her feet deeply through the leaves on the ground. She stopped once to look back and saw that her yard was barely visible now but the great twisting furrow that her feet made wound around like a trail of breadcrumbs. That was good. She knew that she'd be going farther than promised. But not *too* far.

After about ten minutes she came to a place where the trees seemed to spread out more and her eyes picked out what looked like a path.

The leaves were heavily trodden, the dirt showing through in big dark splotches. As she stood on the edge of the path she tried to trace it winding around to the right and the left of her like a giant U.

Emily peered back behind her and saw her own footpath stretching away. The light still didn't penetrate far.

For the first time a bit of worry swelled up inside. She had walked along at a good pace and knew that her house lay a ways behind her. Her mother's warning came crashing back.

But the way she had come was still clearly marked, wasn't it? And someone had walked this way enough to carve out a trail.

Still, she stood there unsure.

The right, or the left?

She put on her best look of determination and practically marched out onto the trail, stamping her feet hard as she followed it around the leftward bend. She pretended to be a young maiden on her way back to court. A princess even. Following behind her, watching and unseen, would be her handsome knight errant who would leap out of the thickets and save her should anything run afoul.

The path didn't wind as much as she had expected and the trees seemed to keep clear of its progress. Sometimes the effect was so uncanny that she thought for sure some of them must have been cut.

There was a loud cracking of branches and leaves from somewhere behind her. Emily stopped, her head snapped to the left as she scanned the forest in vain for the source of the sound.

Now the uneasy feeling seemed to stay, making her want to turn tail and run. But she didn't. Instead she took up a tune and tried to drown the feeling out.

She had walked for another fifteen minutes when the clearing sprang out from a twisted wall of Oak.

The trees had gone wide in a great circle leaving only the thick carpet of leaves. Sunlight poured in from the opening and fell golden at an angle all around her.

In the center of the clearing there was a stone rising out of the ground. It looked like a giant arrowhead with its base buried in the dirt and leaves. Its point was rounded and worn down, reaching toward the sky.

Emily stopped at the edge of the clearing and stared. Even from where she stood she could see that something was carved down the side of it and up toward the top a hole had been cut straight through. The hole looked large enough to stick your head in but the stone was at least three times taller than she.

Slowly Emily approached it. The sense of wonder was fighting fiercely with the desire to get the hell out of there.

As she got closer to the base there were beer cans lying around. She sighed with relief. That explained the path, but as much as it alleviated her fear it also vanquished some of the reverie. Her mysterious kingdom had been tainted. Now she approached with less caution. In fact she half-expected the carving to say something silly like Bobby Loves Sue or maybe something a little more daring like what you found in public rest rooms.

It didn't say anything.

The carving looked old, and well worn like the rest of the stone. It was nothing but a bunch of funny shapes all connected together. They weren't any shapes she could name; they seemed weird and angular and a little nonsensical. But there was something about the way they fit together that seemed familiar. Something. *Like hopscotch.*

That was it. The way they all fell into place reminded her of a hopscotch board. She giggled at the thought. Now the carving seemed silly again.

She was tracing the deep, smooth grooves in the stone when the wind picked up. It came suddenly in a great gust that stirred the dead leaves around her feet into a little whirlwind. There was another sound, too, as the wind continued to blow. It started off low and deep, something not so much heard as felt. Then it rose in pitch to a great empty howl.

Emily whirled around, her heart suddenly thumping in her chest. She spun in a full circle expecting something to spring out at her. Nothing did. As the air continued churning the leaves, the mournful wail continued, too. She turned again more slowly trying to pinpoint the sound that seemed to come from all around her.

It was the stone. She cocked her head and listened closely but now there was no mistaking it. The howl was the wind as it rushed through or over that big hole, like blowing across the top of a soda bottle.

Emily let out a nervous laugh and rubbed at the bumps up and down her arms.

But as the wind died back down and the howling faded away another sound slowly crept up to take its place. It was a soft scrabbling of something making its way through the carpet of dead leaves. Holding her breath she tried to pin down just where it was coming from. There would be a small burst of rustling, then it would stop. Each time it resumed, the sound seemed to be closer.

It wasn't the sound of someone walking. This had more of a dragging, shuffling quality to it.

There was another burst of rustling, this time close.

Then it stopped.

Her heart was beating fast again and she could feel moisture welling up in the corners of her eyes.

Emily stood completely still, afraid to move. Without turning her head she tried to scan along the edge of the clearing where it met with the thicket of trees. She felt like she was being watched. Watched was too gentle a word for it. She could feel the cold penetrating gaze boring into her with anger and malice.

Just when she had finally mustered the courage to turn tail and run, she saw it.

Right beyond the tree line was the shape of someone lying on the ground. At first she could just barely trace the outline of what looked like a woman wearing something long and white, but covered in grime and leaves. She couldn't see her face.

Suddenly the body moved. There was a rustling again as the

thing scrabbled forward a little more. It was crawling. The front arms flew madly at the ground while the rest of the body dragged behind them.

The face was now hidden only by the trunk of a single tree. Emily could see a long dingy red lock of hair spilling down. Slowly the figure began to peer around.

Emily tried to scream but it came out more like a sick croak. All at once her paralyzing fear vanished.

She exploded out of the clearing. Now her feet beat down on the path with a speed and force that made her knees ache. She ran and ran until it felt like her lungs would quit and her heart might burst but still she pressed on. She wouldn't stand still in those woods again. She was sure that beneath her own footfalls was the frantic sound of something terrible crawling after her, but she never looked back.

Finally a wide sea of green peeked in through the trees ahead. Her yard. The skinny grass. Emily thundered out of the woods and didn't stop until she reached the center of her lawn. The forest was at a safe distance but still she eyed it warily, collapsing to the ground, fighting for breath.

When Emily finally managed to choke down enough air she pulled herself up from the grass. She wavered and faltered for a second. The woods were behind her. She hadn't looked back once since collapsing on the lawn.

As she stood there every muscle rigid, the wind did a little dance around her. It pricked at her skin with its cold, dry fingers. From behind Emily could feel the trees towering over her. Their presence was now something dark and vast without an ounce of color or warmth. The hair on the back of her neck stood up as another breeze raked her face.

She couldn't shake the feeling still boring into her. It was the same as back in the clearing. The feeling of being watched.

Her fists clenched and unclenched a couple of times as she stood rooted on her lawn. Finally she balled them up tight and gritted her teeth. She was going to turn and face her fear.

There's nothing back there. Stop being chicken.

Finally, eyes forced wide, she whirled around.

The forest still stood, silent and forbidding. Emily's fists loosened at her sides. She let out the breath that had been locked up in her chest and scanned the woodline a second time. Nothing.

The tension drained out of her neck and shoulders and she decided to go back inside. Everything had only been in her head.

Just as she was turning back for the porch a tiny bit of movement caught her eye. A pale white hand slithered back into hiding behind the trunk of an Oak. She watched in horror as the fingers raked the bark tracing their return through the tall grass and darkness at the edge of the woods. Emily saw nothing else of the figure, but the hand was enough.

She screamed at the top of her lungs. As she screamed the feeling of those cold eyes peering out at her began to slip away.

2

Nick Anderson liked Rockwell. The place had that sleepy, small town charm that almost seemed like it couldn't still exist in a day and age of global networking, cell phones, and commuter trains. It was exactly what he'd been dreaming of all his life.

Simplicity.

Palmdale hadn't been a hellhole by any means, though over the years it began to feel like one. It was a tourist trap. The kind of place where the old, white, and wealthy retired to play golf and die.

It was a place where everything was well groomed and constantly in bloom.

Nick had lived there all his life, but as part of the working class all of the amenities were off-limits.

A lot of people would write to get out of the Rockwells and into the Palmdales he figured. But not him.

When Tangled Web had sold, the first thing the Andersons did was pull up stakes. Everything seemed to fall into place after that.

He stood on the front porch and took in a deep breath. It seemed like nothing could ever shake the smile from his face again. He took a pack of Lucky Strikes out of his pocket and lit one. A piece of tobacco stuck to his lips as he pulled the cigarette out.

He took a drag then exhaled in one long sigh. Three days and everything had been unpacked. Now there was nothing to do but enjoy the fine air, the changing of seasons, and simplicity.

Nick took another deep breath and savored the cool dryness of the air as a light breeze brushed over his cheeks. *The winds of change.*

Emily's scream sounded from the back yard. The cigarette that had dangled from his lips only moments before fell smoldering to the grass as he took off around the house.

3

Even after they had gotten Emily settled down she had seemed spooked for most of the evening. As soon as the sun had set she made Nick go around and close every curtain in the house.

Ordinarily he might have thought differently about humoring her fears, but just this once he supposed it wouldn't hurt. They were in a new town, new house and it was natural for her to be a bit uncomfortable.

He had to admit that as Emily had recounted her story about what happened in the woods, it had given him the creeps, but he locked it away in his imagination for a later date.

"Daddy, I don't want to go to school tomorrow," Emily said

from on the couch next to him.

Rebecca shot him a look from across the room. He knew only too well what it meant. In trying to put out one fire Nick had inadvertently set another.

He had told Emily that the "thing" in the woods had probably been local kids playing a prank on her. As soon as she got to school she would quickly see that she hadn't been at the mercy of some monster, just the butt of someone's bad joke.

"You're going to school and nothing you say is going to get you out of it," he replied.

"What if they laugh at me?"

"Then just be the bigger person and laugh along with them. Tell them they got you good."

"My phone still doesn't work either. I want to go back home."

"I'll get the phones fixed tomorrow. Give it a chance Ems."

Emily spent the rest of the evening sulking, but never strayed too far from either him or Rebecca.

Once they had gotten their daughter bundled up in bed, Nick and Rebecca decided to turn in, too. Rebecca had to be up by six to make it into Devon for the first shift at the hospital and Nick figured he'd get an early start on a fresh week.

He felt good and charged and ready to start writing. He would begin the new book in the morning.

4

It was around one o'clock that Emily awoke.

She had been dreaming when the thumping roused her. As her senses slowly crept back she remained completely still. The sound got a little louder.

The dull, hollow thumping was coming from downstairs. The pounding called up to her, rhythmic and insistent. There were three consecutive knocks, then nothing. Repeat.

Outside her window the wind was shaking the last of the leaves from the big Maple in the front yard. Crawling out of bed she shivered as her feet planted on the cold wood floor. She tiptoed out of her bedroom and paused in the darkness at the top of the stairs.

The sound was coming from down below. Ever so slowly she descended the first five steps, then stopped again.

The utter stillness of the house made a creepy contrast with the loud, hollow sound reverberating off the floors and walls.

Emily took two more steps. Now she was sure where it was coming from. It was the front door. Goosebumps poked out up and down her arms. The pounding continued. As she listened she thought she could even hear the faint sound of the doorknob rattling.

Emily turned to run back upstairs and smacked right into something. As her feet faltered on the steps, two hands shot out of the darkness and caught her by the shoulders.

"Whoa, Ems."

As her panic-wide eyes adjusted to the dark she saw her father leaning over her.

"What are you doing down here?" he asked.

"I heard the sound. Someone's knocking at the door."

Nick laughed.

"Go on up to bed, hon. The door's just loose. Wind's making it rattle. I'll wedge something in there for tonight."

Emily waited in the darkness at the top landing and listened as her father walked across the floor below. With each creak of the floorboard the lump in her throat got bigger until she heard his hands undo the latch. When the door groaned open on its hinges she wanted to scream. But then it shut again, the sound a little muffled.

She retreated back to her room when she heard the slow and steady tread of her father come back up the stairs. At the end of the hall a door closed and she crawled back into bed.

The sheets were pulled up tight under her chin and her eyes

still bulged as she waited. Waited for the knocking.

But it didn't return.

5

Nick Anderson leaned back in his chair and rubbed his eyes. He'd been staring at the computer screen for half of the day and now he needed a break. And a smoke.

Nick saved what he was working on, then got up from his desk. The new book was going even better than he'd hoped and that gave him a good deal of satisfaction.

He walked to the front door and opened it. The rag that he had shut in it fell to the floor. The rag would have to do until he found something better to stop the banging.

Outside, the air was a bit brisker than it had been. Even having lived in Palmdale all his life, Nick knew that it was the feeling of winter coming on. You could almost smell it, that change in the air. He figured it was one of those instinctual things, like a genetic memory.

He took out a Lucky Strike and lit it.

Cauffield Street was quiet from one end to the other. Most of the trees were bare by now but only his yard seemed to have a complete blanket of dead leaves. They had started to scatter and spread out to the surrounding lawns. He figured he'd better rake them soon before the natives got restless.

Nick walked to the end of the drive and peeked in the mailbox. It was empty. The mail probably wouldn't start coming for a few days still and then it would hit like a flood.

A ways down, Cauffield Street curved around to the right. If he followed it, the road would take him right out onto Main and straight into the center of town.

It was only a twenty minute walk, he figured, and the weather was so nice.

Nick looked around for a good place to put out his cigarette. He didn't want to throw it in the road in case one of the new neighbors happened to be looking out. Not finding a good hiding spot, he bent down, stubbed it out in the grass, then looking around quickly, got back up and popped the butt into the open mailbox. He made a mental note to retrieve it when he returned, then set out for town.

Five houses down wouldn't have been much of a jaunt back in Palmdale, but here in Rockwell it amounted to a pretty good stretch. Nick had slowed his pace a bit already and began rethinking a walk all the way into town. Maybe he'd just go down to the bend, then head back.

"Hi there."

The voice caught him by surprise and he jumped a little.

Sitting on the porch to his right was an old man in a rocker. The pipe clenched between his teeth put out little clouds that floated off, leaving a cherry scent behind.

"Hello," Nick said.

"You must be Mr. Anderson. The writer fellow."

Nick nodded in reply and took a few steps closer to the porch.

"I am, but how did you know?"

"No mystery there," the old man replied. "Mary Winston who sold you the place is a friend of mine. Hell, I guess you could say she's a friend of just about everyone. Things are like that in Rockwell, you'll see. Word travels fast."

Nick just nodded again.

"Come on up and sit a spell if you've got the time. The beer's still cold."

The old man slid a six pack out from under his rocker. Nick couldn't help but smile as he mounted the porch. He couldn't have written it any better if he tried.

"Name's Rampart by the way. Wilbur Rampart. But you can just call me Ramp."

Ramp extended his hand and Nick shook it. He may have

been old but he had a hell of a grip.

"I'm Nick Anderson. Pleasure meeting you."

Ramp laughed, a deep and hearty roar.

"All right," he began. "Now that we've got all the formal bullshit out of the way, sit down and grab yourself a beer."

Now Nick couldn't help but laugh, too. Ramp slid the six pack back out and tore off a can, handing it to him.

"So how are you liking Rockwell so far?"

"It's perfect. Everything is. I feel like I've died and gone to heaven."

Ramp laughed again but with a little less mirth.

"Well, it's good that you get to see the place a bit before winter. Sometimes a good winter storm'll take away some of the charm. Betty seems to think we're in for a whopper this year."

"Is Betty your wife?" Nick asked.

Ramp chuckled.

"Nope. Betty happens to be this mangy thing laying over here."

Ramp gestured to a shaggy beige dog lying on the porch that Nick had somehow missed before.

"The missus," Ramp continued, "is over at her bridge meet with the other old biddies. In fact, they're most likely doing the same as we are."

"Drinking beer and shooting the shit?" Nick joked.

"No, talking about you."

Ramp gave him a sideways smile and finished off the can he was drinking, then tore another one loose and popped back the tab. Nick pulled out his cell phone and opened it.

"Hope you aren't expecting a call," Ramp said

"Just checking the time," Nick replied.

"That's about all the good it'll do you. Those damn things don't work around here."

"How's that?"

"I've heard some of the younger ones in town say it's the terrain, maybe a geological thing. Hell I don't know. I'm old enough it doesn't really confront me. I *do* know that you'll be lucky to get a signal before you're halfway to Devon or Bedford Falls," Ramp replied.

Nick and Ramp talked for awhile until the six pack was gone and the sun had dropped lower in the sky.

"I better get moving," Nick said. "I think that's Emily coming down the road."

Ramp eased himself out of the rocker as Nick stood. He offered his hand again and they shook.

"Well, don't be a stranger," Ramp said. "You can just about always catch me and Betty out here in the afternoons. I'll keep the beer cold for you."

Nick thanked him and set off back down Cauffield Street. Emily had already disappeared inside the house.

By the time Rebecca walked in looking tired and rubbing her temples, the sun was creeping down to the horizon and filtering its light through the last of the leaves on the Maple in the front yard, making them burn a fiery red.

"How was work?" Nick asked.

"Saving the world one cold at a time." She smiled weakly and plopped down onto the couch.

"What's for dinner?" she asked.

"I thought maybe we'd order pizza or something. I didn't get a chance to put anything on."

Nick noticed the look she gave him but tried to shrug it off. It was one of those looks that said *do I have to do everything?*

"I met one of our neighbors today," he said.

"Oh yeah?"

"Yeah, old man. His name's Wilbur Rampart but you can call him Ramp. We sat on his porch and talked a bit."

"He nice?"

"Nice as can be. Although he does think his dog can predict the weather. According to Betty we're in for a hell of a winter," he said smiling.

"You know, that's funny. Sharon at the hospital said the same thing. She said it gets bad sometimes in winter. I guess Crosscreek is the only road that goes in or out of here. She said the Devon side of it gets just as bad as the part that runs out to Bedford Falls. Apparently the trees along the road are half-dead from a fire in seventy-eight, and sometimes in a good storm they just fall right over. Sharon said once about five years ago it took a whole week before the road was passable again."

"I guess that's one of the drawbacks to carving your town out of the middle of the forest," Nick said.

Emily was staring up from her homework and listening to them with a curious look.

"Oh honey, I'm sorry. Ems, how was your first day of school?" Rebecca got up from the couch and went over to her.

"It was school," Emily said.

"You make any new friends?"

"I don't know. Maybe one. But I don't know if I can stand her yet. She talks an awful lot."

"What's her name?"

"Annabelle Clem. She's got an older sister and a younger one. They both go to Oakview, too, but I didn't meet either of them. It's just not the same as back home though."

"Give it some time. It'll get better."

"That's what she said."

6

Around two o'clock the next day Nick turned off the computer, grabbed his cigarettes and headed out the door. He thought that maybe he'd catch Ramp again and talk for a bit.

As he neared the house five doors down Nick saw the familiar shape of Ramp sitting in his chair, but someone else was with him. He stopped on the sidewalk in front of the porch.

"Hi there," came the greeting.

"Hey, Ramp. I thought I'd stop by for a bit, but I can come back later," he said.

"Hell no," Ramp yelled down. "Come on up here. I want you to meet Tom Parsons. Tom, this is Nick Anderson. That writer fellow."

Nick walked up the steps and shook hands with Tom. He wasn't quite as old as Ramp but still he was up there. Tom wore an old, dirty mechanics getup covered in grease spots.

"How you doing, Nick?" Tom asked.

"I'm doing well."

Nick pulled up one of the other chairs on the porch and sat down. Betty was lying next to Ramp's rocker and didn't look like she'd moved since the day before.

"Tom was just telling me how his old hound Chester ran off into the woods and hasn't been back."

"That dog's no hound. He's probably got himself lost back in there," Tom replied.

"How far do those woods go on?" Nick asked.

"Don't matter, Chester could get himself lost on my front porch. Sonofabitch woke me up in the middle of the night just yapping and going mad. Damn near choked himself I think before he finally broke off his chain. I just caught sight of him when he went off into the woods," Tom replied.

"Broke through his chain?" Nick said.

"He probably went after some kids messing around back there. Chain wasn't that strong anyways."

"I guess you get a lot of that here? Kids being back in the woods and all. There can't be much for teenagers to do around here," Nick said.

He noticed that Ramp was eyeing him a little curiously. Was he really that transparent?

"Why the sudden interest in the woods?" Ramp asked.

Nick paused for a minute to gauge his response. Emily's tall tale was apparently not tucked away as much as he thought.

"No reason really. My daughter Emily was playing back there and some kids I think were having a little fun with her. I guess there's some sort of big rock? She said it looked like something Indian maybe."

Tom Parsons hissed through his teeth.

"Oh, now you've done it." Ramp shook his head.

"That rock doesn't belong to the damn Indians," Tom started. "White folks built it. They built all of those things back there in the woods. They were here before the Indians, not that you'll ever hear that Red in town admit to it."

"I don't follow," Nick said.

"It's true," Tom went on. "There was a tribe of white people who settled here something like five thousand B.C. You remember that, Ramp, when they found that skeleton?"

Ramp nodded and pulled a beer out from under the rocker.

"How's that possible?" Nick asked.

"I don't know," Tom said. "All I know is that after those kids found the skeleton a bunch of them university types came out here and did a slew of tests. They said that there was a tribe of Caucasian type people who used to live here a long time ago. Anyway, all those rocks and stuff back in the forest belong to them."

"So what happened to all of them? Where did they go?"

Tom shrugged and eased back into his chair.

"Damned if I know, but I'd be willing to bet when those Indians moved in they probably killed them all and ate them."

Ramp continued shaking his head.

Nick sat on the porch for a while longer but heard little of what was said. He wanted to get up and go back home but stayed to be polite.

Finally after another half-hour of local gossip Nick said that he had to be going. Tom and Ramp shook his hand and he was off back down the road.

The whole way home he eyed the great expanse of forest, watching as it sprang into view between houses, then disappeared again.

The second day of school had gone better than the first. Emily met the other two Clems and it seemed that the whole trio had taken a genuine liking to her.

Still feeling good, Emily decided she'd ride her bike over to Carlson Road after school and see what her new friends were up to.

As she rolled onto their street Emily realized that she had no idea which house belonged to the Clems. She decided that she'd ride down the length of it anyways and maybe find it by luck.

She kept her eyes open for any signs of three young girls in occupation, having a pretty good idea of what to look for. As she neared the end of Carlson Road Emily saw that her detective work was all for naught. Out on the sidewalk in front of the very last house the three girls were playing.

"Hey, Emily!"

Anna ran over to greet her as she got off her bike and flipped down the kickstand.

"What are you doing?" Emily asked.

"Well, we were playing hopscotch but Elizabeth says it sucks and hopscotch is too easy and we're too old to be playing it anyways."

Emily crinkled her nose and walked over to the sidewalk. The game had been drawn on it in pink chalk. Hopscotch had never been one of her favorites but she could tell by Anna's voice that the girl actually enjoyed it. As she stood there looking down the sidewalk an idea flashed at her. In her head she could clearly see the massive stone from the woods, standing before her. Every single line carved into its surface stood out.

"I can make it better," Emily said.

Before she even completely realized what she was doing Emily had grabbed the chalk and moved down to a clean stretch of sidewalk. She got down on her hands and knees and began drawing from memory. She drew the funny interconnected shapes, even managing to fill in the strange pictures inside each one. Under each picture she wrote in a number to make it a little more like normal hopscotch.

When she finished Emily got up and brushed off her knees. The new board was at least twice as long as the old one and the numbers ran all the way up to twenty.

"Cool," Elizabeth said from behind her, the aloofness dropping away for a moment.

"Hopscotch is actually based on a Roman military exercise. They used it for training," Emily said.

"How do you know that?" Elizabeth asked.

"I read it," Emily replied.

"Wow!" Riley poked past her sisters to get a look. "Is this Roman?" she asked.

"No, this is something different," Emily said.

She wasn't quite sure why she had drawn it. The stone had still been there on the surface of her memory and somehow it just seemed right. She guessed that more than anything she'd wanted to win over the Clem sisters just a little bit more.

That had done it.

The four of them played, tossing the little piece of chalk since no one could find a rock. The new game proved much more challenging than the old one and soon all were laughing as they stumbled around the board.

It was the first time Emily had honest to goodness, gut-busting fun since before the move.

The wind had grown up around them and dead leaves showered down as they took turns skipping down the walk.

The four girls began making up rhymes as they skipped their way down the board. Some were so ridiculous that Emily felt her sides ache from laughing. She felt good and alive, and the shadow that had been hanging over her since that day in the woods seemed to drift away

The laughter didn't last, though.

Riley had made it almost to the last two shapes when her foot landed on the piece of chalk and skidded. In an instant she lost her balance and came down hard on the sidewalk. The skin on her knee tore open and blood smeared where she fell.

Riley started crying as the other three rushed over to her. Elizabeth bent down to take a look at the wound.

"It isn't that bad. Don't be a baby."

Riley continued to wail.

In between great choking sobs she managed to say, "I want to go inside."

Elizabeth helped Riley hobble in and before she knew it, Emily and Anna had said their goodbyes.

Emily stood staring at the pink shapes and symbols scrawled on the sidewalk and wondered again. *Why?* Suddenly the empty silence of Carlson Road was unnerving. The wind whipped around her and from behind a small branch snapped off of a tree and smacked the back of her head.

Running over to her bike, Emily hopped on and took off down the street. Sometimes as she went the wind would gust and shove into her almost like it wanted to knock her down.

CHAPTER TWO

Jake Blacktree stepped out of the Main Street General Store and sniffed at the air. Overhead grey clouds had thickened in the Rockwell sky. A storm was coming. It would be the first winter storm of the year and Jake knew it was going to be bad.

He crossed the street and opened the passenger door of the old red pickup. With a slow and graceful ease he set the bag of groceries in and closed the door.

Jake looked around at the growing clouds and his eyes narrowed. A storm was coming but something else, too.

Crawling into the cab, he fired up the truck after a couple of tries and soon the pickup was headed just outside of the nicer part of Rockwell. He crossed over the old railroad tracks and ten minutes later arrived at a rundown shack.

The shutters over the windows had once been red like his truck but too many years had made the paint peel and chip. The yard was barren, too, except for a few weeds here and there that poked out of the soil.

Hung over the busted screen door was a piece of wood that said The Reservation. He had put it up as kind of a joke but on days like this it only made him sad and want to rip it down.

Balancing the groceries in one arm, he pulled open the screen door with his foot and used the free hand to open the other door behind it.

He went into the kitchen and set the groceries on the counter. From off in the living room he could hear the sound of the television.

"Momma, I'm back."

There was no answer.

Jake sighed and pulled a cigarette out of the pack on the counter. He lit it and moved into the other room. His mother sat on the couch staring at the television. In the gloom of the house and the grey afternoon, her dark skin almost looked black. The wrinkles on her face were darker too, filled with shadows from the flickering screen in front of her.

His mother was Cree Indian just like him. She had never wanted to move to Rockwell but there had been work and Jake took his breaks where he could get them.

A commercial came on and his mother looked to where he stood in the doorway.

"You can feel it, can't you?" she said.

Jake nodded his head.

"Spirits are stirring," she added before turning back to the television.

Jake went into the kitchen to unload the groceries.

There *was* something funny in the air. It was a coldness that seemed to go deeper than just the weather. There was an empty loneliness hanging over the town, held in place by the darkening skies.

Jake shut the refrigerator and looked out the dirty window, watching as empty branches shook in the breeze. He tried to laugh but the sound wasn't reassuring. She had him spooked alright. Somehow she always managed to get under his skin.

Jake opened the fridge again and pulled out a beer. Leaning against the counter he drained half of it in the first gulp. That was better. Crazy old stories from a crazy old woman. Even if she was his Momma.

2

The Rockwell Tavern was one of the oldest establishments in the city. It was tucked away neatly on First Avenue right off of Main Street and had been the social gathering place for several generations of Rockwell citizens. The red brick façade looked a little better in the dark but not by much. In between the bricks, mortar had chipped away in great big pieces, some so large that if you got up close you could see all the way inside. The front door was a big slab of steel that had once been the vault door in the Northern Commonwealth Bank building before it burned down. Rudy Vitters had gotten it at a good price and put it up in place of the old door which used to have trouble staying shut, making it colder than hell in the winter.

Tom Parsons sat at the first stool inside drinking whiskey on the rocks. He was still wearing his grease-stained shop coveralls even though he'd finished up work five hours before. But then work was never truly done until the drinking commenced and once that job was started he liked to see it through to the end.

Tom had hoped the booze would lift his spirits a bit, but so far it had only served to darken his already despondent mood.

His hound Chester running off had started it, but there was something else, too. Something that made his stomach turn a bit like when he'd go off on a bender with the really cheap stuff.

He drained the glass he was working on and called to Rudy for another when Jake Blacktree walked in. Jake froze for a moment when he saw Tom, then turned his gaze and headed to the other end of the bar.

"Goddamn redskin savage," Tom muttered under his breath, and took a heavy gulp from the new glass.

Seeing Jake Blacktree always pissed Tom off. Jake and his Momma were the only two Indians living in Rockwell but that was two too many in Tom's eyes. He tried to keep the dislike to himself but sometimes he got so fired up that he couldn't help it.

Tom could feel the warm flush as his face reddened a bit and he belted back the rest of the whiskey.

After the kids had found that skeleton and it got carted off to the University in Chesterfield some Indian committee had protested. They said that the body had to be returned to them so it could be buried according to their custom. All of this was even after they said the remains belonged to a white man, or at least a distant relative of one.

They were always prancing around getting special treatment and it pissed him off. In the end the body was returned and no more tests had been done.

They're just afraid of the truth, he thought. Afraid that somebody might find out they weren't the first ones here and all that special treatment would get shitcanned.

Tom looked down the bar to where Jake Blacktree sat joking with Rudy. It was too much for him on top of all the other shit that had happened. Too much to see the way Jake sat there without a care in the world. *Sure is easy when you're special, huh, Red.*

Tom got up from his barstool and planted both hands on the counter to steady himself.

"Rudy," he slurred. "Don't you serve that goddamn savage another drink. You know how those people get. You give him enough liquor and he's liable to go crazy and kill us all in our sleep. Ain't that right, Red."

The few other patrons in the bar had grown silent. Now the only sound was a dull murmur and Louis Armstrong crooning on the jukebox. Jake stared straight ahead at his glass of beer.

"Ain't that right," Tom said again. "Kill us all, then you and that Momma of yours can eat us for supper."

Jake had enough. Quick as lighting and with an easy grace in his tall frame, he was up from the stool. Rudy was even quicker, and sensing trouble, had hopped over the bar to place himself between the two men.

"You know I've had enough of your racist hillbilly shit," Jake sputtered. "From day one you've given me nothing but trouble and I've never been anything but nice to you. You know what? You'll be the first one I eat."

There was a little gasp from one of the tables at the back. Rudy had moved closer to Tom now and had started into his placate-the-drunk routine.

"Come on, Tom, no trouble here. Why don't you go home and cool off. Come on now. No trouble."

Suddenly the last glass of whiskey had seemed to catch up with him and all at once the fight had gone out of Tom. He was tired and didn't give a shit now. Besides, he would have other days.

"Goddamn savage," he muttered under his breath raking his keys off the counter.

As he shouldered his weight into that great slab of a door, the bar behind him stayed quiet, all except for the juke.

Ten minutes later and he was on Crosscreek just outside of town. The few lights had softened and were barely a twinkle now, like stars dusting the horizon. Here the forest closed in tight on either side of the road, but up just a stretch it cleared out and he would soon see the faded sign for Shady Acres, the little pariah of a trailer park he lived behind.

It was only another five minutes away but Tom wasn't sure he could make it that long. Since leaving the Rockwell Tavern the pressure in his bladder had built up fast. Now it was full and threatened to pop if he hit one of the big potholes that scarred the blacktop.

Tom pulled his truck off the road and got out quickly. The wind was blowing hard and cold air nipped at him making the feeling like he was going to piss himself shrink back for a second. But only for a second. Quickly he stumbled to the side of the road and fought with the zipper on his coveralls in a drunken daze.

He sighed with relief as the steaming stream leapt from him and splattered on the bark of a tall Maple. It felt like just about the longest piss he'd ever taken and somewhere in the middle of it a sound grabbed his attention. It was a low howl, almost like a wail. The sound seemed to come from nowhere and all around him. It was a hollow, mournful sound but even still carried a hint of menace. He shook himself off and zipped back up quickly but a little prematurely, he realized, as a warm trickle went down his leg, soaking into the faded blue shop clothes. Tom turned around fast and, just as he did, thought that he caught a glimpse of something shoot across the road, illuminated for a second by his high beams.

Just one of those goddamn rocks. They howl like that sometimes in the wind. But had he seen something? Tom felt his heart thudding and some of the fuzziness from the whiskey went away in a flash.

He wanted to bolt for the open door of his truck but his limbs betrayed him. Instead he put one foot forward and took a small deliberate step in front of the truck. Although his mind screamed *run*, his body demanded caution.

The fury of the wind lessened a bit and the moaning died away with it. Tom was now standing right in front of the truck, his body splashed with the cold light of his high beams. He could see every breath he took puff out in a little ragged white mist.

Despite the coldness all about him he could feel a damp sweat building inside his work clothes. As much as he wanted to round the corner of the hood, he still found himself rooted to the spot. *There's something over there. Waiting.*

The idea was ridiculous but he just couldn't shake it. Even though the headlights blinded him to anything behind their arc, he felt safer standing in the pool of light.

Tom picked up his other foot to take another tentative step when all of a sudden he was plunged into darkness. The pickup truck died. In that instant he almost fell to the ground. His eyes tried desperately to adjust to the blackness as the ghost images of headlights clouded his vision.

The night was completely dark and quiet now. The branches of the forest scraped their skeleton fingers together making a soft rustle.

The cold began digging in, chilling the layer of sweat all over his body. In the blackness he could see his truck again.

Tom took another careful step forward, instinctively balling his fists as he did so. Then another step. Just one more and he'd be able to see whatever was waiting for him on the other side. He took a deep breath and made his move, quickly this time.

His eyes were wide and ready, but there was nothing to see. The door stood ajar just as he left it, but there was no man nor beast waiting to spring on him.

As he released the air clenched in his chest he couldn't help but feel a fool.

Tom climbed back into the cab of his truck and slammed the door. The loud bang of it shutting steeled his nerves. He turned the keys in the ignition but nothing happened.

"Son of a bitch!" he swore as he opened the door and popped the hood.

Not wanting to think about the feeling of dread still deep within his bones, he tried whistling as he went to his toolbox in back. The tune came out thin and shaky and died on his lips almost as soon as it began.

From the toolbox he pulled out a small flashlight. Light in hand, he made his way back up front. He clicked on the pale beam and shone it down on the engine block. The light bounced around unsteadily in his hand. He felt naked and exposed with his back to the open night and his face buried under the hood.

At first nothing seemed to be amiss but then a noise mixed in with the clicks and pops of the engine cooling caught his ear. It was faint at first. A low raspy, almost gurgling sound. He leaned in closer and tried to pinpoint the source. The sound grew louder, wet and choked.

Tom's eyes went wide in horror and the flashlight slipped

from his fingers, tumbling into the open maw of the hood.

The sound was coming from behind him.

As he spun around, two hands shot out of the darkness and sank into his face like talons. Tom screamed.

He continued screaming even as he felt his thoughts cloud over, even as he felt fingers tearing at his tongue. Soon his own cries were nothing more than a choked gurgle.

As Tom Parsons lay on the freezing blacktop bleeding and dying, his body grew numb and colder. With the last of his life pouring out into the darkness he hoped for release, but the empty pervasive fear only dug into his final thoughts.

From over him came the low raspy noise again. The warm wetness of tears mixed with the heat of blood came spilling out of his eyes and down the sides of his face.

3

Jake was out of bed and over to the door almost after the third rap had landed. He opened it and found Sheriff Rawley standing there scratching at his sizeable belly with one hand while the other remained curled into a ball in mid-air.

"Sorry to bother you so early, Jake, but I've got to ask you a couple of questions."

Jake stood back from the door and opened it a little wider to let the man pass.

"It's about Tom Parsons," he continued as Jake tried to suppress a scowl. "Rudy says you two got into it a bit last night." Jake nodded. "Rudy also says that some words were said and some of them none too nice." Jake merely nodded again. "Well, you see, Wilma Stevens said that you maybe threatened old Tom. Something about killing him and eating him?" Sheriff Rawley cocked an eyebrow at Jake.

"It wasn't a threat, Sheriff. You know Tom's been on my case since day one. I just got a little fed up with it is all."

"Fed up like how?"

"I just thought I'd give him what he wanted to hear. He was going on and on about me killing everyone in their sleep and so I told him he'd be the first one I got. I didn't mean anything by it. I was pissed, you know?"

"Well, like I said, Jake, I just have to ask the questions. It's part of my job, comes with the badge I guess. I don't really think you could have done something like this but l have to ask."

"Something like what?" Jake asked.

Rawley dropped his head a little and his face set itself grim.

"Tom was found next to his pickup this morning about a mile down from Shady Acres. Something had tore him up real good. Not like anything I ever seen, and I consider myself keen on the ways of the woods up here, if you know what I mean. This didn't look like an animal got a hold of him. Awful."

"Jesus," Jake said, white as a ghost.

"Well, look, like I said, I don't think you figure in it, but all the same let me know if you have to leave Rockwell for any reason. I may have to come back and ask you some more questions. Just the job, that's all Jake. Just the job."

Jake said goodbye to Sheriff Rawley and closed the front door. He'd never gotten even the slightest satisfaction hearing that Tom was dead. Even though the mean old bastard had been a constant thorn in his side, he never wished him dead

Jake walked into the kitchen and pulled a cigarette out of the pack on the counter. He took a deep long drag off of it, then nearly choked when the voice called out from behind him. The cigarette fell out of his hand and tumbled onto the floor sending off little red sparks.

"Jake, what was all that?"

"It was nothing, Momma."

And he hoped like hell it was true.

4

The Sunnyside was Terry Haggart's own little kingdom. Granted, it was a kingdom that smelled constantly of coffee, eggs, and bacon frying in its own grease, not to mention the rich and sickly sweet smell of syrup, but it was her own. The Sunnyside had been her father's creation before his death.

The diner had been open for thirty years and Terry always felt pleased when her thoughts lingered on her father, knowing he would have been proud with how well she had held up the fort.

The Sunnyside was about the only regular all-day eatery in town unless you counted Mrs. Ellington's sandwich shop, but the only breakfast served over there were pastries and muffins, and slow-cooked Irish oats.

Terry had been running around like crazy that morning, sweat beading up on her brow as she tried to make up for Molly Carter's incompetence waiting tables.

Molly had dropped out of high school the year before and Terry had hired the bubbly seventeen-year-old hoping to give her a break. But now it was Terry who felt broken.

She'd been pondering the best way to let Molly go during one of the lulls in the morning rush. Even though Terry wasn't quite twice the girl's age she'd always possessed a great deal of urgency and sense of responsibility that Molly would never have, no matter how old.

Outside the stretch of windows that made up the front wall of the Sunnyside, the sky hovered in an early morning grey. Somewhere high up behind it the sun must have been shining but not a single ray peeked through and none of its warmth would be felt in the ever colder day.

It was while pondering Molly and the onset of winter that she saw him. Jake Blacktree was climbing out of his dusty old pickup and heading up to the door. His long black hair shined dully and the tan skin seemed an ashy color in the morning's gloomy light.

Terry picked up one of the glossy little menus off of the counter and tried to get a glimpse of herself in the laminated surface. Her long chestnut curls seemed all right, but there was no way to tell how the makeup held. Her hand went up and wiped the sweat off her brow, then her moistened fingers dropped and kneaded into her apron.

Jake seemed troubled as he walked in but the look disappeared when his eyes locked with Terry's, a thin smile taking its place.

"Morning, Jake," she said as he took a seat at the counter and she wondered again about the makeup.

"Hard to tell with the weather being like this," he said.

"Tell what?"

"That it's morning."

There was something somber in his demeanor, something that Terry wasn't used to seeing. His eyes seemed hollow and he sat there like a man with a great weight upon his soul. She was worried about him and the sick little flutter in her stomach betrayed her truer feelings deep inside.

"I heard about Tom," she said quietly. "How are you holding up?"

"I'll be fine," he said.

"Let me get you some coffee." She smiled.

Terry had been hearing the small town buzz all morning. It hummed low and constant like power lines before a storm. Most everyone in Rockwell liked Jake and had known plenty of the way Tom had treated him ever since he first arrived, but this was a serious matter. And old Tom Parsons had been one of their own.

As she set the coffee down in front of Jake she was aware of the quieting in the diner. The conversations had taken on a hushed tone. Here and there a face peered over uneasily. She tried to meet their gazes with a look of defiance and, catching that look, no one stared long.

Things were going to get ugly in Rockwell, she could feel it.

Outside a page from somebody's discarded newspaper was grabbed by the wind and smacked up against one of the diner's windows. The people sitting in the booths around it jumped and somewhere a coffee spoon rattled to the floor.

CHAPTER THREE

On Harland Avenue back behind the White's Dry Cleaning building, a plastic sack floated around in the air. It went unnoticed by the Whites who were busy opening up shop for a new day of business. For five minutes it floated around, sometimes spinning in circles and sometimes filling up like a balloon and drifting up high before it settled back down. Then the sack took off in a straight line zipping through the air four feet off the ground. The two plastic handles jutted forward as the bag inflated behind them like someone running with a tiny open parachute. A moment later it stopped and sank to the pavement unmoving.

2

In front of the Rockwell Township Courthouse on Main Street a large flock of sparrows took off from the leafless trees. They climbed into the sky squawking, fifty of them moving as one. The birds turned south where they seemed to stop in mid-air, little wings still beating hard, then all at once went backwards in one great swoop as if blown off-course. The sparrows smashed into the side of the courthouse building leaving splatters of red where they hit. The great white front steps of the building were littered with their shattered bodies. Here and there a small voice cried out and a wing fluttered.

3

On Rockwell Court a child's tricycle rolled up the driveway on its own. Right before running into the garage it fell on its side, one back wheel still spinning.

And that was how things started to change.

4

He had been rubbing his eyes and staring blankly at the computer screen when the noise first grabbed his attention. The book had been going well but then slowed to a dead crawl over the last two weeks, almost like it was in time with the changing weather. Now his brain churned, far away, and the pale white glow from the monitor seemed to echo the growing gloom outside.

At first Nick had barely noticed it. His mind was still locked in a battle with the words on screen when the noise came again, loud and above him.

His eyes flicked over to the little clock on his desk. It was half past one and the house would still be empty for a couple hours until Emily got home from school.

From upstairs came the sound of something thumping and rolling on the hardwood floor. It seemed to be right above his head in Emily's room.

Gooesbumps broke out on his arms. He sat there quiet and motionless, trying to place the noises. There just wasn't any explanation he could think of.

His imagination was running in overdrive now. Quickly his eyes scanned the little office and settled on a letter opener gleaming silver on his desk. It would have to do.

Nick Anderson got out of his chair and walked slowly to the door. He thrust the letter opener out in front of him like a talisman or some sort of holy relic.

The living room was empty.

As he moved toward the staircase every step became slow and deliberate. He tried to move as silently as possible. On the one hand he wanted the element of surprise, but on the other he wished he could just thunder up the stairs and let whatever was up there know he was coming.

On reaching the fifth step from the top the sounds stopped suddenly. He waited, his breathing fast and hard. Instead of the thumping on the hardwood floor a new sound took its place, the soft and tinny version of Fur Elise coming from one of Emily's music boxes.

Nick resumed his ascent. When he reached the landing one of the boards groaned out beneath his feet. From Emily's room there was a crash and the music stopped. He moved faster now and covered the remaining distance in several strides.

With one hand still brandishing the letter opener he used his foot to push the bedroom door open all of the way.

The room was empty.

In the middle of the floor lay the remains of the music box. It had been smashed to pieces as if someone had stomped on it. Nick's eyes darted around the room again nervously. He went to the closet door and threw it wide open. Nothing. Then taking great care to position himself where he could still see the door, Nick bent down to look under the bed. The room was empty.

Taking the trashcan from underneath his daughter's desk, Nick began picking up the pieces of the music box. He would dispose of it and hope she didn't notice. If she did he'd be forced to make up a story. There was no way in hell he wanted to tell her the truth. Of course, he had no idea what really happened; he only knew how it would sound. And how she would take it.

He picked up the letter opener and gave the room one more glance before heading back to the stairs. As soon as he put his foot on the first step there was another crash, this one from below in the kitchen.

A great choking fear welled up inside, making it hard to swallow as he moved downward. From the landing he could see a bit into the kitchen, but only a small stretch of counter and the stainless steel sink under the window.

Nick abandoned all stealth this time as he as crossed the living room and rounded the corner of the kitchen.

The hand clutching the letter opener fell by his side. Every single drawer and cabinet door was standing wide open. On the counter were the remains of two broken glasses.

There was nowhere to hide in the kitchen.

5

In light of his afternoon scare, Nick had wanted to get out of the house. He put on a jacket and snatched his cigarettes from the desk, then walked down the road to see if Ramp was about. When he got there the front porch was deserted and the house looked shut up tight. Betty was nowhere to be seen either and he figured the weather-watching dog must have hidden away some place warmer.

Pulling his jacket on even tighter, Nick shoved his hands deep in its pockets and set off for town.

Arriving in front of the Sunnyside Café on Main he saw Ramp standing a little ways off down the sidewalk talking to a cop. Nick lit a cigarette and strolled down to say hello.

"Hey there, Nick," Ramp bellowed when he saw Nick approaching.

He walked up and shook hands with Ramp, then gave the officer a nod.

"I didn't catch you out on the porch today so I thought I'd head into town."

"I'm afraid today's no good for sitting on porches, Nick."

Then he paused. "Have you met Sheriff Rawley yet? Sheriff, this is Nick Anderson."

"Ah the writer," Rawley said and extended a hand. "Well, I'm sorry your introduction to Rockwell had to be like this. Things don't normally go this way around here."

"We did get a little bit of the fall before it got nasty," Nick said and motioned to the sky.

"I wasn't meaning the weather," Rawley said.

"You remember Tom? Met him over at my place not long ago?" Ramp started.

"Sure. Yeah, I remember."

"Someone killed him last night out on Crosscreek."

"Jesus," Nick whispered.

"Now, Ramp, I never said a person did this. For sure I'm keeping the idea open but I can't imagine anyone in Rockwell capable of-" Rawley trailed off.

"What happened to him?" Nick asked.

"Old Tom was laid out there next to his pickup. His face was messed up pretty bad and something took his tongue clean out of his mouth. Bled to death in the middle of the road," Rawley answered.

"Jesus," Nick said again.

The radio on Rawley's hip crackled and a woman's voice came through.

"Walt, Chrissy Hendricks just called. Says she thinks she might have a prowler. Guess she heard some noises in her house, then she says she saw some strange folks out in the back yard."

"Copy that. I'll drive over and take a look."

Rawley holstered the radio back on his belt.

"Nick, it was good meeting you. Ramp, I'll let you know if anything turns up about Tom. Damn strange, it is."

The Sheriff got in his car, then headed north up Main.

Both Nick and Ramp stood in silence for a moment as the Sheriff's car disappeared down the road and out of sight. As they watched it fade into the distance an old dirty red pickup came down the road toward them. It really wasn't red anymore so much as it was rust and primer grey.

"That there's Jake Blacktree," Ramp said nodding in the direction of the truck. "He and Tom got into it last night over at Rudy's. That was the last time anyone saw Tom before-"

"Does Rawley think Jake did it?"

"I'm sure not. Jake's a peaceable fellow. Cree Indian. He and his Momma live just a little out of town across the old railroad tracks. It's no secret there was some bad blood between him and Tom, but that's no fault of Jake's. He just had the misfortune of not being white."

Nick remembered the conversation on Ramp's porch, the way Tom's face had flushed and spittle flecked at the corners of his mouth.

Tom had been the one main blemish on the entire Rockwell experience so far, and now Tom was— well, he was dead. *Murdered?*

The muse had begun flittering around in his brain before he could tell himself not to read too much into it. Suddenly the real world had begun to take on the bizarre feel of fiction. It was more than just Tom, though. It was the whole town. He sensed things were stranger on some deeper level than the surface showed.

"You okay?" Ramp asked.

"Yeah, fine. Just thinking."

Jake Blacktree's pickup had moved on down the other side of Main, no longer in sight.

"I've got to get going I'm afraid. Mabel's waiting for me over in the drug store. Why don't you and the family come over for supper tonight. The missus has been dying to meet you."

"Sure, will do," Nick said in a voice still far away.

The two men shook and said goodbye, then Nick was left standing alone again. For a weekday Main Street seemed utterly deserted. He could see the patrons of the Sunnyside eating in their booths, but out on the road he was the only one in sight. The weather must be keeping everyone in, he figured.

A blast of icy wind rushed past him and with it the sound of children laughing. Nick turned a full circle where he stood. Main Street remained empty.

6

Colin Green was the Chief Medical Examiner in Rockwell, a title that amused him because of its phony sense of loft. He was the only medical examiner in Rockwell, and he owned and operated the only funeral home in the town, too. Death wasn't a big business there; in fact Tom Parsons was the first stiff he'd gotten in over a year, the last being the little Hawkins kid who drowned in Evans Pond.

Now that there was another body to deal with he felt inconvenienced and a little pissed at having to waste half of his day off. Since death was just small potatoes in Rockwell he also set type for the *Rockwell Times*. It was steadier work for sure, but not by much.

The *Times* still came out once a week but only amounted to about four pages usually, and half of that was the Swap Meet section. By Thursday night he always had the type done, which gave Henry Mack Friday and Saturday to run off all hundred and twenty copies.

Sitting with a corpse on a perfectly good Friday afternoon seemed like a waste.

Colin stared at the metal door to one of the two refrigerated vaults. He hadn't done the examination yet and from what he heard from Rawley, didn't want to.

He could picture the body lying in there still wrapped in the bag on one of the slide-out drawers in the vault. He could almost see the eyes wide open and bulging from their sockets, the face mangled and disfigured, the bloody stump that used to be a tongue. Nothing but cold sticky meat. He shuddered.

And just what made him qualified to deal with shit like this anyways? He'd been appointed the job because he had been Doc Green's son and because he'd taken some nursing classes over at the community college in Devon. Now his Dad had been dead two years, his practice still closed up, and his fuck-up son got to run the chop shop and casket business.

Colin walked over to the heavy steel door that concealed Tom Parsons and threw it wide open. He slid out the drawer where the old man's body lay wrapped in one of the town's two grey body bags. Now that it sat there, a big nasty bulk under his gaze, he went about the work more quickly.

State law required that the body be kept for three days before cremation could occur, but he just wanted to be done with it and rid of the goddamn thing. He thought maybe when it was over he'd stop in the Sunnyside for a bite to eat and maybe check out Terry Haggart's tits. She had a great set on her and just thinking about the way they swelled up behind her apron made him hard.

He whistled a little tune now as he cranked up the furnace and moved the body, bag and all, to the oversized industrial gurney. The town wouldn't miss the bag and it sure as hell beat taking Tom out and moving him to a box.

He wheeled the gurney over to the metal ramp and waited for the temperature to climb.

When the furnace got up to speed he opened the door and struggled with the body as it rolled its way into the flames.

As long as the afterburner didn't give him any trouble, no one would be the wiser. Besides, what's the difference in a couple of days?

From deep inside the burner there was a sound not unlike a scream. *Bodies do that sometimes. Gasses escaping and what not.*

Colin suddenly felt uneasy down there and decided he'd go have that bite to eat while Tom Parsons burned.

7

David Turner pulled a beer from the twelve pack in the trunk of his Packard and zipped his leather jacket tight around him. As he lifted the bottle to his lips, the smell of gasoline hit him, first tickling his nostrils, then burning them. It was a smell that he couldn't seem to shake.

On the short dirt road that ran off of Crosscreek and into the thicket of forest, he waited for Molly Carter to come cruising up to tell him about how bad her day had been.

Truth to be told, he didn't really give a shit about her day, or about her feelings, but he knew they would end up screwing if he pretended to listen long enough and that, along with the beer in his trunk, was about all he wanted.

He looked at his watch again.

"Fucking bitch," he muttered.

If she only knew the shit he had to go through to ditch out of work early. He had to listen to Rick Hendricks rattle on for fifteen minutes about responsibility before he was finally off the hook and free from the Pump n' Pay for the afternoon.

The dark looming clouds overhead had made the day seem shorter than usual, and somehow all of those leafless trees stacked up around him made it feel even colder. It already felt like the temperature had dropped by ten degrees since morning.

David opened the driver side door, leaned in and turned the heater up. If they were going to fuck, there was no way they'd be doing it out in the cold.

As he got back out of the car and shut the door, the wind whipped up in an incredible gust. Dry dead leaves whirled all around him and from behind in the thicket of trees branches broke off and snapped loudly.

The beer bottle dropped from his hand and smacked the dirt

at his feet spraying a stream of suds onto his blue jeans and soaking into the ground.

"Fuck."

He started to stoop to save the bottle but realized it was a goner and headed back for the trunk instead.

David glanced at his watch and saw that he had been out there waiting for at least twenty minutes. Molly Carter could be a real fucking pain sometimes. He could almost picture her, taking her time, primping her hair. It got him a little pissed. He almost had the thought to drive off and forget about her, but just where the hell would he go? His piece of shit Dad would be well into a monster binge by now and the idea of going back to Shady Acres only to get in a pissing contest with the man didn't do much for him. He would wait for her.

He didn't like waiting.

Behind the wall of Oak and Maple more branches snapped seeming to echo loudly in spite of the roaring wind. David glanced nervously at the edge of the forest, the open trunk door resting in his hand.

Something was moving in there. The snapping, breaking sounds were getting closer but that wasn't all. He noticed the odor, too, something old, mossy, musty, and maybe a hint of ozone danced around him and made the scent of gasoline dim. Most of all, though, he could feel it, whatever it was, looming out of the blackness toward him, cold and angry.

David looked hard into the trees to his left. He felt like he was being watched. He *knew* he was being watched.

The thought of jumping back into the Packard and hauling ass never occurred to him. He wouldn't dare turn away from those trees even for a second. Slowly he began to back away past the car and toward the thicket of trees on the other side.

Another branch popped so loudly that he jumped. For a second he became tangled in his own feet and before he knew it was falling straight back on his ass. His body hit the ground hard and the air in his chest rushed out. As he tried to regain his breath he scrabbled backwards on his hands.

There was another volley of branches cracking.

From underneath the Packard he could see where the trees met the gravel on the other side of the road. A hand emerged from the scrubby growth next to the road and smacked down on the gravel. Next another hand did the same. He watched in horror as the hands led to arms, then knees and legs. It was a person. Crawling out of the trees. His view under the car was narrow, just enough to see those hands, arms, and legs as they scrabbled forward in short spasmodic bursts. It was a woman, that much he could tell. Her skin was bone white, mottled with dirt and snakes of bright blue veins ran under the surface.

When she reached the car, the figure stopped. The only thing that stood between them was that big black hunk of metal.

David Turner was paralyzed with fear. He could feel the coldness and malice boring into him from those unseen eyes. In fact, he was sure that she was looking right at him. Even through the car.

There was a wet almost choking sound from the other side. Slowly a bit of dark coppery hair appeared dangling down. The hair touched the ground and started making a neat little pile there before he realized what was happening. She, it, was bending down.

His fingers dug into the dirt road like they were claws and a warm patch began spreading through the crotch of his jeans. He could feel the tears in his eyes now, and his lips were trembling.

Ever so slowly a pale white sliver of cheek began emerging from under the car. Now the corner of an eye.

Like a twisted half-moon the left side of a face peered at him through the undercarriage. The eye was like a black hole, it was so dark and sunken. The skin on her face was stretched tight over the bone. Her cheek stood out sharp and angular from the gaunt face. Her mouth began to open and the wet gurgling issued from it. He could see that inside a dark scabby mass moved around uselessly where there should have been a tongue.

All at once the empty features pinched up and contorted into a mask of rage. Her face was hate in its purest form. The black and purple remains of her tongue flopped around wildly as the choking grew louder.

In that instant of complete and total terror, something snapped inside of David. His reason shut off completely and his body went into survival mode. He was back on his feet in an instant and crashing headlong into the trees.

His feet hammered down on branches and undergrowth, away from Crosscreek and the car, only knowing that he had to get far from her, and fast.

As he ran faster something came crashing into the trees behind him. Tears were flying out of his eyes feeling like little ice chips on his cheek as they hit the cold air. Below him the wetness was spreading from the crotch of his pants and down into the legs of his jeans. He barely noticed. He just had to run.

He'd been going good and hard for a long stint before rational thought began creeping back. He didn't know how far he had gone into the woods, but his legs were beginning to weaken and his stride became wobbly. As his mind began to worry and his body began to wear down it became impossible to navigate the maze of trees at full speed.

David Turner was just realizing this as his foot smashed into a rotten log. His boot sunk in up to his ankle and he pitched forward with full momentum.

The blinding white flash behind his eyes came at the same moment as the loud crack that echoed in his skull. It was the sound of his head connecting with the trunk of an Oak.

His body dropped to the ground like a ragdoll. His consciousness held just long enough to hear the snapping of branches somewhere close by. Then he was gone.

8

Sheriff Rawley thumbed absentmindedly at his temples with one hand while the other held the cruiser steady. It had been one long goddamn miserable day and now he wanted nothing more than to call it quits, head over to the tavern and suck down a couple cold ones.

First Tom, then Chrissy, and now this. Eileen had called him over the radio just as he was finishing his last cruise around town. She'd been getting ready to close down the station for the day when Molly Carter came busting in. Apparently that dingbat boyfriend of hers had gone missing.

Christ almighty, what a day.

Rawley eased the cruiser down the dirt road that forked off of Crosscreek and in the gathering twilight could already make out David Turner's Packard sitting cold and black in the arc of his headlights.

He fished a flashlight out of the glovebox and got out of the car. It wasn't dark yet but his eyes were getting old and weren't worth a shit around dusk.

The flashlight clicked on and made a glowing path as Sheriff Rawley spit a brown stream of tobacco onto the loose dirt and made his way to the dark open maw of the Packard's trunk.

Light bounced off the ten brown bottles that sat there inside on a piece of plywood which covered the rusted out holes left by road salt and too many winters.

Rawley opened the driver's door and stuck his head in. The car's interior was in slightly better shape than the trunk but layers of ash had streaked the upholstery grey and, sniffing once or twice, he was sure he could smell pot.

Pulling himself back out of the car he stretched and spat again. On either side, the forest loomed like great, black, boney walls. It was a little intimidating looking at them like that. They almost seemed like they could come together and crush you.

Rawley diverted his eyes to the ground and that was when he saw the footprints.

He meandered around the car for a minute, trying to follow the tracks as best he could in the dimness. Something didn't seem to sit right, though. He circled around the car again and paid closer attention this time. There were bootmarks all over to the left of the Packard and this was where Rawley figured the boy must have been while waiting for Molly. But there was also a set of prints coming from the woods and leading up to the right side of the car. They were the same tread as the other ones, but there were no marks leading to the woods. How could he come out of the trees if he never went in?

Rawley bent down and groaned as his weight shifted and muscles tightened in his calves and thighs. He held the flashlight close to the ground and studied the tracks more closely. The impression of the heel was deep, much deeper than the toes, and deeper than you'd expect just from the shape of the boot. *He was walking backwards.*

Rawley straightened and glanced around nervously. David was backing away from something, but what? The remaining light in the sky had turned to a faint ashen glow and the beam of the flashlight seemed to darken everything it didn't touch.

The Sheriff took a tentative step to the edge of the trees and peered at the ground. Sure enough there were deep impressions in the soft dirt. These, however, led into the woods. It was one print specifically that bothered him. Overlaid on top of one of David Turner's boot marks was the unmistakable outline of a hand. This time Rawley wheezed as he settled on his haunches. He reached out and placed his own palm over the top of the print. It was much smaller and thinner than his own. Not a child's, but maybe a woman's. As he pulled back his arm he noticed it was shaking and the hairs were standing on end.

On the surface none of it seemed to make any sense. A cold breeze came up suddenly and half-startled the Sheriff as he got back to his feet. Around him the darkness had all but settled in.

He walked slowly away from the tree line and back toward the Packard. With every step he scrutinized the light and dusty prints on the gravely surface of the road and sure enough there was another one. Not just one; there was a whole set he'd missed the first time. They were faint but unmistakable if you were looking for them.

Handprints. He followed them to the side of the car where they actually continued on underneath the vehicle and then all the way into the forest on the other side.

Somewhere behind him a branch snapped and all at once every hair on his body stood on end. Rawley suddenly felt like he was being watched. He wasn't a man who spooked easily but at that very instant he was scared shitless.

He hurried back to the cruiser without ever turning around. The flashlight in his hand remained on and blazing until his car was started and the headlights were on and cutting a path through the darkness. Only then did he turn it off.

The cruiser shot back in reverse, kicking up clouds of dust as it turned onto Crosscreek and sped toward town. Rawley was shaky and cold but he didn't think it had much to do with the weather. It had been one strange, long, miserable goddamn day and now it looked like it wasn't quite over.

It was times like this that he wished there were more to Rockwell's peace force than just himself. What he wouldn't give just to have a deputy again.

CHAPTER FOUR

Tom Parsons had been dead three days when the Andersons finally met Mabel Rampart and had dinner five doors down.

Emily and Rebecca had taken a shining to the old couple as quickly as Nick had his very first meeting with Ramp. They were about as perfect a pair as you could imagine.

After dinner the five of them had sat around in the living room where Mabel dished out the latest town gossip, always taking care to avoid the more unpleasant subjects of late. All in all the evening had been a good and uplifting break for Nick. He'd almost been able to push Tom Parsons and the strange goings on in his house out of his mind for a bit. Almost.

As the Andersons were saying their goodbyes there was a single loud thump upstairs right over everyone's head. It was quick but loud enough to command silence from the group. Nick noticed the expression on Ramp's face change a bit.

"It's probably just Betty," Mabel said. "Her eyes aren't what they used to be. Always going around and knocking into stuff. Poor sweet thing."

Nick bundled Emily up in her coat and stole another glance at Ramp whose eyes were still fixed on the ceiling.

As the trio walked home the wind shoved at them relentlessly. Somewhere behind the sound of rushing air Nick thought he could hear a faint howl. Emily moved closer and closer to him with each step. By the time they reached their own house she was practically walking on his feet. Nick pretended not to notice.

2

Rick Hendricks was leading one of the search parties out looking for David Turner. The kid had been kind of a twit but somehow he still felt a little responsible for the boy, almost fatherly. *And just where in the hell was his father?* Getting tossed and sloppy with a quart of Wild Turkey in back of Shady Acres probably.

When David never turned up Sheriff Rawley had gotten together a group of men to go out and look for him.

Back in town Chrissy would be running the Pump 'n Pay with Molly Carter to help her. He figured it would be a good diversion for both of them. Chrissy had seemed battier and battier lately, always thinking she was hearing things during the day, seeing people.

He knew, though, that it was all a ploy for attention. The only things she'd been seeing were the buckets of Blue Bonnet ice cream and the afternoon soaps.

The two search parties had set out into the woods earlier that morning, each plunging in on different sides of the little dirt road. After a few hours Rick had almost forgotten what the hell they were out there for in the first place.

He liked the feeling of winter. He liked the grey unbroken clouds overhead. Liked the way the air felt cold and sharp as he drew it into his nostrils, and the crunching of dry leaves under foot.

"Ricky, come look at this." Rudy Vitters was motioning him over.

Rick remembered again what they were doing out there in the woods and headed over to Rudy with a bit of trepidation.

"What do you got?"

"Look at this."

Rudy was pointing to an old fallen log half-hidden by dead leaves. The bark had gone black and soft, and in places a fine spray of green covered the surface. For a minute Rick just stood there waiting.

"No, look down here. Those look like teeth marks to you?"

At first he almost laughed thinking that Vitters must have been joking but then, yeah, he saw them. It looked like something had been chewing on the log in places but that wasn't the strange part. The strange thing was the teeth marks left behind. They reminded him of the way an apple looked when you took a good, deep bite out of it.

"Now why would you want to chomp on something like that?" Rudy asked.

Rick just shook his head and muttered, "Animals."

The party had moved on but saw nothing in the rest of the day that seemed to scream out *David Was Here*. As they had gone deeper into the woods the thick carpet of leaves had obscured the footprints. They had blanketed the woods in one great sweep circling deep into the trees, then turning their course back for the road.

As the afternoon light had begun to wane the men's jackets had gotten wrapped tighter about their bodies. The wind had been blowing strong for half an hour. Every now and again someone would yell out David's name, either from their party or the one with Sheriff Rawley.

Rick had just emerged from the thicket of trees and back out onto the dirt road when someone cried out.

"Quiet now! You hear that?"

Some of the other men were now threading out behind him, and from across the way he could see Mark Devlin from Rawley's patrol coming out of the woods, too.

Then from somewhere behind came the small sounds of branches snapping, followed by a loud crack as if someone had fallen.

No one made a move. All just stood there jaws open for a

minute until the uneasy glances turned into even uneasier laughter.

By now all of the men from Rick's party had gotten out of the treeline and were standing along the edge of the road as Rawley's group made their way out.

In the trees behind them there was more snapping and the soft crackle of dead leaves being crushed. They had all gotten a little jumpy and now slowly heads turned back to the dark wall of forest. The breaking and snapping continued in a slow and steady pattern. Rick did a quick head count but everyone was there.

They could just start to make out a figure now shambling slowly toward them from inside the trees. It moved with a jerkiness like a puppet dancing from strings and made Rick think suddenly of *Night of the Living Dead* and the slow disjointed amble of zombies.

As the first bit of light splashed on the figure everyone seemed to gasp as one.

It was David Turner.

He walked out of the trees with that slow and convulsive gait almost as if he were just learning to stand on his own two legs. His eyes were ringed in dark circles and his face seemed kind of gaunt. There was a bit of something mossy and green hanging from one corner of his mouth, and as he opened it to speak, Rick saw that pieces of something black were stuck in and around his teeth.

"I heard you calling me, boss. Heard you calling and I came." Then he collapsed to the ground unconscious.

3

Annabelle and Riley Clem had been home from school for three days with a case of the winter-time flu. Elizabeth and their parents had so far proven too tough to be brought down with the bug, which left the girls alone to their own devices.

Both fevers had broken at about the same time the night before and by morning most of the aches and sniffles and tiredness had gone.

"Let's get out of here," Anna said.

"Mom and Dad will kill us."

"Well, I'm feeling better and I'm tired of being cooped up in here and besides Mom and Dad won't be home for another couple of hours," Anna rattled off.

"I don't know," Riley answered, unsure. "What if Elizabeth gets home?"

"She won't be here anytime soon. Remember she's going over to what's her name's house. The snotty one with the pigtails."

"Ichhh!"

Both girls sat quietly for a moment and thought the whole thing over.

"Where will we go?" Riley asked.

"We can go over to Emily's. We'll ride our bikes."

Riley was still wary of the whole idea but there would be no stopping Anna. Now that just a fraction of her energy had returned she was just busting at the seams to use some of it.

Both girls bundled in warm clothes then headed to the living room. Anna checked the grandfather clock against her watch to make sure they both agreed.

"I'll leave a note," Riley began to say but Anna was already bounding out the door. She stood there for a moment torn between doing what she knew was right and the idea of getting left behind.

Riley pulled on her gloves and ran out of the house after Anna.

By the time the girls got to Cauffield their noses were bright red and cold trickles of snot had to be sucked back up constantly before it could drip out onto their upper lips.

"I don't think anyone's home," Riley said.

Even though it was still afternoon the house should have had some lights on to fight off the lingering grey. The windows stared back, though, dark and empty.

Anna had begun to move around to the side of the house trying to catch a glimpse of some movement inside. The movement that caught her eye, however, didn't come from within, but from the backyard.

"There she is," Anna said and took off running. "Emily! Hey, Emily!"

Riley watched as her sister spun off around the corner, then she adjusted her gloves and followed. Behind the house, the Anderson's yard was much bigger than their own backyard. It stretched out, a great yawning field of green that stopped suddenly and violently at the base of the towering trees.

Anna was half-way to the woods already, and Riley could see just ahead of her as the dark-haired girl plunged into the thicket in front of them.

Even with the thick pink wool of her gloves for protection, Riley's fingers began to feel stiff and numb. The greatest discomfort didn't come from the cold, however. It came from the thought that kept crawling around her mind. The dark-haired girl was much too tall to be Emily.

4

By the time the Andersons got home night had fallen and overhead the thick dark clouds had knotted themselves together so tightly that not a single speck of star or moon peeked through.

They had gone to dinner and then to a movie over in Devon. Emily hadn't cared much for the film. It was one of those a little too cutesy type flicks that her parents had never realized she had outgrown.

The Plymouth turned into the driveway, then stopped so quickly Emily had to hold out her hands to keep from smacking into the back of the front seat.

"Jesus, Nick!" her mother yelled.

Sitting in the middle of the driveway were two bicycles. Her Dad slammed on the brakes to avoid plowing them over.

"What the hell," he was muttering as he got out of the car. He moved them off of the driveway, got back in, then pulled the car the rest of the way forward.

As the Plymouth rolled parallel next them, Emily saw that they were indeed girls' bikes, and for a second she thought of the Clems but dismissed the idea just as quickly. There had been only two bikes not three, and she knew that Anna and Riley were sick with the flu.

The Andersons stood next to the car and puzzled over the scene.

"Are these your friends'?" her mother asked.

"I don't think so," Emily said, still unsure.

"It probably just got too cold and dark," her father was saying. "Parents probably picked them up. I'm sure they'll be back for the bikes tomorrow."

The Andersons went inside and got ready to bed down for the night.

Emily had been asleep for hours when something made her eyes fly wide open.

It was the pounding. The dry rhythmic thudding came calling up the stairs and into her room.

The fear didn't overwhelm her this time as she tiptoed down from the landing. Her dad must have forgotten to put the rag back in.

Without the moon cascading through the windows the house was so dark that Emily had to bump her way around blindly for a minute before she finally found the front door. The hammering was quite loud now. She fumbled on the ground trying to find the rag but came up empty-handed. She would have to improvise.

One sock came off and her now bare foot hit the floor sending a little shock through her body as the cold connected with her warm flesh. She shivered, then reached out to grope for the knob. Something soft brushed against her fingers and quick as lightning Emily's hand flew back to her side. Images of huge hairy spiders came rushing through her head and she almost gave up and ran back upstairs, but the hollow thud was so insistent.

Slowly and cautiously her fingers probed the darkness again. This time when the something soft brushed against them she didn't recoil.

It wasn't a spider at all. It was the rag, stuffed in tight between the frame and the door.

But the knocking?

Now she backed up quickly, the chilly tingle of fear taking hold. Emily took a deep breath and moved to the front window with the greatest of stealth. With a shaky hand she reached to pull the curtains apart just a little to peer out. Just as her fingertips brushed the fabric the knocking suddenly stopped. The silence pressed in around her so completely as the last echo faded that she instinctively held her breath. The pounding was bad but the stillness was worse.

Emily moved her face closer to the curtains and with trembling fingers pinched together a small bit of material and pulled it aside.

The peephole she had made was small, just about the size of her eye. She tried to focus past the pane of glass but still could see nothing. There was only the image of her own eye staring back at her, dark and unmoving. She tried even harder to see past the reflection but it was useless. Just as she was about to give up and make her retreat she noticed something. The eye in the window blinked. *Can you see yourself blink?* Still uncomprehending she moved a little to the side but the image in the window stayed.

Emily started shaking from head to toe and a scream welled up, sticking somewhere in her throat. From the other side of the glass came a noise like dried out branches scraping against the window. She let go of the curtain reflexively and scurried backwards. The eye peering in at her was no longer visible but she could still feel it staring. The scraping against the glass grew louder and more frantic.

The tightness in her chest finally burst and out poured the loudest, throat-tearing cry she could muster.

5

Jake had wanted to join the other men in the search for David Turner but had stayed behind at Terry's request.

"Things are different now, Jake," she had said. "I hear the talk in here all day long. God I wish I didn't but it's impossible not to. Ever since Tom- well the others don't quite trust you."

The words had struck him hard but he didn't show any signs of it. He'd known that things were getting ugly but had hoped for the best all the same.

Finding the Turner kid had helped matters some. If he had been dead instead of alive there might have been the chance that suspicions and old fears would have gotten carried away.

He *had* been alive, though.

Jake had been there when they brought him back into town and the image of seeing David like that haunted him still.

The boy had been dirty and thin, his eyes set back deep in dark sockets. There was something in those eyes that shone, fierce and feral.

Jake had gotten within five feet of the gathered onlookers and smelled him like something dank and mossy. That was when David looked at him. Those eyes had gleamed with the glassy luster of a fish's, cold and dead.

Jake had turned and walked out of there as fast as he could manage without breaking into a run.

That had been the day before.

Now as he sat in the Sunnyside, Terry stroked his hand and tried her best to shake off his despairing mood. The sun of a new day was hidden behind the clouds and the café was almost completely dead. It was times like this that she allowed herself to be more open and affectionate. Usually Jake waited patiently for these moments and they had always meant the world to him. But not today.

He felt trapped. His mind was muddy with thoughts that made his head spin as he tried to sort through them.

The little bell above the front door chimed as Sheriff Rawley walked in.

"Terry. Jake." Rawley gave them each a nod as he approached the counter.

"What can I get you, Sheriff?" Terry asked.

"I'm afraid I'm here on business, not pleasure, ma'am."

Rawley wasn't looking at Terry anymore and Jake could feel the man's stare drilling into his head. Rawley sighed.

"Jake, I'm afraid I'm going to have to take you in. You have the right to remain silent-" Terry cut him off.

"Whoa, wait a second, Walt. just what the hell is this? If this is about Tom-"

"It isn't just about Tom anymore," Rawley said. "Now it's about the Turner kid, too."

"How is he?" Terry asked.

"He's pulling through. Rick and Chrissy took him in until he gets back on his feet. Nothing a little rest and food won't fix, I imagine. Trouble is, he isn't saying much yet. When we asked him what happened all he could say was *the Indian*."

"Sheriff, you can't possibly believe-" Terry had begun.

Rawley held up a hand to silence her.

"I'm not saying I believe anything. All I know is that

accusations are flying and I have certain protocols to follow. It'll be better for everyone if Jake cools it over with me at the jail until all of this can get sorted out."

"This is bullshit!" Terry said defiantly.

During the entire exchange Jake had remained silent. He had known something like this was coming. It hadn't exactly played out like he'd suspected but all the same it was no surprise.

He got up from the stool, towering over Rawley who took a step back from him.

"Will you do me a favor and check on Momma?" he asked Terry.

"Jake. No."

He had already turned to walk out and now Rawley led him from the Sunnyside and into the cold.

6

By the time Nick crawled out of bed yawning and groggy, it was a quarter past eleven. He'd been vaguely aware of Emily and Rebecca getting up for school and work, but the images were fleeting like snippets of a dream.

The cold, grey, winter light made it seem much later in the day as Nick crawled out of the soft warmth of bed. Whenever he awoke with them long gone he would sometimes get that feeling that it was *everyone* and not just Emily and Rebecca who were gone. Outside, the streets would be empty, the town deserted and silent. That was how it felt at least.

He winced for a second as his feet touched the chilly wood floors, then moved over to the dresser and grabbed a pair of jeans and a sweatshirt.

For a split second as he walked across the landing a quick flash of movement drew his eyes to the partially opened door of Emily's room. All at once he shivered and stopped in his tracks.

He suddenly remembered why he was so tired, why he'd been up consoling his daughter until the wee hours of morning. Emily had seen something.

Nick had once again dismissed his daughter's fears as nothing more than her imagination. But he had *heard* something himself only days before. And now. *Did I see something?*

With slow and careful steps he moved down the hall to Emily's room. The sense of déjà vu was overwhelming as he placed each footfall methodically and silently. When he reached the door he pushed it open with his right foot, keeping both hands at ready to defend.

Inside, the curtains were drawn tight and the wan grey light that seeped around their edges created more shadows than illumination. He stood there unmoving, holding in his breath. He listened and waited for the slightest trace of movement to betray a presence lurking somewhere in the gloom. There was nothing.

Nick finally exhaled and took a step backwards. It wasn't the first time his imagination had run away on him and it wouldn't be the last. All the same he decided to walk backwards toward the stairs.

Just as he made it past the threshold of his daughter's room Nick stopped and looked at the floor. There was dirt on the little rug inside her door.

"Shit," he muttered and lifted his feet one at a time to inspect them. They were clean. Now he stooped to take a closer look. What he had first taken for footprints were nothing of the sort. The dirty marks had been made by hands.

After taking the small Handvac to the rug Nick went downstairs and into his office. From his top desk drawer he pulled out a pack of Lucky Strikes and stuffed them into the pocket of his sweatshirt.

He didn't feel like writing. His brain was too busy churning out ghosts and goblins to sit and focus on the book. He grabbed the knob firmly in his hand and shook. The door banged and rattled noisily in its frame.

Pulling the hood of his sweatshirt over his head, Nick stepped out into the cold. It was times like this that he wished they owned more than one car. On his more ambitious days the walk to the hardware store would seem a brisk little jaunt, but today the task was more daunting.

He stopped a little ways down the street in front of Ramp's house, but neither Betty nor her old master were on the porch. He considered going up and knocking but decided to stop in on his way home instead. He could probably use a beer break by then.

Down at the very end of Cauffield where the road went around a bend and curved off toward Main, Nick stopped to take a breather. He'd been walking at a fairly good pace but now he slowed and fished the pack of cigarettes out of his pocket. He popped one between his lips and lit it.

The familiar buzz of the day's first smoke hit him but instead of feeling warm and fuzzy like usual he felt uneasy. Nick looked at the houses surrounding him.

Across the street was a house similar to his own. The curtains in the front window were thrown wide open and a man was standing there looking at the street, looking, it seemed, right at him. Nick offered a small wave but the man didn't move. He had the stony lifelessness of a corpse or one of those figures in a wax museum. As he walked away Nick stole another quick glance at the man in the window. His body hadn't moved a bit but his head seemed to follow Nick as he moved down the road.

7

As Sheriff Rawley leaned back in his chair it groaned out in protest. There was a sharp clank and he felt the whole thing jerk as if it were about to come apart.

He had been at his desk most of the morning doing what he considered to be the worst part of his job. Paperwork. The recent events with Tom Parsons and David Turner had only made the mountain of forms even bigger.

Several times during the endless pencil pushing he'd decided to go back and check on Jake but in the end he'd stayed put, determined to get it done. Jake didn't need anyone looking in on him anyways. It wasn't like he was locked up in a cell. Rawley had put him up in one of the back offices with a couch, TV, and water cooler. Plus, he was allowed to roam about freely so long as he didn't leave the building.

Rawley shifted the mound on his desk a little to the right and in doing so upset the whole thing. Papers and folders went cascading to the ground.

"You rotten sonofabitch," he growled to the room.

He bent over and wheezed as he pushed past his stomach to grab the things closest to his feet. There was a folder, some papers, and a few scattered Polaroids all belonging to Tom's case in a little ring around his right foot. In one big sweep he managed to get them all in his grip before sitting back up and taking in a good long breath.

As he sat there about to stuff everything back into its file the top photo caught his eye. It was a closeup of the inside of Tom Parson's mouth.

Having always been a cop in a small town Rawley had never gotten hardened and desensitized the way he might have in a bigger city. Even over in Devon he would've had more than his fill of death and nastiness, but in Rockwell things had always been fairly tame and pleasant.

The bloody and mangled hole that had once been a mouth made his stomach do a flip. Even though it was only a picture, the effect was almost as bad as it had been when he took the snapshot.

He thumbed through the seven photos quickly before

coming back to that first one. Narrowing his eyes, he held it close to his face.

Rawley had never considered himself a master sleuth but he had always thought his instinct was sharp as a razor. It had been his instinct that bothered him at the crime scene and it was that same little murmur in the back of his head that bothered him now.

In the closeup of Tom's mouth the first thing that grabbed your attention was the lack of a tongue. In fact, it was hard as hell to see anything past that torn and scabby looking stump. There *was* something else, though, something that Rawley hadn't seen until now.

Embedded half-way into the gums was something white and crescent-shaped. He looked down for a second at his hands, then back at the photo. Thumbing through the batch quickly, he pulled another snapshot out. This one showed Tom's hands. In it, the middle finger of his right hand stretched out, capped with a dark purplish splotch. The fingernails on all other digits were plain as day. All except that one.

Rawley suddenly shivered and the chair beneath him groaned out as if in understanding.

Could a man rip out his own tongue?

The idea was ridiculous. In fact, it was so far beyond ridiculous that he wasn't sure how he could even entertain it. The only problem was, it felt right.

There was more and more in Rockwell that just didn't fit the bill but Rawley was beginning to think he had better start paying attention, damn close attention.

He put the photos back in the file and got up from the desk. Even though the body was cremated he hoped like hell that Colin Green had at least given a thorough once-over before sending Tom Parsons up in smoke.

8

Just as Nick exited the hardware store, Ramp's station wagon pulled to the curb right next to him. Nick walked over and opened the door. From inside the deep voice boomed out. "Are you a damn fool or is this just how you Southern boys take to the cold?" Ramp laughed.

"Are you kidding? This is great! I never thought it was actually possible to freeze your balls off."

"I'm on my way home if you want to hop in."

Nick didn't wait to exchange any more witty banter. He climbed in quickly and shut the door.

"Jesus, Ramp, it's no better in here."

"Oh! Forgot to tell you the heater's broken. I can guarantee you the trip is much faster, though."

The trip *was* much faster and in less than a minute they were pulling into Ramp's drive. As the old man shifted the station wagon into park he invited Nick up for a beer.

"I don't know," he replied. "Do you have any warm ones?"

Ramp laughed and the two ascended the porch. Inside Betty was waiting for them, her tail beating a rhythm on the little table by the door. She backed up a little as they approached and bumped the table hard enough to knock a small figurine to the ground. Luckily it didn't break.

Nick remembered the night they'd come over for dinner and the sound he'd heard from upstairs. *Maybe it was just the dog.* But what about his house?

He took a seat on the couch and settled back while Ramp went into the kitchen. When the old man returned he was carrying two beers. He tossed one to Nick who caught it, but just barely.

For a few minutes neither spoke as the warm air slowly worked its magic. It was Nick who finally broke the silence.

"So what were the people like who used to live in my

house?" he asked.

Ramp gave him a funny look as if he'd just snapped out of a dream.

"Your house?"

"Yeah, I mean, why did they sell it? Did somebody die?"

"Die? No, let me see. The last couple who lived there was fairly young. I think he ended up getting a job in Bedford Falls and they moved. They were just renting of course. Before that there were a few others. Nothing remarkable as far as I can remember. In fact, even old Harold only lived there long enough to get the place built. It's had nothing but renters ever since. After he died, his daughter put it on the market and there you have it."

"So Harold died?"

"Sure but not in the house. What's this all about anyways?"

Nick was about to dismiss it all until he saw the look Ramp was giving him. He realized then that he would never get off so easily.

"Well, you'll probably think I'm crazy but I've been hearing some strange things."

The look on Ramp's face changed again, but this time only for a second before he had managed to get it back under control. That second had been enough. All at once Nick understood that it wasn't just *his* house.

9

When her mother finally walked through the door Emily felt a small bit of relief. Since finishing her homework she and her father had been playing what he called the memory game. It wasn't much of a game, really, and after half an hour she usually felt herself growing bored of it and a little uncomfortable. Sometimes she felt like a dog doing tricks.

She had always had what her mother called a *special memory*. After looking at something once she could recall the image without fail whenever she wanted. The memory game usually consisted of her father reading names out of the phone book and her reciting back the numbers. He never seemed to tire of it.

"Hey, you two," her mother said as she unslung her purse.

Emily breathed a sigh of relief as she watched her father close the Rockwell phone directory.

"How was school?" Rebecca asked.

"It sucked," Emily replied. "Anna and Riley are still out sick and Elizabeth is gone now, too."

"Just hope you don't get sick," her mother said. "There's a nasty flu going around. I don't know how many people I saw today who had it. For that matter I hope I don't get it."

Rebecca took off her shoes and undid the top button of her uniform then dropped onto the couch next to Nick. Emily sat at the dining room table doodling on a piece of paper.

"I fixed the door today," Nick said, getting up from the couch.

He went over and took the knob in his hand, then gave a small demonstration.

"See? No more banging."

"Thank God. It was making a bunch of noise again this morning when I got up. I was so sure that someone was knocking that I actually had to go over and open it."

Emily's eyes went wide and the pencil slipped from her fingers, rapping once on the hardwood floor. Neither of her parents noticed. She felt her arms prickle with goosebumps as her eyes drifted warily to the top of the stairs.

Somehow just the very idea of opening the door for the knocker chilled her. It was as if just that act alone were like an invitation. Now whatever had been lurking outside could come and go as it pleased.

Ghosts and monsters don't have to be invited. She tried to reassure herself but then remembered that in fact some things *did* have to be let in. Vampires, for one. If vampires needed an invite, then why not other things, too?

She was so lost in her own thoughts that at first she didn't notice her mother was talking to her.

"Earth to Em's."

"Hmm?"

"I said that there's a good chance it'll snow tonight. How about that? You've never seen snow before."

"That'd be cool," Emily replied with fake enthusiasm.

For the rest of the evening she remained vacant and detached. Her mind was running in overdrive trying to think of ways she could get out of sleeping in her room. All of the solutions she came up with were weak, however. The best any of her plans might do would wind her up having to sleep on the couch for the night and that was no better.

When the time for bed finally came her father gave her a kiss on the forehead, then she headed upstairs with her mother. She changed into sleep clothes while her mother pulled pillows and stuffed animals off the bed.

Instead of completing the nightly ritual by hopping in bed she went over to the closet and threw the doors wide open. Behind her Rebecca let out a small gasp.

"Em's! My God, you about gave me a heart attack. What are you doing? It's time for bed."

"Sorry. I was looking for something."

She left the closet open and crawled beneath her covers. At least if something *had* been hiding in there her mother would've seen it, too.

Rebecca kissed her daughter goodnight, then clicked off the light and began shutting the door.

"Can you leave it open?" Emily asked.

"How are you going to sleep with all that light and noise?"

"It'll be okay."

"Goodnight."

Then she was gone.

Emily pulled the covers up tight under her chin, then waited for her eyes to adjust to the darkness. Once they had done so she scanned the bedroom carefully and took note of every shape and shadow. She tucked them away in her mind for comparison later. If anything was there that shouldn't be, she would know.

She had drifted off long before her parents went to bed, but when she awoke her room was pitch black. At first she panicked thinking that her door had been shut, but as her eyes grew accustomed she realized it was still standing open. There was no way to know what time it was without getting out of bed and fetching the watch off her dresser, but she guessed it was quite late.

Calling up the image of her room from earlier, Emily took a quick look to make sure there were no extra shadows lurking about. Everything appeared normal.

What woke you then? It wasn't like it was weird to wake up in the middle of the night but still something nagged at her subconscious. She *knew* that *something* had awakened her.

Just then there was a soft scratching sound at the foot of her bed. Emily felt her heart do a flip in her chest and her fingers instinctively clutched at the sheets. The sound was slow and irregular, like something raking over the wood floor. When it stopped suddenly, she gasped.

At the foot of her bed something popped into view. It stayed there unmoving. Emily only needed a second to figure out what she was seeing. It was the top of a head. Just the dark mass of hair barely rising above her mattress.

She watched in complete terror as the head began to move slowly along the foot of the bed. As the shape inched along she could hear the soft padding of hands moving along the floor. Each muffled thump brought it closer to the open side of the bed.

All in one quick movement Emily pinched her eyes shut,

screamed at the top of her lungs, and scooted into the corner of her bed where the headboard met the wall.

Through her closed eyes she could still see an instant later when her bedroom light came on. She didn't dare open them until she felt the reassuring grip of her father's hands and heard his voice.

"Wake up, honey, it's just a dream."

He gave her a little shake and she finally opened her eyes.

"I wasn't dreaming!" she managed through hysterical sobs. "I was awake, and there was someone by my bed."

With a shaking hand she pointed to the foot of the bed. Her father actually went over and looked, much to her surprise. For a second his brow furrowed as he looked at the floor.

"What? What is it?" she yelled."

He only shook his head and walked back over to her.

"Emily, look, you had a nightmare. You were still asleep when I walked in. Now for the sake of all of us getting some rest you can sleep in our room for tonight. Only tonight. Got it?"

She nodded solemnly and wiped at her eyes. In a flash she was out of bed and through the door before her father could even turn around.

10

Rudy Vitters set down his whiskey and stared at the static on his TV set. He watched the white noise for five minutes before finally getting out of his chair.

"Shit," he muttered under his breath.

His house lay on the outskirts of Rockwell where the nearest neighbors were a short drive down the road and the underground lines for cable had never quite reached.

Out in the back yard far off by the edge of the forest stood the tall antenna he had erected for the television. It usually got great reception unless the wind picked up really strong. Then, more often than not, the cable that ran from the house and out to the tower would come loose and everything would go snowy.

Rudy paced up and down the living room still muttering. "Singapore Sling, one ounce gin, half-ounce cherry brandy, teaspoon of sugar, soda."

It was a little trick he used to keep his mind where he wanted it. He couldn't quite remember when it had started but it was a hell of a way to keep your thoughts from wandering.

"Mexican Coffee, half-ounce tequila, one ounce Kahlua, one ounce coffee, one ounce cream."

Sometimes he didn't know what day it was, but he could tell you every single drink in the Bartender's Bible. He had memorized it, all of it from A to Z. It was about the closest he'd come to achieving something admirable in his entire life.

Rudy tried to tune into the sound of the static for reassurance but the constant, sharp hiss only made things worse. He needed to get the picture back.

Not having been much of a sleeper for years now, the television had always just been something to space out with, images and sound to occupy the time when he was awake but his brain had already shut off.

Lately, though, it had been the only thing that made him feel safe. Without it the place would be quiet and empty. Then he'd be at the mercy of every little noise and creak the house made, and some it didn't make.

Rudy stopped pacing for a moment and grabbed the glass of whiskey, draining it in one quick gulp. He was just as scared of what might be outside as he was of what he might hear if he stayed in.

"Melon Ball, one ounce vodka, two ounces melon liqueur, four ounces pineapple."

There wasn't a mind trick strong enough to make him forget the sound of his basement steps creaking or the soft scratching at the cellar door. That had gone on for two nights before he finally just cranked up the TV and tried to ignore it.

He had checked during the day and found no signs of anything down below, but at night whatever it was would return. If he had to hear it one more time he thought he might just snap.

Rudy set down the glass and walked to the hall closet. He tried to make as much noise as possible with every little movement. From inside the closet he grabbed a coat and a flashlight. He clicked the flashlight on and off a couple of times to make sure it had enough juice, then headed toward the door in the kitchen that led out back.

Turning the light on once more he reached out and placed his hand on the knob. It was freezing cold. Rudy clicked the flashlight back off and turned back to the kitchen. Quickly and loudly he went over to one of the drawers and pulled out a fresh pack of batteries. He replaced the ones already in the flashlight then tested it again.

"Belmont, two ounces gin, half-ounce raspberry, three quarters cream."

This time when his fingers wrapped around the knob, he turned it hard and stepped out into the cold, inky night.

Aiming the beam straight ahead he moved it a little to the left then to the right until the light reflected back off the antenna tower.

Rudy took off in a straight line at a pace that was damn near a run. Off to his right something stirred the carpet of dead leaves. He froze in his tracks swinging the light in that direction as he tried not to topple from momentum.

There was a figure standing just outside of the beams penetration.

"H-Hello?"

Even though he couldn't see them, he could feel eyes boring into him. The figure took a few slow and awkward steps forward until the farthest fingers of light managed to light on its face.

It was Johnny Carter from up the road, Molly Carter's Pop.

"Jesus Christ, Johnny! You just about scared the shit out of me!"

There was no reply.

"Hey. Is everything all right?" Rudy asked. "Are you okay?"

It had just dawned on him that there was no reason for Johnny Carter to be in his back yard especially not at three in the morning.

Still there was no reply.

Rudy took a couple of tentative steps toward him and shone the light directly into his face. It looked like Johnny alright, but only if he were dead and someone had propped him up in the back yard.

His face was pale and sunken, his eyes dead and glassy. Suddenly the figure began moving forward. Rudy watched for a second, not sure what to do as his neighbor began ambling toward him. He was moving much faster now, but he was unsteady. Suddenly Johnny stopped and made a choking sound then coughed out a spray of blood onto the ground.

Rudy turned and ran back into the house. He flew in a straight line, through the kitchen and into the hall. Not stopping, he grabbed his keys from the hook on the wall and half-slammed into the front door as he skidded to a stop. In seconds he managed to get it open. As he bolted out the front of his house Rudy took a fleeting glance back over his shoulder. Johnny Carter was nowhere in sight but the basement door was shaking hard. The wood around the hinges looked ready to splinter and break any second.

Rudy hopped into the cab of his truck and had it in reverse before he could even shut his door. The pickup smashed the tin mailbox by the side of the road, then fishtailed as he swung it around and into drive.

As much as he loathed the idea, he would drive up to the Carter place and check it out. Maybe Molly and Sarah needed his help. *Maybe they were dead.*

Flying down Harland Pass he tried not to think of what he'd just seen or what he was about to see, and for a minute he managed. There was something else, though, begging for his attention. Instead of thinking about Johnny he conjured images of David Turner walking out of the woods. Walking much like Johnny had.

The driveway to the Carter place seemed to spring out of the blackness so fast that Rudy had to fight with the wheel to make the turn. His tires kicked up a cloud of gravel and fought for traction before shooting him up to the house.

His headlights cut through the dust in the air and splashed the front of the house with a cold, white light.

Inside, everything was black. The front door stood wide open and to the right of it jagged teeth of glass shimmered where a window had been.

Rudy threw the truck in reverse and headed for town.

"Tom Collins, two ounces gin, one ounce-" He made a fist and pounded it against the steering wheel. "One ounce lemon, teaspoon of sugar, club soda."

He would stay the night in the tavern he decided. Then first thing the next morning he'd check on Rick and Chrissy.

11

Terry had driven out to Jake's house the morning after the first snow of winter blanketed the town quietly in the night.

It had come softly and small like someone walking on tiptoes. The sky had cleared up and even in the early morning light she could see great patches of blue and sunshine beaming down.

The ground and trees still held their light covering of snow but she knew it would start to thaw and melt once the sun warmed it.

Terry had brought along a bag of food which she set down to open the rickety screen door. She had only knocked twice before Momma Blacktree answered the door. She stood small and wrinkled, with an old shawl wrapped around her shoulders. The little old lady smiled when she saw Terry and waved her inside.

"How is my Jake doing?" she asked.

"He's fine, Momma. He's doing just fine," Terry answered.

"This is some nasty business," the old woman said with a sweep of her arm.

Terry noticed then how terribly cold it was inside the house. Little white wisps of breath curled out from her lips when she spoke. She looked around and saw that the kitchen windows were standing wide open.

"Momma, you shouldn't leave these open. You'll catch your death in this weather," Terry said as she went over to close them.

"It doesn't do any good to shut them. They just come back and open them again."

Terry felt her stomach flutter and turned to look back at Momma Blacktree.

"Who comes back and opens them?" she asked.

"Those nasty little girls. The little golden-haired ones. I shut the windows and they come back and open them. All night long they do this."

The hair on Terry's neck and arms stood on end.

"Kids did this?"

The old woman shook her head solemnly.

"No not kids," she replied.

"Momma, please, you really need to call me when something like this happens. Or call Sheriff Rawley."

Momma Blacktree pretended to spit upon the ground.

"That fat sheriff who arrests my Jake? You don't worry about me. I have medicine for this kind of thing."

With her wrinkled fingers she clasped a small cloth bag hanging around her neck.

"Strong medicine," she said and smiled.

Before heading back into town Terry circled the little clapboard house and studied the snow. It was surrounded by hundreds of little footprints all crossed over each other and messy in the fine carpet of white. She didn't know what it meant but she didn't like it either. Terry decided that as soon as business slowed for the afternoon she'd close up the Sunnyside and go over to see Jake.

12

When the sound of feet marched up the front steps, Ramp didn't immediately go for the door. He waited for the knock, but even then hesitated before walking to the window. It hadn't been the first time in the last several days that this same thing had happened, except usually there was no one there.

Ramp peered out through the curtains and saw Nick Anderson standing in front of the doorway. He sighed with relief and went over to open the door.

"Hello Nick," he said but with less enthusiasm than usual.

"Jesus, Ramp, you look like shit," Nick joked.

"It's the weather. Makes every damn bone in me get all creaky. You're not looking so hot yourself."

Nick came in and took a seat on the sofa. He looked exhausted. His eyes had that glassy sheen of too little sleep, red with a growing darkness about the edges.

"It's Emily again. This time she said there was something in her room."

Ramp simply nodded. The day before both of them had told each other their ghost stories over a couple of beers. Each had agreed to keep the other filled in on any new happenings but

Ramp had never expected news this soon.

Rockwell had been his home for seventy years and Ramp was more than familiar with its comings and goings, its secrets and doings. There was something different about it now, something about the town that almost made him feel like a stranger taking it in for the first time, and the weirdness hadn't just stayed outdoors.

Things were going bump in the night and he didn't like it one bit.

"Emily said whoever was in her room was doing something at the foot of her bed," Nick said. "After what happened to me I couldn't just discount it, so I took a look."

Nick reached into his pocket and pulled out a little piece of paper with something scrawled on it. For a second he stared at it, then handed the scrap over to Ramp.

"This was scratched into her floor. Right at the foot of the bed. I guess she could've done it herself but I just don't think so. What do you make of it?"

Ramp studied the symbol drawn on the scrap of paper. It didn't set off any buzzers, but at the same time it *did* seem familiar.

"You say it was scratched into the floor?"

"Yeah. Not real deep, but I know it wasn't there yesterday morning."

"Well, I haven't been back in the woods since I was a boy. Never really felt like they belonged to me, you know. This thing here reminds me of that stuff. The standing stones."

"Why's it showing up in my house is what I want to know."

Ramp shook his head and handed the piece of paper back.

"I'm afraid I'm just as much in the dark as you. The only person who might have any clue is Jake Blacktree. He knows more about those woods than anyone else."

"Do you think we could ask him?"

"I don't see why not. Word has it that Rawley's got him over at the jail. Seems some of the townsfolk are a little nervous after

Tom, and then when David Turner came out of the woods and kept on about *the Indian*, I guess the Sheriff is just trying to keep the peace."

Fifteen minutes later the two of them were shivering beneath their coats in the front seat of Ramp's station wagon.

They pulled into the Pump 'n Pay because the old car was close to empty. The building was dark and still locked up.

"Never seen the station closed before," Ramp said uneasily.

"Is there another place to fill up?" Nick asked.

"There's the Amoco on the way to Devon. Little far to be worrying about just now, though."

They got back in the car and headed toward the courthouse on Main.

The Sheriff's office and jail were both housed in a little brick outcropping off to the side of the courthouse.

When they walked through the green wooden door that led inside, Eileen Wilcox jumped a little. Eileen sat behind her desk which was littered with papers and disposable coffee cups from the Sunnyside. A radio crackled out on her left and over it came all of the official drama from over in Devon.

"Hey there, Ramp. You startled me," she said in a cheery voice.

"Hey Eileen. This is my friend Nick Anderson."

Nick extended his hand and she shook it.

"Anderson. Oh yeah, Walt was telling me about you," she said.

"Look, Eileen," Ramp continued. "I heard that Rawley's got Jake Blacktree locked up in here. Was hoping I could have a chat with him."

"Sure you can. He's probably ready for some company. Go on back. You can find him in the last room on the left."

The two men walked down the hall, found the room, and went in.

Jake Blacktree sat in a high-backed chair behind an old oak desk. He was reading a book when they entered.

Ramp had always liked Jake. The man had a sort of quiet grace about him, the kind that made you feel immediately at ease.

Now Jake was looking up at the two of them curiously.

Ramp made the introductions.

"Guess Rawley doesn't think you're too much of a threat," Ramp had tried to joke. "Didn't even put you in a cell. Hell, didn't even lock the door."

Jake actually smiled at this and got up, shaking Ramp's hand square and hard.

"How's it going, old timer?" he said.

They talked for a few minutes trying to keep the conversation light and away from the more troubling present, but eventually the pleasantries had to end.

"Jake," Ramp said. "We wanted to pick your brain about some things."

The smile vanished from the Jake's face and it seemed to go a little slack. He leaned back in the chair and folded his hands on top of the desk.

"Sure. What's on your mind," he replied.

13

Jake twisted in his chair and thought for a moment before speaking. In his hand he still held the scrap of paper Nick Anderson had given him. Across the desk from him Ramp and Nick looked on with anticipation.

The symbol on the paper was no mystery. The thing that had his mind busy was why they had brought it to him. He could understand Nick's interest but Ramp should've already known. There was something more than what they were telling him. He decided he'd have to draw them out.

Jake cleared his throat, then set the scrap down on the desk.

"I can't tell you what the marking means but I can tell you where it came from. Ramp should know most of this story already though.

"Tal Teh Thule is the name the Canasak gave them when they first migrated to this region. The name in its literal meaning is Eaters of Moss. They were fair-skinned, red-haired people who had settled this area long before the first Amerind tribes moved in.

"It's not something you'll read about in any history book because the idea is still controversial. In fact, most Native American groups completely denounce the idea that there were people of Nordic or European descent living here before the first great migration.

"To me it doesn't matter so much who was here first. This land is big enough to belong to all of us," Jake said.

"So what happened to the Moss Eaters?" Nick asked. "If all of this is true, wouldn't there still be some modern day lineage or culture?"

"The only knowledge we have of what became of these people comes mostly from the accounts of tribes that first encountered them.

"The Paiute in the Southwest have stories about a war-like race of red-haired natives. In 1940 a mummified body was found in Spirit Cave in Nevada that lent some truth to their legends. You'll find similar cases in at least four other states.

"As far as the Tal Teh Thule there's a strong oral tradition of the Canasak people that tells of their encounter with them.

"The Canasak tried to live peacefully alongside the Moss Eaters but these strange natives were territorial and would bear no one else in their lands.

"During their first winter in this region the Canasak realized that if they were to survive, they must get rid of them. By the first thaw of spring all traces of the Tal Teh Thule were gone. All except the standing stones."

"So that marking is from one of the stones?" Nick asked.

"I can't tell you for sure, but it does look like their writing," Jake replied.

Nick and Ramp both settled back into the chairs and for a minute no one spoke.

Jake studied their faces, trying to find any hint of meaning in their visit. It was Ramp who finally broke the silence.

"Didn't you say your daughter went back to the stone behind your house?" he asked.

"Yeah."

"So she had to have seen the markings then."

"But how would she have known about the hair? The red hair," Nick replied.

There was another long pause as Nick seemed to mull the whole thing over. Jake still had no idea what the two were driving at.

"Do you want to tell me why you came here?" Jake asked. "If you had found this back on one of the stones, you guys wouldn't be here asking me what it was. Am I right?"

"It was on the floor in my daughter's room," Nick said.

"On the floor?" Jake asked.

"Yeah. It was scratched into the wood."

"Look, Jake," Ramp began. "I'm getting up in my years, and maybe Nick here has an overactive imagination, but frankly there have been things going on that I just can't explain. There's more to it than just Tom and David Turner. I'm talking about things I've heard with my own ears, seen with my own eyes,"

"Why don't the two of you tell me what's happened so we can be on the same page," Jake said.

After they'd finished telling their tales Jake noticed that the hairs on his arms were standing on end. Spirits weren't the realm of fantasy for him. He'd been raised in a landscape full of spirits. Some were good, some were to be feared, and not all were those of the dead.

When the dead did cross over to the realm of the living it was always for a reason. The thing that bothered him most was that *this* reason didn't seem benign.

"So what do you think?" Ramp asked. "Time for the padded rooms?"

"I hope so," Jake answered. "But just in case, maybe someone should check on David Turner. He saw something, too. Something that changed him."

CHAPTER FIVE

Chrissy Hendricks tried to listen to the sounds below over the frantic beating of her heart. There was a loud crash as something broke in the living room. It wasn't the noises that bothered her as much as it was the silence. When everything grew quiet she would have to strain to figure out where he was. The silence terrified her. She was certain that any minute she'd hear him again, this time right behind her.

Another tear spilled down her cheek in the darkness of the attic. There was now little doubt that the man downstairs was not her husband.

In the eight years she and Rick had been married she had seen every side there was to him. She'd been there through his drinking before he quit, and she'd been there when his mother died and he relapsed. No matter how different he became when on a binge, she could always see the real Rick buried beneath it all.

Now she was certain that all traces of that man were gone.

Out of the silence there came a heavy thud, followed by another. He was walking up the stairs now, slowly.

Chrissy tried to stand and move to the farthest corner of the attic. Her legs wobbled badly and she wasn't sure if they could even support her anymore. She wanted to collapse right then and lose all control. She wanted to give up and just die already.

There was silence once more from below. She'd been counting his steps and knew he couldn't have reached the landing yet, but somehow the thought of why he'd stopped was the most terrifying yet.

In her mind she could still see him clearly, shambling about as if he were learning to walk again after a long convalescence. Or worst yet she could see him crawling the way he did that morning when he came down the stairs.

He'd been in bed sick for the last couple of days and when she saw him coming down the stairs on all fours she rushed over immediately, fearing the worst.

No, not the worst. She could have never dreamed the worst in a million years.

All of a sudden Chrissy felt her head go light, and little black spots began to dot the edge of her vision. She was getting weaker fast. With her left hand she reached out for a rafter to steady herself. For a moment she almost forgot and reached out with her right as well. At the last second she closed her fingers back around the handle of the kitchen knife before it dropped to the ground.

Not a single movement reached her ears from down below. The image of him standing there, listening, stayed at the forefront of her mind.

The little black spots began moving in tighter now.

As slowly as she could, Chrissy lowered herself back to her knees. The fogginess in her head cleared some and the blackness retreated again.

The muffled tread of footsteps worked its way back up to her. Something wasn't right. This time they were moving away. He was going back downstairs. *But why?*

Sensing that this might be her only chance, she began sliding over to the access panel that opened down into the bedroom closet. As she pulled herself along, her fingers ran through the cold sticky trail of her own blood.

When she reached the square opening she stopped again to listen. There was a groan of wood. He'd reached the bottom step. All of a sudden there was a loud rapping toward the front of the house. It startled her so much that she had to clasp a hand over her mouth to keep from crying out.

Someone was there. Knocking at the door.

Now was her only chance. Quickly pulling aside the panel, she stuck one foot down into the opening, then the other. It took a second of flailing around before they finally gained purchase on the closet shelves.

Her whole body trembled as she tried to lower herself from the attic. The blood-streaked heel of her right foot skidded over the wood and connected with a box of photos, sending it toppling to the ground.

Her time was up.

Abandoning all stealth now, she released her hold and went crashing down. The knife stayed firmly in her grip and just missed slicing through her arm as she landed in a tangle.

This time the black spots weren't going to leave. The exertion had been too much.

Looking much like her husband had earlier that morning, Chrissy Hendricks crawled across their bedroom floor leaving a trail of red deep in the beige carpet.

She scrambled like mad for the window. All she had to do was reach it and yell to whomever was below, and she might be saved.

Finally one hand grasped the window sill. Still holding the knife in the other, she tried to pull herself up. Her body had all but given up and couldn't do it. She made a stabbing motion at the glass but the blade glanced off of it with a weak tap.

Outside she could hear as a car door shut and the vehicle backed out of the driveway. It was over.

Chrissy gave in and slumped to the floor. There was a creak from the doorway. Turning her head, she saw what she had already known was there.

The man who had once been her husband crawled toward her with his cold, glassy eyes full of hate. When he was nearly on top of her she used every last ounce of strength and brought the knife upward until it sank into the bottom of his jaw.

Blood sprayed into her eyes and mouth as he toppled off to the side.

Lying there listening to the spattering and gurgling of her husband bleeding out, Chrissy felt something changing inside of her even as the blackness stole away her sight.

Part of her was still aware she was dying. Part of her still felt the pain, and still tasted his foul blood in her own mouth. But another part, a quickly growing part, was consumed with rage.

Like ghost lights flickering out in the fields at night, brief visions clouded her dying thoughts.

Someone smashed her ankles with a stone. People were laughing at her. She felt agonizing hunger. Terrible pain. She was an animal. Tethered.

The last thing she felt was pure hate. Then Chrissy Hendricks was dead.

2

Nick caught himself chewing nervously at his fingernails as Ramp drove them out to the Hendricks' place. He thrust both hands under his legs like a child and stared vacantly out the window. It almost seemed impossible to think about doom and gloom when the world all around them shone so bright and beautiful.

With the first snow of the season melting softly on the ground, everything was clean and crisp. Even the sky was sunny and blue, no hint of the grey ceiling that had covered them for weeks.

Again Nick chewed at his nails. He didn't know what they'd find when they looked in on David Turner, but his imagination was already running like a freight train.

Ramp eased the wagon into the drive of a fairly nice two-story house. He shifted to park, and for a moment the two of them said nothing. Nick saw three little sets of eyes peering back at them from the snow on the front lawn. It was a family of stone rabbits that followed the bend of the front walk. For a second he found himself smiling.

"I guess I'll go on up and see if anyone's even home," Ramp said.

The old man climbed out of the car a little slowly, then proceeded up the walk. Nick watched as he lifted the brass knocker on the front door.

Finally after no answer Ramp shrugged and shuffled back to the station wagon.

"Maybe we should head out to Shady Acres. They might have taken him back to his dad's," Ramp said as he got back in.

They drove on out to the Amoco off Crosscreek and filled up before doubling back toward Shady Acres. Neither said much the entire time, and somehow that false sense of everything being okay melted away as quickly as the powder under beaming sun.

Shady Acres had the empty cast-out feel of a deserted gypsy camp. The better looking dwellings were old Airstream trailers and from there they went downhill. An occasional camper or two with out-of-state plates sat nestled between the more permanent residents.

The people who lived in Shady Acres were seldom seen in town. For the most part they kept to themselves, either working at the paper mill, or staying just long enough to construct the new Mega Mall in Devon.

As they drove in on the twisty concrete road that wound its way around back, Nick couldn't help but feel that the place was like a mole in the center of your back. It was ugly and you knew it was there, but you could just barely see it, just a little out of reach.

"Here we are," Ramp said and shifted to park.

They had pulled up in front of what had once been an RV.

She had probably been a real beauty at some point in time, one with all the bells and whistles, but now it didn't even have wheels. The whole thing sat on rusted rims that sank into the ground. Underneath at least fifty or more concrete blocks were wedged between its belly and the earth. A small set of wooden steps led to the door.

Ramp knocked off and on for a minute or more.

"Guess the boy's not home. If that waste of a father is, he's probably still passed out drunk."

Ramp had started back down the stairs and Nick turned to follow. He almost fell down when one of his bootlaces caught between the wooden risers. Catching his balance, he bent over to tug himself loose. Then he saw it.

"Ramp! Wait a minute."

The old man turned around and walked back up to him.

"There's blood here on the step. It's still wet."

Neither had noticed it on the way up. If the awning over the door hadn't diverted most of the snow from the walkway it would have been more obvious. It would have flashed out at them bright and pink.

"Might be nothing," Ramp said.

"Yeah, and it might be *something* too. That's why we're here, isn't it? To have a look."

Ramp nodded his head silently.

Nick stood up and tried the latch on the door.

"We can't just go busting in there," Ramp said.

"We aren't busting in. See? It's open. Besides, someone might be hurt."

Inside, the air smelled rank. It wasn't so much rotten as it was musty and dank. The blinds were all pulled down tight, making it hard to navigate by the pale light that passed through them.

From the doorway it was a straight line right through the place. First, the living area, then the kitchen, bathroom, then a bedroom at the back. It was like a shotgun shack on wheels.

Nick started in, slowly weaving his way through toward the

closed door in back. His eyes had adjusted enough now to see that most of the stuff in his path turned out to be piles of beer cans and whiskey bottles.

When he reached the bedroom door, Ramp's hand fell on his shoulder almost in a plea for him not to open it. He turned the knob and threw the door wide before he could lose his nerve.

"Holy fuck!" Nick cried.

The hand on his shoulder tightened its grip so hard that Nick winced with pain.

Inside, David Turner's father lay tangled in a mess of blood-soaked sheets. Large chunks of flesh had been torn out of his arms and one piece taken from the side of his face. Where there had once been two cataract-swirled eyes, dark and empty blood-black sockets stared at them.

Nick and Ramp bolted from the room and from the RV, Ramp almost slipping on the bottom step.

"Jesus!" Nick said, still winded. "We've got to call Rawley."

Ramp's face had gone an ashy white and his lips tinged a little blue. For a moment he looked more like ninety than seventy.

"Hey, Ramp, are you okay?"

The old man held out a hand and nodded.

"You sure?"

"Sure as shit," he wheezed in reply.

"Wait here a minute and catch your breath," Nick said. "I'm going to try to find a phone."

Nick knocked on at least ten doors before finally giving up. It was a weekday and probably all of the residents of Shady Acres were already gone to work.

"Any luck?" Ramp asked when he got back.

"No. Are you okay to drive?"

Ramp shot him a look of reproach.

They both took one long glance back at the RV, then drove like hell into town.

3

Rawley was sitting in the back room with Terry Haggart and Jake when the writer and old Ramp busted in. He'd been considering taking a drive out to Jake's place just to check things out. Something had Terry spooked and he didn't like it. The girl was usually more level headed than that.

"Walt, there's been trouble out at Shady Acres," Ramp said slightly out of breath as the door swung wide.

Rawley felt that sinking feeling again and wished like hell he could just cover his ears and ignore everyone.

"What kind of trouble?" he asked, finally resigned.

"It's that old drunk Turner. He's been killed," Ramp said.

"Not just killed," Nick added. "Somebody mangled him, took out his eyes.

There was a gasp from across the desk and Rawley saw Terry shudder.

The room was silent and all eyes were burning into the Sheriff's head. He closed his *own* eyes for a moment and thumbed at his temples.

"This means Jake can go, doesn't it?" Terry had regained her composure. "He sure as hell couldn't have done this, and if what they say is true then whoever killed Tom is still out there."

Rawley raised a hand in the air.

"Now hush on up just a minute," he said. "Hush up and Jesus H. Christ let me think. Nobody is leaving here until I say so. Now, Jake isn't locked up for killing Tom, he's in here cause of what David Turner said. I'll be the first to admit I think the whole thing is a load of horseshit, but he's staying here until this gets sorted out. I'll go out to Shady Acres and have Eileen make some calls to see if anyone's seen David. Nick, Ramp, I'd like it if you rode out with me."

"But-" Terry began.

"No buts. You can wait here with Jake if you like until we get back, but he's not going anywhere."

Rawley pulled himself up from the chair and started out the door.

A wordless look was passed between Jake, Terry, Nick, and Ramp, then the two turned and followed Rawley out.

4

At the Rockwell Tavern Rudy Vitters was sweating in spite of the chill in the air. Not being a man who was handy with anything but a tap, the project which he figured would only take a few hours had turned into an all-day affair.

The afternoon was growing late. All around him most of the snow from the night before had melted, leaving the world with a wet glassy look. The clouds had begun to form again in the sky, a thick wall of them moving in from the west. That morning had only been a reprieve, the calm *before* the storm.

Rudy hadn't noticed that he was shaking until the trowel slipped from his fingers. Occasionally a car would pass by and he'd stop to wonder just how ridiculous he really looked.

As the sun began to hide and the temperature slowly dropped, the mortar seemed harder and harder to work with. The trowel slipped again, this time leaving a crusty grey trail down the side of his jeans.

"Fuck!"

He had started patching the holes in the mortar earlier that day and by now had progressed to fixing the window.

Is all of this really necessary?

He stopped for a minute and thought about it. If somebody had told him he'd be bricking up the only goddamn window in his bar, he would've said they were nuts. Probably exactly what *they* now said about him when they motored their way down First Avenue. Would you look at that, old Rudy's lost his shit.

But they hadn't seen. They didn't have a clue.

"Rum Gimlet," he muttered under his breath. "Two ounces rum, half-ounce Rose's lime juice. Gin Cooler, Two ounces gin, two ounces club soda, teaspoon of sugar, ginger ale."

Something was terribly wrong in Rockwell and the only thing he could think to do was hide. At least the Tavern was close to other people, unlike his house far off on the outskirts of town.

With the place sealed up tight the only way something was getting in was if he let it. That was the only thought that restored some of the confidence he'd lost the night before.

Rudy tried to put the last brick in place. It didn't quite fit so he knocked a quarter of it off, then patched the hole with mortar.

He took a few steps back to survey his handiwork. It wasn't bad, especially since he didn't know a damn thing about laying brick. You could clearly make out where the window *had* been; the new bricks were a bright red next to the old ones. The pattern in the block didn't quite match either. But he hadn't put it up for looks.

Without the neon signs for Budweiser and Early Times on display, the Rockwell Tavern looked more like a fort. Looked like one all the way up to the bank vault door. The door no longer struck him as a novelty like it used to. Now it seemed like a godsend.

Rudy went inside and bolted the steel door in place before going behind the bar and pouring himself a drink. He felt safe now, but not good.

One word kept repeating in his mind over and over like a mantra. *Coward.* He downed his drink, then poured another.

He *was* a coward, hiding in his bar while something happened to the town, to his friends and neighbors. It was all adding up to more than he could handle.

Tom Parsons, the Carters, David, the noises at night, the thing in his cellar, the way the streets seemed emptier and emptier every day, these were the reasons he hid.

Something was stealing over Rockwell. It was moving fast and unseen behind the closed doors of every house on every street.

He didn't want to be a hero; he just wanted to survive.

5

"Eileen you'd better come take a look at this," Terry was standing in the little five car parking area next to the jail and hoping she'd yelled loud enough.

Seconds later Eileen came breaking through the front door in a run. Terry stood in front pointing to the tires of Eileen's little blue Chevy.

"Shit!" Eileen knelt with her back to the jail and examined her front tire. There was a deep slash in it toward the bottom and it sat flat and misshapen on the ground, rim resting on the blacktop. The back tire was in no better shape.

"These goddamn kids! They get worse and worse every year. Oh, Charlie's going to pitch a fit about this."

"I'm really sorry. Can I give you a lift to pick up a couple of new ones?"

"No, but thanks. I can't leave till Walt gets back. I'll just have to call Charlie and have him bring me his spare when he gets off. I think my spare's okay."

"Well, you know where to find me if you change your mind," Terry offered.

"Nice of you, but I'll be fine."

Eileen went back into the building and Terry got into her Volkswagen, started the engine, then waited. Moments later Jake walked out cautiously from behind the courthouse building. He ran over to the idling car in one silent sweep and got in. It was hard for him to scrunch down out of sight but he managed his best as they backed out of the parking lot and headed for the outskirts of town.

By the time they got to the old railroad tracks, Jake had taken a normal position again in his seat. Terry glanced over and saw the faraway look in his eyes. Jake wasn't just worried; he was outright scared. She slipped her right hand over the top of his and gave it a squeeze.

If they got out there to the *Reservation* and something had happened she didn't know if he'd ever forgive her, didn't know if she could forgive herself.

All of these black thoughts fogged her mind and she tried her best to fight off the miserable tears building in the corners of her eyes.

When they finally pulled into the gravel drive, the first thing she noticed were the windows. All on the front of the house stood wide open.

Jake was out of the car and running almost before she had shifted to park. Terry leapt out after him.

"Momma!" Jake was yelling from inside.

The screen door caught as she tried to throw it open, and in those few seconds that she fought with it the tears had begun to spill wet and warm down her cheeks.

"Jake!" She was sobbing now.

Finally the screen unhooked and she pushed past it, a tiny sliver of metal from the frame cut into her shoulder as she went through.

"Momma!" Jake was still yelling.

He came running out of the back bedroom, eyes wild, his chest heaving with quickened breath.

"She isn't here," he said.

The image of him blurred as he darted past her again and out the front door. She followed blindly and stumbling as the tears rolled out of her eyes.

They went all around the house but there was nothing. No signs. Just the open windows where the curtains flicked in and out like dirty white tongues.

Jake dropped to his knees five yards in front of her. His head hung low but she couldn't see his face behind the long black hair that framed it like a curtain. She stood there frozen for a minute and watched as his body rippled with little tremors.

Slowly she walked over and knelt beside him. He turned his head toward her as she put her hand on his shoulder. His cheeks were just as wet as hers and he looked at her with those soft grey eyes she'd always loved.

"She's gone," he said in almost a whisper. "It's all my fault, and she's gone."

"She's not gone," Terry stammered. "We'll go inside and call Eileen. We'll tell her to get Rawley out here and we'll find her, Jake. All of us."

"Rawley's got other things to worry about. We'll look ourselves," he said and slowly got on his feet.

The strong determination she was so used to from him was gone. There was something else in its place. If she hadn't known him better she would've almost thought it was fear.

6

The snow had already begun falling by the time Nick and Ramp got back to Cauffield Street. Somewhere behind the dark bonnet of clouds the sun was setting, and somewhere it was probably a hell of a sight, too. Wind was hammering the soft, white flakes out of the sky in a rage.

Ramp pulled the station wagon into Nick's driveway behind the Plymouth which was gathering its own winter coat. Off to one side of the yard two bicycles still remained, forgotten and unclaimed.

The day had been long and their nerves were raw. Nick didn't get out immediately and neither said a word as if a conversation were taking place in the silence.

They had gone back to Shady Acres with Sheriff Rawley and helped load the body into its grey bag before finally seeing it over to the Green Funeral Home. The task had almost proved too much for Ramp, and more than once while bagging the body Nick had thrown up on the ash-stained carpet of the RV.

Now both of them sat there like two soldiers home from war.

"You make sure and keep in tonight. All of you. And seal the house up tight. There's more than bad deeds coming our way. There's bad weather, too," Ramp said.

Nick nodded.

Inside the house Emily was watching television. Nick stood in the doorway and felt the weariness sink deeper into his bones. He had decided not to mention anything that had happened. Not yet at least. Where would he even begin? What could he say?

"Hey there, pumpkin. How was school?"

"It sucks," Emily said never taking her eyes off the screen. "Anna, Riley, and Elizabeth are still out sick."

"Where's your mother?"

"She's upstairs in bed. She's sick, too."

Rebecca was indeed lying in bed. Her nose was red and her face was puffy and a thin layer of sweat glistened on her forehead.

At first he thought she was sleeping but her eyes opened to slits when he walked in.

"How're you feeling?" he asked.

"I feel awful. I started the day with just a little sniffle and now I think I'm burning up."

He reached over and put a hand to her head.

"You feel pretty warm."

She rolled more to her side and moaned.

"We don't have anything to take anywhere in the house. I think I threw most of it away before the move. Can you run down to the store before the weather gets too bad?"

"Sure, you just sit tight until I get back. I'll even grab dinner. How does that sound?"

"I'm not really hungry."

Nick went around to every door in the house before putting his coat and shoes back on.

"What're you doing?" Emily asked him.

"Just making my rounds before I go out." He forced a smile.

"Where are you going?"

"The store, to get some medicine for Mom."

Emily's eyes lit up.

"Can I come? I want to get some ice cream."

"Ice cream? It's freezing outside and you want ice cream?"

Nick felt the first tinge of happiness in the entire day. Emily ran upstairs and fetched her coat, then bounded back down in a flash.

He had to practically keep the Plymouth at a crawl as they drove down Cauffield into town. The snow was coming down in great white sheets, the windshield wipers could barely keep pace and the headlights penetrated only a few feet or so.

As soon as they got in to the General Store Nick was greeted by a scene he knew all too well. Back in Palmdale it happened every couple of years whenever one of the bigger hurricanes would plot its course straight for land.

The few customers had carts loaded down with candles, batteries, water, and canned goods. There were great big bare spots on many of the shelves.

Nick realized that maybe he lacked some foresight into the nature of a bad winter storm, so he and Emily went about picking what scant provisions were left to them.

They had shopped for about twenty minutes before wheeling the woefully under-burdened cart into the checkout lane. There were three other shoppers waiting by the front window of the store. Their carts were full of groceries already bagged. Nick only recognized two of them, Regina White and Rudy Vitters.

Outside, the wind howled and shook the door so hard that

the electronic chime kept going off. Snow was already stacked at least a foot and a half in front of the door where it would smack into the wall and settle into an ever growing pile.

Nick and Emily paid for the groceries, bagged them, then joined the others by the window.

The cashier, a plain looking girl of about sixteen came up behind them.

"Give it a little bit and it'll die down," she said cheerily.

"I've really got to get home. My wife is sick," Nick said.

"You don't want to go out now, you might never get home," she replied.

Nick could feel Emily stiffen a little by his side.

"She's right," Rudy said. "There's no passing through a squall like this."

The look on Rudy's face seemed to echo Nick's own.

"Can I use your phone then and tell her we'll be delayed?" he asked the girl.

"Sure thing. It's over here."

She led them to a little office on the side of the store. Sitting on a desk half-buried behind papers was a black rotary phone. He picked it up, dialed, then waited. By the fifth ring, his fingers had begun to drum nervously on the side of the desk.

Six rings, no answer.

Seven.

Finally a nasal sounding voice came over the line.

"Hello?"

"Hey, sweetie, it's me," he said, finally taking a breath.

"Nick? Where are you?"

"We're at the store but the storm is blowing like hell. We're going to have to wait it out a bit until it dies down some."

"Emily's with you?"

"Yeah, she's right here."

"Must have left the TV on. I thought she was still downstairs. How long do you think you'll be?"

"I don't know. The first break I see, we'll take it."

"Okay. Love you."

"Love you, too."

Nick hung up the phone and walked back out front, Emily trailing behind. Rudy, Regina, the cashier, and the woman he didn't know were still waiting patiently by the glass.

"Can I have my ice cream now?" Emily asked from beside him.

"Sure, why not." He glanced at the cashier's name tag. "Maybe Tracy here can help you find a spoon."

At the sound of her name the girl looked at him, then broke into a wide smile.

"Of course I can," she said to Emily. Then in a mock whisper, "I bet we can even find something to sprinkle on top of it."

The two girls vanished, skipping off down an aisle. Nick tuned back into the conversation between the other three. Regina White was saying something about how the storm must be letting up because she could see someone moving around out there.

Nick noticed Rudy tense up and take a couple steps back. It was then that the thought occurred to him and panic began playing chords up and down his spine. He whipped his head around and scanned the aisles for Tracy and his daughter. When the two finally appeared around a corner, he practically ran to them.

A look of concern spread over Emily's face.

"Ems, honey, was the TV on when we left?"

"No. I turned it off. Why?"

"Are you positive?"

She nodded slowly.

"Shit! Shit! Shit!"

Nick took off sprinting for the office. He picked up the phone but had to redial three times because his fingers kept messing up the rotary.

The line was busy.

"Shit!"

Emily was standing in the doorway with huge, wet eyes.

"Dad?" Her voice quavered. Tracy, the cashier, was standing behind her.

"Tracy, can you watch Emily for me? I have to run to the house."

"Sure, but"

Nick was already running for the front of the store. Emily was crying hard and running after him, Tracy bringing up the rear.

"Don't leave me here! I want to go!" She was almost hysterical.

In the front of the store the others had turned away from the window and were now staring at him as he made for the door.

"Look, Ems, I'll be right back. Promise. I'm going to get Mom and bring her here."

Before Emily could have a chance to reply he'd thrown open the door and stepped half outside. He had to fight as the wind tried to wrench the door out of his fingers. From behind, an arm seized him by the shoulder. It was Rudy.

"Look, man, you're not doing your wife or your daughter any good by going out there. I know what's out there."

"So do I, and Rebecca's by herself."

He tore free of Rudy's grip and barreled out into the storm, head down, snow and ice stinging the side of his face.

He stopped and tried to remember where they had parked the Plymouth. It had gotten so bad that the General Store was only a vague glow ten feet behind him. *This is nuts! Can't see a goddamn thing. Rudy's right; I can't make it.*

Tears were spilling out of his eyes. They turned to frosty crystals as soon as the air touched them.

There was no way he could make it to Rebecca. It was too far. And what if something happened back at the store while he was gone? What if something happened to Emily?

He ran back to the glow of the front windows. Inside, a

figure jumped back as his dark shape loomed in the glass. The little chime dinged as he opened the door and shoved inside, one wet foot slipping and dropping him to his knees.

"I need a phonebook. I've got to call Wilbur Rampart." His breathing was ragged. "Can somebody please get me a-"

Emily rattled off the number. He looked at her. She wasn't crying now but her bottom lip still trembled.

Nick got up off the ground and jogged to the office once more. Icy clumps fell off of him as he went, making little splatting sounds behind him.

7

The furnace was cranked up and blazing in the Green Funeral Home. The steel door above the rolling ramp was open partway. Heat rolled out of it and settled into every corner of the room. Colin Green was still shivering though.

He had lit the oven early to take some of the chill out of the basement. With a trembling hand Colin raised the whiskey bottle to his lips, took a swig, and grimaced. The whiskey was for warmth, but it was also to steel his nerves.

The grey bag containing the body of David Turner's father rested, zipped up on the industrial gurney. He would have to take him out of there before burning. The other bag had gotten cooked up with Tom Parsons and torching both of them in one month would be bad form.

He set the bottle down on the concrete floor and walked over to the body. His hand shook so badly that he missed the oversized zipper the first time he reached for it. Seizing it finally, he yanked it down in one stroke before it caught somewhere about chest level.

"Jesus!"

Before he knew it was coming, Colin leaned over and heaved.

Whiskey, bile, and the burrito he'd eaten earlier that day, splashed around his feet. When the worst of it was over he straightened and wiped his mouth on his sleeve.

He'd wanted to make this quick but, turning back to the body, he found he could no longer make himself reach toward it.

The blood in what had once been eyes still glistened deep within the sockets. There were little ropy cords of something down in there, too. The rest of the blood had dried into a flaky, scabby-looking, maroon. Colin thought he might puke again.

He didn't want to keep staring but a sick fascination held him. *Breathe in and out, in and out.* Deep in the still glistening parts of the sockets the shredded connective tissue had started to look funny. It almost looked like there was movement in there.

Colin cautiously leaned over the body and peered into the two dark cavities.

Cold, sticky meat. But at least it wasn't *really* moving.

Off behind him an electronic chime rang out. The chime was connected to the doorbell up top. He figured it was probably that big bastard Rawley coming back to make more work for him.

He forced himself to look away from the corpse and peeled the latex gloves from his hands. Taking the steps two at a time, he swore the whole way up.

Upstairs, the front parlor was lit only by the small table lamp that he kept on at night. Outside the front door he could see that the storm had finally gotten up to speed.

Colin moved over to the glass and peered out. He could barely see more than a couple feet past the door, but there was no one out there. He was in no mood to be screwed with.

Completely ignoring the freezing wind and snow he threw open the door and stepped out. As he did, he thought for sure that he saw someone disappear around the side of the building. It was impossible to be positive but by now he'd gotten himself worked up. *Someone sure as hell rang the bell.*

"You better hope I don't catch you!" he yelled into the wind as he took off around the corner. "I'm not in the mood for this shit!"

By the time he made it back to the front of the building his nose was running and his hands had gone completely numb.

He took one last look before going back inside. There had been no one out there. As he locked the door behind him an uneasy thought crossed his mind. Someone could have circled the building and gotten in before he made it all the way around.

The building was quiet except for the rattle of the furnace from deep down below. There was no other sound to betray the presence of someone hiding.

Colin went over to the fireplace in the front parlor and snatched up the black iron poker that lay in front of the hearth. By now some of the bravado had left him and he no longer wanted to catch somebody, especially not inside. He just wanted to finish the work and get the hell out of there.

Brandishing the poker in front of him, Colin descended the steps to the basement. In the darkness of the stairwell he could feel his skin prickle with fear. A thin line of light spilled from underneath the door that led to the work room. Staring at that small patch of amber glow he took a deep breath and reached out. Just as he placed his palm on the door and began to push, a shadow obscured the light for a second.

He almost dropped the poker as he took two quick steps back.

Most people have a defense for fear; Colin's was to get mad. Suddenly he could picture himself cowering in the darkness of the stairwell quivering like a child, and it pissed him off. Whoever had decided to jerk his chain had picked a bad fucking night to do it.

Gripping the poker like a baseball bat, he kicked at the door, sending it flying open. In the same motion he charged into the room, stopping suddenly.

Standing next to the corpse on the gurney were two children,

THE DEAD OF WINTER

a boy and a girl. They were peering over at the body, the little girl poking at the bloody flesh around the eye sockets.

Colin dropped the poker. The impact sounded with a sharp metallic clang that echoed loudly in the basement room. The two children spun around quickly to face him.

Their little faces were pale and twisted with hate. Glassy grey eyes bore into him from dark sunken holes.

Colin tore up the stairs. He wanted out. Out of that place, and out of that town.

The wind blew the front door back at him so hard that the impact sent his nose gushing blood. For a moment the pain was blinding. Blood was still coming when he got behind the wheel of his truck and threw it into drive.

He groped around on the seat next to him and pulled up an old rag. With one hand he held the rag to his nose and with the other he steered.

Plowing on with almost instinct alone he sped through the streets of Rockwell, driving faster than he should, occasionally fishtailing, but somehow keeping it under control.

He was on Crosscreek trying to make a break for Devon when the great wall of white shot up in the short arc of his headlights. He slammed on the brakes and skidded. The front end of the truck smacked into something hard and he heard the sound of his headlights shattering.

The trees. Oh Christ, the trees have come down.

His nose had stopped bleeding and fortunately the impact of the crash hadn't been too bad. The truck was still running.

This time as he turned around to head back into town, his progress slowed by the two destroyed headlights.

8

When the phone had first started ringing Ramp felt his

stomach jump and do a sick little roll. He knew the ringing could only mean trouble. There had been some hope that maybe the night would pass by uneventful, giving pause for planning and settling of the old nerves. It wasn't looking that way.

By the time he'd set the phone back down on the cradle his hands were slick with sweat. He was afraid again but this time it wasn't so much a fear of whatever was out there, as it was of him being able to rise to the occasion.

His mind was ready to wage war but his body had seen far better days. *I'm too old.* But old or not it was up to him to help Rebecca Anderson. If he wasn't up to the task, at least he'd go down trying.

Mabel walked in as he was pulling bullets out of the bureau drawer and stuffing them into his service revolver.

"Wil? What's all this? What's going on."

"I don't have time to explain. Go on and get some warm clothes on you. We've got to go fetch Mrs. Anderson and head into the General Store."

"But Wil, the storm."

"I know. Believe me, I know. Go on now."

Ramp's eyes weren't quite what they used to be and in the blinding white fury he'd almost driven right over the Anderson's mailbox before even realizing they had reached the house.

Ramp parked the car and looked over at Mabel. Her forehead and the corners of her eyes were creased deeply with worry. He gave her hand a little squeeze.

"I promise as soon as we get to the store I'll tell you all about it. In the meantime, though, I'd feel better if you stuck with me."

He pulled out the revolver and held it in one hand while grasping the door release with the other.

"Okay, let's go," he said, bolting from the car.

When he and Mabel made it to the front porch the first thing they saw was the window standing wide open. Mabel might not have known what was happening in Rockwell, but nobody needed to explain to her that this was a bad sign.

Ramp tried the doorknob but it was locked. He looked at the window but knew it was too high to go crawling into. Without another thought he leveled the pistol at the doorknob and fired. The report was deafening and somewhere in the midst of the ringing he heard Mabel scream. It had done the trick. The lock was busted.

The two of them hurried inside. Everything looked to be normal within. As Ramp did a quick search of the downstairs he kept calling out Rebecca's name. There was no answer.

They moved on up to the landing, first checking Emily's room and then the other. The Anderson's bedroom was trashed. The window was broken and jagged pieces of glass covered parts of the floor. There was blood on the floor, too.

Mabel's trembling hands were on him now. "Wil, what is this? What's going on?" Her voice was trembling, just past the verge of tears.

As he stood there not knowing what to do, a rustling sounded from the closet. He leveled the revolver at it and crept over to the wooden bi-fold doors. His hands were shaking badly now. As he reached out and tore the doors wide open, a scream roared out and he jumped back just in time as something swiped at his leg.

It wasn't something. It was Rebecca. She cowered in the corner of the closet, her arms a mess of long red scratches.

"Jesus Christ! Are you okay? We came as soon as Nick called us but"

"The woman. She attacked me. I thought it was Emily downstairs but then she- I pushed her- out the window."

Ramp rushed over to look out the shattered frame. There was no one on the ground that he could see. When he turned back, Mabel was wrapping Rebecca in a thick heavy coat from the closet.

"Now I know you're hurting, dear, but we can't stay here.

You've got to see your husband and little girl in town," Mabel said. She helped the woman to her feet and together, the three of them made a slow and careful trek back out to the car. Rebecca was still shaken and sniffling when the station wagon eased back out onto Cauffield.

The storm had grown so terrible that Ramp had to keep his foot on the brake, barely letting the wagon crawl forward at an idle.

When they reached the intersection where they would cross over to Main, Ramp let the car coast out into it. Ordinarily the General Store could be seen sitting two buildings down from the corner but the gale had erased all signs of it.

Just as they straddled the road, wheels slowly turning to Main, something smashed into the passenger side so hard that the car began to roll.

The next few seconds were wild and disjointed like a dream. One minute they were right side up, the next they were coming down on their heads. There was a horrible screech of rending and twisting metal. Glass exploded all around them and sprayed in like a shower of razors.

In those topsy-turvey seconds Ramp saw a pickup, then sky, then ground. His head smashed into something hard and the screaming all around him took on a muted quality as a blinding white flashed behind his eyes.

His thoughts turned muddy and his vision began to blur, first softening, then fading to black.

CHAPTER SIX

Terry and Jake had been holed up in the Sunnyside's back room since the snow had begun falling again. They hadn't found his Momma but they *had* found enough to make them realize things were much worse than they could have imagined.

Their search had taken them through a Rockwell that neither were familiar with. People they had lived amongst for years regarded them with fear and suspicion every time they knocked upon a door. Even worse than their encounters with others were the empty houses, open doors, and broken windows.

By the time evening had begun to darken the already somber skies, Jake and Terry sought shelter in the Sunnyside.

As the waning dusk faded into night Jake filled Terry in on his conversation with Ramp and Nick Anderson. He'd expected her to laugh at him or say that he was crazy, but she did neither. Instead she sat there, face grim, and listened to the whole damn thing.

"So what do we do?" she had asked when he finished.

"I don't know," he replied.

As the darkness crept in through the front windows and blanketed the diner with its embrace, he found himself thinking of her again, thinking of Momma. He tried to push the sorrow deep into his mind. There would be time to grieve later and for now he needed all of his wits about him.

The two had eventually dozed off into a shallow and fitful sleep. Terry had wrapped herself around Jake's tall frame, her head resting on his shoulder.

Then there was a crash.

Jake's head whipped up and his eyes snapped open just as the last tinkling of broken glass reached his ears. Terry hadn't moved but, glancing down, he saw her eyes were open, too. Wide open.

"That was the front window," she whispered. "I'm sure of it."

Quickly and quietly they got to their feet. Jake glanced around the small room and tried to take stock. There was nothing, absolutely nothing he could use for a weapon.

Now there were shuffling noises from the front of the diner, feet tramping over the broken glass.

Jake took Terry by the hand and started for the office door. Her palm was slick and sweaty inside his. Before reaching out for the knob he clicked off the light switch, plunging them into darkness. Shaky hand upon the knob, he turned it and slowly pushed the door out, praying that it would glide silently on its hinges.

The Sunnyside was pitch black. All of the lights had been off since the afternoon, when they had first hidden in the office.

Jake took a tentative step into the darkness and pulled Terry along behind him. The office opened directly into the kitchen, which sat behind a little pass-through window behind the front counter. He cocked his head and listened. The storm was howling outside but it was loud inside, too. One of the windows was definitely broken. Every second or so the crunch of shoes on glass floated through to the kitchen.

Eyes now adjusting to the dark, he could see the outline of someone moving around by the booths. The figure was stooped and seemed to be bumping around blindly, hands out for support. It suddenly stopped moving. Jake and Terry also froze in their tracks.

Now there was another sound buried under the roar of the wind. At first he thought it was breathing, raspy, harsh intakes of air. And to a degree that's exactly what it was. But not just breathing, he realized. It was sniffing. The person out there was smelling for them, and it seemed to catch something that it liked.

Suddenly the figure ambled forward, smacked into the counter, then proceeded to crawl over it. Jake still stood frozen as it bounded into the wall separating the diner from the kitchen. A gnarled-looking hand shot through the window and groped about.

That was when Terry screamed.

The hand had startled both of them, but not as much as the face. It was Peter White, the owner of the dry cleaners on First and Main. His face was pale and gaunt, his features almost distorted by the grimace that seemed to be stretching every muscle to the breaking point. The eyes had really done it.

Sitting under those two unblinking lids they seemed to cut straight through the darkness with a chilling ferocity that froze Terry where she stood.

When Terry screamed he pulled her hard and ran to the back of the kitchen. From behind them they could hear the scrabbling sounds as what had once been Peter White pulled itself through the window.

There wasn't anyplace left for them to run. They had reached the back of the kitchen where boxes were stacked high against the walk-in cooler. They were trapped.

Peter smashed into a rack of pots, sending them clanging and scattering to the ground. He was closer now.

Beside him Terry was shaking hard. There was nothing left to do but fight. Instead of waiting for him to get any closer Jake took the offensive and charged. Just before he plowed into Peter, Jake dropped low and rammed him in the chest with his shoulder. Both men went flying to the ground. As soon as his body touched the floor Jake went into a roll. He was back on his feet before Peter White had even gotten to his knees. The man lashed out like an animal.

Jake grabbed one of the pots off the counter next to him

and swung it at Peter's head. The blow connected with a hollow metallic gong before dropping him to the ground.

"Open the cooler," Jake yelled.

Behind him he could hear the whoosh as Terry broke the seal on the big walk-in. Cold air rushed out and played about his ankles as Jake grabbed Peter White by the feet.

He'd just gotten the body inside when a hand clamped around his ankle and pulled with such a force that his foot went out from under him, and he dropped to the ground.

Jake was up in a flash, slamming the door shut hard. It was only seconds before he felt the metal shudder beneath him as it was struck from the other side.

"Can we lock this?" he yelled to Terry who was still crouching in the corner.

"I-I don't know. They're built so you can't get stuck inside."

The door pushed open a crack then slammed shut again as Jake shouldered all of his weight into it. A dry and rattling yell echoed from within.

He began to panic as the door shoved back out again, his feet giving way a little on the floor.

"We've got to block it with something," he yelled.

Terry sprung out of the corner in a flash. She stood there, chest heaving. Terry looked around. Jake did the same. Everything large in the kitchen was too heavy to move.

The door pushed out a little more and Jake let up for a second then slammed his body hard against the metal. His whole side screamed out in pain, but there was a little click as the latch slipped back into place. Still bracing the door, he slid one hand down to it.

There was a hole that overlapped a catch.

"Do you have a lock or a screwdriver?" he asked.

Terry didn't reply but ran off instead. He heard clanging a few feet away. She was back in a flash with an ice pick in hand.

Jake snatched it and slid the pick down into the hole. Not sure if it would hold, he let go of the door reluctantly. The ice pick bent a little and wobbled as the thundering blows continued inside.

He grabbed Terry's hand and began running with her to the front of the diner. They made their way past the counter and stopped by the door. A single coat hung on the rack next to it, and he pulled it so hard that the little brass hooks popped loose from the drywall. Wrapping it around Terry he zipped it tight then hugged her close. She was trembling hard. He didn't know if it was fear or the cold, but suspected it was both.

Jake bent down and kissed her forehead. The shaking eased up a little. She looked up at him, her eyes moist with tears. She started to say something but he put a finger over her lips. Then he did something he hadn't done in weeks. He smiled.

2

The first thought that crossed Colin's mind was that he was blind. The second was that every bone in his body must be broken.

He rolled onto his back as the snow beat down on him and soaked into his clothes. He blinked and for a moment caught a glimpse of the raging whiteness that surrounded him. He wasn't blind but his eyes were filled and gummy. In an effort that seemed almost impossible he brought both hands to his face and rubbed. When he pulled them away they were red. He was bleeding, and badly.

Colin tried to roll back over and get to his knees. Every limb screamed in protest but they all still seemed to work. Nothing broken either.

Somewhere in the drifts behind him the truck sat cold and dead. It was impossible to see how far he'd been thrown when it crashed. And what did he hit? As much as he tried to shove the image from his mind, he could still see the car and for a brief second the faces inside, screaming.

Some small part of him said crawl back there, but the voice went unheeded. Instead he pulled himself forward, slowly, on his hands and knees. Palms and fingers began to go numb as they sunk deep into the snow. Everything hurt so bad that he wanted to stop and give up, just roll over and hope that he froze quickly. He didn't, though.

After what seemed an eternity, the pad of one hand scraped hard against concrete. It tore the flesh but he was too cold to notice.

The concrete was part of the curb. He'd reached the sidewalk. Even slower now, he pulled his body forward knowing that any second he would feel the rough wet bricks of a storefront.

Through the terrible howl of the wind he could hear the crunching of footsteps next to him. Colin stopped his progression and looked to his right. There was a man looming up over him.

In the very instant that the figure seemed ready to pounce another shape flew out of the maelstrom slamming into the man. Colin could just make out two people now beating each other on the sidewalk only feet from where he lay. Now that he'd stopped moving it seemed all the more impossible to start again but he didn't want to wait for the victor to come after him.

Pulling himself along a couple feet at a time he realized that he'd never escape. Behind him there was a loud smack that reminded him of bone breaking, then a wet choking cough.

He had only crawled another foot when the crunching sounds came back. This time there seemed to be more and they were coming much faster. His arms gave out and he fell to his stomach with a force that shoved the air right out of his lungs.

Two sets of feet appeared next to his head. Groaning he rolled to his side and through the blood-snow film over his eyes he could see another man looming over him. This one was dressed differently, though. And there was a woman with him.

"Christ, it's Colin Green," the woman said. "Do you think he's okay or is he changed?"

The giant bent over him and two strong hands pulled him off the ground and set him against a wall.

"I wouldn't say he's okay, but he's not one of those," the giant replied.

There was something familiar about them. The girl, he knew her but with the cold freezing the marrow in his bones and blood pouring out of his head everything seemed distant and vague.

They were saying something else but he couldn't understand. Suddenly his stomach lurched and did a little back flip as he felt himself go upside-down in the air. He was being carried. He only hoped it was to someplace warm. Behind him the sidewalk receded upside down. He could just make out the shapes of two bodies lying there in a dark patch that crept out, engulfing more and more of the white as he watched.

3

"What the hell was that?"

Rudy was the first to speak but Nick and the other four by the General Store window were all thinking the same thing.

The sound, and Rudy's comment, forced Nick into the real world again. Ever since hanging up with Ramp he'd been far away and obsessing. *Where were they? Was everything all right? What was taking so long?* It took every ounce of restraint to not head off out of the store, running for Cauffield.

Whatever was going on outside had sounded like thunder. There was a great crash followed by other sounds he couldn't make out. He'd heard it all, but his head had been so far away that none of it really registered until Rudy spoke up. Now he pressed his face to the window with the others and cupped his hands around his eyes to block out the light of the store.

"I think there's a light out there," Rudy said. "See it? Over there in front of the video rental."

Nick strained his eyes and then in one of the quieter seconds of the storm, he *did* see it. There was a single beam, strong, cutting through the whiteness. It almost reminded him of a headlight. Maybe a motorcycle?

Nick felt his heart stop dead in his chest. The sound, and the headlight.

"Oh shit."

Rudy and the others had turned toward him now. His skin had gone as white as the world outside.

"We've got to get out there," he said. "Emily wait here."

Nick took off down one of the aisles running like mad. His hands flew over the shelves and pulled down a flashlight, then some batteries. Once he got the light loaded and working he bolted for the door. Without ever taking a look back he was gone deep into the maelstrom once more.

"Christ, slow down. I can barely see you." Rudy was yelling from behind him.

Somewhere beneath the panic there was a glimmer of joy at knowing that he wouldn't have to do this alone.

Nick had to stop for a moment to get his bearings. Rudy came up beside him. There was another small break in the driving wind and for a second the headlight shone out like a beacon. They were off again.

The station wagon was lying on its roof. Nearby a smashed up truck still sat on all fours. Both Rudy and Nick stopped dead in their tracks for a moment when they came upon the twisted masses of metal. It was like turning a corner and stepping out face to face with some childhood monster. But this was worse. This was so much worse. And it was real.

Rudy was the first to break the stalemate and practically dove at the crunched-in windows. Nick was fast behind. At first he thought Rudy was talking to someone in the car but as he, too, got down on his knees he realized that the man was reciting drinks. Measure for measure.

Already the snow had piled up around the windows. Nick thrust an arm into it and drew back, screaming. A large jagged piece of glass had sliced him from wrist to elbow. Ignoring the pain and the queasy feeling in his stomach, he pulled more and more snow out of the hole where the window had been.

It was Ramp whom he finally saw twisted and wedged up in there upside-down. His eyes were closed and his face was bloody. Nick reached in and grabbed the last few pieces of glass that stuck up out of the frame like wicked teeth. He snapped them off with his fingers, then took hold of Ramp by the shirt.

The man was heavy and all at once, adrenaline or not, he realized there was no way in hell he could pull him out by himself.

"Rudy! Rudy! I need some help."

Rudy didn't answer so he got up and crawled to the other side of the car. Rudy had already pulled Mabel out from one window, her body stretched out on the snow battered and lifeless, eyes staring into the terrible sky. Now Rudy was struggling with another body and Nick wanted to look away. In that second it was more than he could take. He shut down and dropped to his knees. Tears sprang to the corners of his eyes and seemed to freeze there. The queasy feeling was stronger now, so strong that he leaned over and heaved into the snow.

Suddenly there was a cry of pain next to him, but the cry wasn't Rudy's.

"Nick! For fuck's sake, give me a hand. She's stuck. Her foot is caught on something."

Rebecca was screaming now, her back arching up away from the snow. Nick threw himself into the window Mable had come out of and tried to see what Rebecca was hung up on. Her foot was bent back at an unnatural angle and stuck between the door and the seat. He immediately reached out and tried to pull it loose as she continued to cry out in pain. He was so focused on getting the foot out that he had never even noticed the leg until finally getting her out of her shoe.

A bone was sticking out through her calf, broken and splintered. He only had a second to register it before it went flying past him and out the remains of the window.

One of the hardest things he'd ever done was leave her howling there on the snow. If it hadn't been for Ramp though, and the dead body of Mabel, he never would've been able to do it. The fact of the matter was that Rebecca was alive, Mabel wasn't, and they wouldn't know about Ramp unless he and Rudy worked together to fish him out.

When they did finally pull the old man from the wreckage, both feared the worst. But then his eyes twitched and his mouth moved slowly.

"Run back and bring the others to help us get them into the store," Nick yelled.

Rudy was off and he crawled back to where Rebecca lay sobbing. He cradled her head in his lap and tried to keep the snow from falling into her eyes.

"We're going to be alright. We'll get through this, I promise," he said, stroking her blood-wet hair.

4

When Rudy returned with the others in tow Nick saw with great relief that Tracy and Emily weren't with them. Rebecca's cries of pain had settled into a delirious murmur as they began get hold of the bodies and carry them away.

Regina White and the other woman were struggling with the lifeless Mabel Rampart, while Rudy and Nick tried to figure out a way of taking Rebecca without hurting her even more. They had managed to lift her into the air without too much protest when two forms came toward them out of the snow. Nick saw Rudy's eyes go wide and for a second feared that he would let go and send Rebecca crashing to the ground. Rudy held firm though.

Nick turned his head just as Jake and Terry came hustling toward him. Jake had someone draped over his shoulder.

Terry let out a gasp as she finally took in the scene.

"What happened?" she yelled over the din of the storm. Jake had set down the body he'd been carrying and rushed over to help. Regina White and the other woman were back now, too.

"We've got her, I think," Nick yelled. "See if you can get Ramp inside now."

Colin Green had managed to pull himself up off the ground during the commotion. As soon as he saw the others he had begun trying to get to his feet.

Jake, Terry, and Regina all strained together, finally getting Ramp off the ground. Slowly the procession started toward the General Store. Colin brought up the lead moving faster now but limping badly.

When they had gotten back inside the store Nick's ears hurt from the stinging cold and everything seemed to be ringing. Emily was bawling and Tracy had the girl hugged tight against her.

Carefully, they set Ramp and Rebecca on the ground. Rebecca let out a single sharp yell as her leg settled into place.

"Mommy!" Emily screamed and tore from Tracy's grip. She rushed over to her mother's side and knelt down, big sloppy tears spilling onto the floor.

Ramp was still unconscious. Colin Green had slid up against the wall, half-sitting, half-falling over.

Between all of the injured, the floor of the General Store had turned slick and red. The whole scene looked even more garish under the glow of the florescent lights.

"Somebody call an ambulance," Nick yelled.

"Won't do any good," Colin started. "Road to Devon's out of

service. The trees are down."

Everyone stared at him silently for a moment. This meant more than just not getting to the hospital. This meant they might very well be trapped.

Nick had started to tell them to call anyways for Christ's sake, when Regina White spoke up. "Wait a minute," she said. "We're missing one."

In all of the commotion no one had even noticed that the other woman had never come back inside. Her shopping cart was still parked by the front window with all of its groceries.

Jake and Rudy were already making for the door. Terry grabbed Jake by the arm and tried to hold him back.

"Jake, you can't go back out there," she cried.

"I have to," was all he said.

Rudy followed him out, but Nick remained behind trying to cradle his wife's head and soothe his daughter at the same time.

Now it was Regina who was losing her cool.

"What is all this? What's going on? There's something more than a car wreck here. What is it?"

No one said a word.

"Goddamn it, I want to know! What is going on here?"

Terry turned away from the store window and looked at her.

"Look," Terry said. "Hysterics aren't going to help any of us here. I don't know what's going on but there's something out there more dangerous than this storm, okay?"

Regina had quieted and now studied the faces on everyone else for confirmation.

"But Pete," she said softly.

Nick watched Regina for a moment and began to feel uneasy. He didn't like the look in her eyes. It was a look that said reason was going, and going fast.

Then it was gone.

"Terry, stop her!"

It was already too late. Regina was out the door, the little electronic chime ringing stupidly behind her. Terry reached for the handle but Nick called her back.

"Rudy and Jake will catch her," he said.

It was at least five minutes before the two men came bounding back into the store.

"We couldn't find her," Jake said.

"What about Regina?" Terry asked.

"What do you mean what about Regina?" Rudy asked back.

"She ran out not a minute after you guys."

"Christ almighty!" Rudy stamped his foot.

Jake had moved over to the door now and flipped the little lock in place.

"No one is going back out there unless we all go together," he said. "It isn't safe to keep splitting up like this."

Rebecca moaned as Nick rested her head back on the floor. He stood and addressed the others.

"Look, I'm going to call for help. Even if the roads are down maybe they can send a helicopter or something."

"Whirly birds won't fly in weather like this," Colin said with a cracked grin.

Nick wanted to run over there and throttle him but he didn't.

"I don't really fucking care," he said. "At least someone will know we're in trouble."

He had started off toward the office without waiting for a response. He felt like getting sick again as he passed by the body of Mabel Rampart and then old Ramp himself. Ramp was still alive, and the cut on his head didn't look all that bad, but the man was out cold. Walking past Mabel, Nick had wondered if maybe it would truly be better if he never did wake up.

He'd gotten just about half-way to the office when the fluorescents overhead dimmed a little. There was a whirring noise as the fans in the produce cooler ground down, and suddenly they were plunged into darkness.

From the front of the store he could hear startled cries. One of those might have even been his own for all he knew. Nick realized then that he had left the flashlight either out in the snow or in front of the store. It didn't matter. The office should be in almost a straight line from him.

5

When the lights went out, Jake held his guard against the front door. After a few startled cries the room had grown silent. It almost seemed like he could feel everyone's hearts sink with the lights. There was a shuffling in the blackness next to him and the soft tread of Terry's fingers brushed against his sleeve. She didn't speak a word, just held on tight.

From off in the store came the sound of footsteps returning. There was a crash as Nick bumped into something, swore, then pressed on. Jake still couldn't see him but the sound of his feet had stopped across the room.

"The phones are dead," he said.

Terry's grip on his arm tightened a bit but still no one spoke a word. Now they truly were trapped, completely cut off from the rest of the world. There was a chance that Crosscreek would still be passable on the way out to Bedford Falls but he didn't hold high hopes of it. In fact, it seemed almost a certainty that the trees would be down there as well. He supposed they would have to take the chance eventually but for now their situation wouldn't allow it.

"Tracy," he called into the darkness.

For a second the girl said nothing, then a small and trembling voice answered.

"Yes?"

"You know this store better than anyone else. Do you think you can find some candles?"

She was quiet again and he could almost see the dread she felt for going off alone even if it was only deeper into the store.

"Mrs. White bought a whole bunch," she said finally. Her

voice seemed to pick up a bit. "Her cart is still up here, by the window."

His eyes had begun to adjust a little now and as he moved forward he saw that Nick did the same. Together the two of them fished through the three shopping carts in front of the store. There was a little flicker of light as Nick struck his lighter and soon the pale glow of a candle spread over the room.

Jake now found what he was looking for and lit a couple more. Soon they had candles burning on top of everything and the gruesome display all around them came back into focus.

Nick was standing over Rebecca again. Emily was crouched next to her mother, shaking and sniffling. Jake took a candle and went over to check her out.

A dark pool of blood had spilled out around the wound in Rebecca Anderson's leg. By candlelight it looked thick and black.

"We've got to do something about this or she'll bleed to death," he said.

Nick was staring down at him with wide eyes as the full import of what had just been said began to sink in.

"Take Tracy and the two of you find something to bandage her up with. I'll take care of the bone."

Nick blinked twice rapidly and his mouth hung open a little, then he turned and took Tracy by the arm leading her off into the aisles.

Rebecca's leg was in bad shape. There was no way of getting the bone back in without causing her considerable pain. He looked up at her face and was shocked to see her staring at him with big eyes. The fevered and delirious look was gone now and in its place was a look of comprehension. Her hand slid over the top of his and she gave it a weak squeeze, then she closed her eyes and nodded.

Jake took a deep breath and clenched his teeth as his hands moved into position. As quickly as he could, he grabbed her leg like a vice and forced.

The scream was terrible and once it started Emily took up

the cry, too. They were like a couple of dogs howling at the moon.

The feeling of bone sliding back into its sheath of flesh made his stomach turn. His hands were sticky with her blood.

"Nick!" he yelled.

"Right here."

Nick and Tracy had returned laden with arms full of bandages. Jake grabbed a roll of gauze and quickly began to swathe Rebecca's leg in it. Something clattered to the ground next to him. It was the broken-off handles of a couple of brooms, and a roll of duct tape. He taped the splints into place over the top of the gauze, then began wrapping a thicker Ace bandage over that. When he finished, the whole mess was tightened with a few more passes of the tape.

Rebecca had stopped crying, having passed out from the pain. Emily's chest still rose and fell with great wracking sobs.

Jake stood and wiped his hands on his pants.

"That should work for now," he said to Nick but Nick wasn't looking at him.

Jake Blacktree followed his gaze over to Colin Green against the wall. Colin's eyes were closed again, but Nick wasn't staring at him out of concern. There was a deep set anger and loathing etched into his face. He had apparently made the connection.

Jake reached out a hand and set it on Nick's shoulder. The muscles tensed underneath his palm.

"Leave it," he said.

Nick turned to face him again, eyes wide, then he looked down at Rebecca and his features softened.

"Christ!" Rudy called out behind them. "Come here, Ramp's coming around."

They hurried over to where Rudy and Terry were already kneeling beside the man. Ramp groaned and in the pale golden glow of the candles his eyes flicked open, glassy. The old man shuddered and for a moment seemed as if he were about to bolt upright, but then a painful wheeze rattled out and he fell back to the floor.

"Mabel," he murmured softly. The a little louder, "Mabel."

Nick had taken one of the man's hands inside of his. He opened his mouth to say something but couldn't. Instead he just slowly shook his head. Ramp's eyes pinched shut and he sucked in a quick breath. Wet streams rolled out of the corners of his eyes and cascaded down his cheeks. They mixed with the congealing blood and plinked to the floor in little red splats that made it look as if he were crying blood.

After a minute of this Ramp opened his eyes and spoke again. His voice was tired and empty of the deep boom it used to hold.

"What about Rebecca?" he asked.

"She'll be fine. Her leg's broken but I think she'll be fine," Nick answered. Then he added, "Thank you."

Ramp nodded then slowly tried to struggle up from the ground. Terry tried to hold him in place but he shrugged her off and got into a sitting position. He turned his head to where Mabel lay next to him and his eyes closed again. He sighed deeply, then looked away from the body of his wife.

Jake recognized the change that overtook the old man in the next few seconds. He knew it because it was the same change that had occurred to him after finding Momma gone. Ramp was building a wall between himself and the grief. When the wall finally came down it would be something terrible, but for now he wanted to survive. And maybe Ramp wasn't holding on just for himself either. Maybe he wasn't even doing it for himself at all.

"I think all of us need to talk," Ramp said. A little of the old force had returned to his voice.

Terry and Rudy helped him to his feet, then the five of them moved off closer to the door and away from Mabel Rampart.

"Who else is here?" Ramp asked.

"My daughter, Rebecca, Tracy the cashier, and Colin Green," Nick replied.

At the mention of Colin's name Ramp gave Nick a peculiar look but it faded quickly. Jake almost wasn't sure that he'd seen it at all, but it troubled him nonetheless. He was going to have to keep a careful eye on the two of them, and on Colin. There was bad blood in there waiting like a snake to strike. He only hoped it wouldn't make things worse than they already were.

6

Nick checked on Rebecca and Emily. Both were still sleeping, and both trembled from time to time as they dozed.

"What's happening to everybody?" Tracy asked in a frail sounding voice.

"I don't know," Terry answered. "I really don't know."

Nick took a seat in one of the check-out aisles pushing his back up against the magazines and tabloids that were racked there. The others milled about quietly with little being said between them. Every face he saw seemed to carry the same hazy look of confusion.

Making sure that he kept his eyes on the front windows Nick leaned back his head and tried to make sense of it all. He thought that maybe by putting all of the fragments together he might somehow conjure a story or framework to hold it in. At this point even fiction was better than nothing and events had become so strange that rational, straight-laced thinking might not be able to encompass them.

The problem he found was that there didn't seem to be a common thread connecting any of it. First Tom Parsons had been murdered, then David Turner went missing,. People were hearing strange things and seeing even worse but no one had gotten hurt from their spectral encounters. Then you had the Others, the people who were different now, changed. *But what happened to them?*

He threw his head back and sighed in frustration. There was a commotion up front as everyone moved away from the windows, tripping and falling over each other.

"Shit!" Rudy exclaimed. "What is it?"

Nick was back on his feet in a flash and next to the others in two strides. Even Colin Green had joined in for this.

At first he thought it was an animal roaming around the wind-raked and snow-covered parking lot. If so, then it was wounded for sure. The thing moved quickly, low to the ground, and in short awkward spurts.

"Put out the lights," Jake said in a commanding voice.

"Are you crazy!" Rudy answered.

It was Ramp, though, moving faster than he had in days that put the group back in total blackness. As they stood huddled together waiting for their eyes to adjust everyone shifted instinctively closer together until they had formed a tight brick of themselves.

A hand grabbed onto Nick's elbow making him jump until he realized it was Tracy the cashier. From off to his right he could still hear the shallow and irregular breathing of his wife and daughter. For that he was thankful. There was a sinking feeling in the pit of his stomach that made him think this would be something they didn't need to see.

Outside, what he had first hoped was an animal was beginning to take shape as his vision adapted to the dark.

It was a person. Crawling.

He didn't even need to see anymore after that, his mind filled in the details from Emily's description. In his head the mass of hair that hung down trailing the snow like fingers was a dark and dingy red. The hands that were leaving their prints through the carpet of white would be almost the same color as the snow, but dirty and mottled with thickets of blue veins.

Nick suddenly realized that he was shaking, hard. It wasn't him; it was Tracy with her iron grip on him.

There was a low murmur among the group almost as if

everyone were speaking to themselves. The effect it had was unnerving, like an unintelligible, disembodied voice floating about the room.

"Shit! Shit! Shit!" Rudy said loudly and took a sharp step back that in turn carried the others with him. "She's coming for us!"

Even in the darkness Nick could see as Jake grabbed ahold of the man by his shoulders, keeping him in check. In that split second before Jake had moved, Nick was sure that Rudy was gone. He already had the image of him running out into the storm, screaming stamped in his mind.

She *was* closer, though. Outside in the sea of blowing white, the figure had stopped just far enough away to be indistinct. Nick could feel her staring in at them. It was a feeling of pure anger, hate, and chilling rage that he'd never come close to experiencing before.

From within the throng of bodies there was a stifled sob which seemed amazingly to come from Terry and not the cashier.

They all feel it then.

Suddenly the figure was back in motion and moving for the window so quickly they all jumped back, stepping on each other and smashing into checkout stands.

Just as the woman outside had crawled close enough to *really* be seen, she was gone. Nothing. It had almost seemed to happen in the blink of an eye, but not before Nick had gotten a good look at that face. If he lived through this, that face would still haunt him for the rest of his life. *Those eyes. And that mouth, open in a silent scream.*

There was a great deal of crashing and banging about as the group suddenly broke apart. Everyone was moving now but no one was going anywhere. Beside him Tracy was crying, big wrenching sobs that shook her entire body. Not even realizing what he was doing, Nick put an arm around her and pulled her close. He didn't say anything. He didn't tell her it was going to be all right, because he now believed no such thing.

7

Jake at first tried to disengage himself from the frantic voices and undirected questions of the others in the aftermath of what happened.

Now he'd seen with his own eyes something that made his blood run as cold as the winter snow outside. After that everything fell into place.

He wasn't quite sure how to convey what he felt to the others. Having been raised to accept much more of the unseen world than the modern mind allowed he didn't need to question the existence of spirits or things supernatural. He believed in them with same sense of "real" that others reserved for the likes of gravity, global warming, and cancer.

"Jake, please don't space out on me now," Terry was saying.

He hadn't noticed her at first. He hadn't noticed any of them. The panic and confusion had subsided mostly and now all eyes seemed to be on him. They were waiting, hoping, that he had answers. In the back of his mind he still wished for the opposite to be true.

"Sorry," he said. "I was thinking."

"What was that?" Rudy asked, his voice still trembling.

At first Jake said nothing. Looking at the searching and expectant eyes that met his own, however, he decided to go ahead and try.

"It was a spirit," he replied.

"You mean like a ghost?" Rudy asked.

There was another silence.

"She was one of them, wasn't she?" Nick finally said. "One of the Moss Eaters, the Tal Teh Thule."

Jake nodded and saw the puzzled and curious expressions everyone wore. Everyone except Nick and Ramp. The others remained silent, listening, and hoping that their questions would be answered.

Ramp moved in a bit closer and spoke with a voice that was soft and tired. Had he not been looking right at him, Jake might not have recognized old Ramp as the owner of it.

"Why do you think she's here? What does she want?"

"I think she wants to take back what belongs to her."

"What is that?" Nick asked.

"This land," Jake replied solemnly.

One by one the others began taking seats all around him. Tracy's face was still red and tear-stained but for now she had stopped crying. Colin Green didn't sit but remained close to the others, standing just a little bit back. Farther off behind Colin, Jake could make out two more eyes shining in the cast-off glow of the candles. It was Emily, sitting up, wide eyed and silent.

The questions he'd expected didn't come. Instead, the others kept up with fresh ones as if everyone were already on the same page. Maybe explanations weren't necessary at this point. Understanding yes, but perhaps not all of the details.

"What about the others?" Rudy asked. "I saw Johnny Carter last night and he wasn't a ghost, but he wasn't Johnny anymore either."

"I don't know for sure," Jake said. "Spirits can interact with this world to a small degree. They draw energy from whatever's around them and use that to take shape but they can't act on things the same way we can.

"Momma used to tell me stories of the old spirits in this land, the ones that were here long before man. They have the power to influence and control people. Use them as flesh and blood, eyes, ears, and hands. If the will of a spirit is strong enough, its influence might be great."

"So you think everyone's possessed?" Rudy asked.

"No, not possessed. Influenced. Her will is spreading out like a virus, bending and breaking others to it. They're swept up in her anger and hate, and carried away by it until that's all they can think or feel."

"I don't know," Nick said shaking his head. "It isn't that I don't believe it. I'd buy anything after seeing that, but it seems too, simple don't you think? The single, vengeful spirit idea is fine for a haunted house, but not a whole town. Besides, I've heard children laughing who weren't really there, Ramp saw an old man who just vanished in his dining room, and I'm willing to bet that others have seen or heard stuff that wasn't that thing out there in the snow."

Jake sighed and lowered his head. It was hard trying to explain the things that he took for granted. Harder still was putting all of the pieces before them so they could see it all fit and make sense.

"I truly don't know any more than the rest of you," he began.

"The land is a living breathing thing just as we are. It gives and takes, and it remembers. I believe that in some places the land holds onto things, especially in places where great events have left their stain. This place that we know as Rockwell has had a dark and strange past. I think something has triggered a release of all of that memory.

"There are some places men were never meant to settle. My people call them the Lonely Places. I think that perhaps the Tal Teh Thule were the only ones meant for this land.

"After the Canasak had killed them off they realized the place was sour. It didn't welcome them. Ever since, people have been coming here and trying to claim this land for themselves but all ended up lost or dead. What makes us any different?"

He watched as the group tried to digest what he'd just said. He didn't know if any of it would stick or not. He didn't even know if there were any truth in even a word of it. All he knew was that he believed.

When Terry finally broke the silence he held out hope.

"I'm willing to believe that maybe this place has stored up all of this energy, held on to all of these spirits. And maybe there's an entity seeking revenge, infecting the people of Rockwell until we're all dead and gone.

"If that's true," Terry continued. "Then what are we doing still sitting here, in front of some big damn windows, with nothing to defend ourselves with? If they might come at any time, and might come in force, don't you think this is a pretty bad spot to be?"

"She's right," Ramp said. "At this point I don't even care about the how's or why's. All I know is that unless we do something to protect ourselves we won't last the night. There are people out there who some of us have known our entire lives that would kill us where we stand. Does it really matter why?"

"If we can make it over to the Tavern," Rudy chimed in. "I've got that place sealed up like a fortress. In fact that was where I was heading when the storm stuck me in here. No windows, bricked them up. And of course I've got the door."

"I don't know if we should chance it while it's still dark," Jake replied. "Even if the storm doesn't let up by daybreak we should be able to see a bit better. If we can find anything to use as a weapon we might be able to hold up here just fine until then."

"What if they come before sunup?" Terry asked.

They all fell silent again. On the one hand Jake thought they should just break for the tavern now. First Avenue was just at the end of the block and even weighed down with injuries they could make it in fifteen minutes. But then again, now that the power was out it would be complete and swirling darkness out there. What if they got lost? What if something was waiting?

Regina White and the other woman had never come back. Did they make it someplace safe or did something snatch them up?

All of them were torn. There was no clear-cut choice, too

many variables.

"If we do stay here what the hell are we supposed to defend ourselves with?" Terry asked.

"There's some kitchen knives back in aisle four," Tracy replied.

"What about the hardware store across the street?" Rudy asked. "I know Clark's got all sorts of guns and ammo there in the back. He's even got a bunch of camping gear, too. Maybe we could use a sleeping bag or something for Rebecca, you know, like a stretcher. If we're preparing for the worst, then I say a couple of us go over there and get some provisions. Whoever stays behind can load up with food and stuff and then we can go over and hold up in the tavern."

"He's got a point," Nick said. "We don't know what we're up against or how long the storm might last. If we prepare ourselves for a long haul then we can wait out the weather someplace safe. I'd rather face this town when I can actually see it again."

"Well, who's going to go across the street?" Ramp asked. "I'm afraid I won't be much good out there."

"I'll do it," Jake said.

"I will, too."

Nick jumped as Colin spoke from right behind him.

When all had finally agreed that only Colin and Jake would be leaving, they set about making preparations for the expedition.

Terry and Tracy went off in search of the kitchen knives, while Nick and Rudy loaded up several flashlights.

Soon the two men were bundled up and overburdened, standing by the door.

Nick clapped a hand on Jake's shoulder and told him to be careful. Terry, who was holding one of Jake's hands, stood on her toes and kissed him. Then quietly so Colin wouldn't hear she said, "Watch your back, Jake. I don't trust him."

Jake simply nodded.

Now the two stood shoulder to shoulder in front of the door, looking like patchwork soldiers, all pieced together and ill equipped, wearing everyone else's warmest clothes.

Jake undid the latch and opened the door. The wind took it and tore it from his grasp. Snow flew in all around, and a gust of wind tried to shove them back.

"Wait a second," Ramp said. "I almost forgot."

From his coat pocket he produced a ball of twine.

"It isn't great, but it might do. I'll make sure one end stays tied to the door here," he said.

Ramp fastened the loose end of the twine to the metal rung on the door, then handed the ball over to Jake.

CHAPTER SEVEN

Colin was swearing to himself only seconds after they were out the door. As the cold bit into his face he stopped and thought of turning back. He looked around behind him but the ghost-like faces pressed against the glass changed his mind.

When he looked away Jake was already disappearing into the gale.

"Goddamn it! Slow down, you son of a bitch!" he yelled.

He took another step forward and felt the twine pulled taut against his coat. With one hand he grasped it and followed along until he came up next to Jake.

"I'm a little fucking beat up, you know," he muttered at the tall shade of the Indian.

Jake took off again but slower. Colin trailed along. From somewhere to their right a peal of childish laughter broke out. They stopped dead in their tracks. Colin spun around with his knife held out at arm's length. The laughter came at them quickly now and Jake too brandished his blade.

All at once it seemed to rush past them with a blast of air. He didn't see anything, only heard the girlish giggles pass on.

Jake said something about restless spirits and began to press forward again. This time Colin made sure he kept right at his side.

They reached the other side of the street quickly and had the good fortune that their blind path through the snow put them right in front of the hardware store.

Jake took the flashlight in his hand and brought it down hard across the glass storefront. For a second the beam reflected off of thousands of tiny pieces of glass as it completed its arc, then it went out. Jake pulled another one out of his jacket then began clearing away the slivers that were still sticking out of the frame.

They entered slowly each with their knives firmly in hand.

"I'll go grab the guns from in back," Jake said. "See if you can find anything else we could use, sleeping bags, lanterns, anything."

Then he was gone.

Colin stood there for a minute feeling a little pissed. Why the fuck did he have to go crawling around the store by himself looking for shit? Jake had it easy. All of the guns and ammunition were displayed across the back wall. Everyone knew that. He'd been back there and admired the pieces countless times. Where in the hell was he supposed to find *useful* stuff? And what the fuck did that mean anyways?

He began going aisle by aisle and was lucky enough to stumble across a couple of sleeping bags first. He unrolled one of them, still zipped up, and began throwing in everything else he could find like it was a great big gunny sack.

By the time Jake made it back with two bags of his own, he had thrown in a couple lanterns, some hammers, a single burner Coleman stove, and a myriad of other shit just to cover bases. Now the sleeping bag trailed behind him like a giant, green, overstuffed caterpillar. A damn heavy one, too.

Jake went out the window first and Colin handed him the bulging gym bags one by one. The barrels of what looked like five or six shotguns poked through the zippers of each. Jake took one of the guns out, pumped it once, then slung the bag over his shoulder.

Colin had gotten out the window now and was struggling to pull the big green worm out behind him. When he finally got it through, the sleeping bag crashed to the ground and something shattered inside. *Fucking lanterns.*

The progress back to the General Store was slower because

of their new burdens, but at least they were sure of the way. Jake had tied the roll of twine to one of the shelves in the hardware store and now it stretched out tight across the road.

Colin had to lean forward at a ridiculous angle just to keep the bag moving through the deep drifts of snow. Up ahead of him Jake seemed to be making better speed. He thought about yelling at him again but decided it was a waste of breath.

A low throaty growl startled him just then and his fingers let go of their cargo. He spun around but not fast enough. Something came bounding out of the blackness and hit him so hard that he flew back off of his feet. Instinctively he threw his hands up to block his face, and whatever was on him sunk its teeth deep into his arm. Colin screamed. He managed to get a knee up between himself and his attacker as he heard Jake's footsteps come thundering toward him. Steely fingers made their way under his jacket and then punched hard into his chest. He felt the wind go out as the fingers pushed through his skin and into the meat of him like talons.

Now he couldn't scream and all at once it didn't seem to matter because he was going to die.

There was a deafening roar and a flash of light from the muzzle as Jake's shotgun went off. The thing on top of Colin flew off shrieking, an all too human wail. Besides the burning in his chest he also felt some of the buckshot bury itself into his shoulder.

He was still struggling for breath and suddenly it came to him, filling his lungs so fast they felt as if they might burst. That first lungful seemed funny and acrid somehow. There was an odor of rot that stung his nose, and the taste of something like dirt or bark in his mouth. He suddenly felt light-headed as Jake ran over and knelt next to him.

"Are you okay?" he asked.

"You fucking shot me!" Colin screamed at him.

"Let me see."

Jake looked at the nasty chunk taken out of his arm, then at his shoulder where a tiny bit of shot *had* peppered him.

"It isn't that bad," Jake said. "It'll smart a lot less than being eaten. Let's get back and we can patch you up."

As Jake helped him to his feet, Colin didn't mention the hole in his chest. Already there seemed to be a warmth spreading from it but not from blood. This was another kind of warmth, one that made the pain go away.

He grabbed his bag again and started back off after Jake. Now as the wind whipped around his head it sounded different. It sounded like voices, whispers too quiet to understand, but in time he knew he would.

2

Had Rudy and Nick not restrained her, Terry would have been out the door as soon as the gunshot echoed back. She had fought and turned on them with a fury that was not at all like her.

"Let me go, you bastards," she had screamed.

The hands that held her wouldn't relent and as quickly as the burst had come it blew itself out, too. She had gone a little limp then and was actually thankful for the hands still holding her.

The only thing she could think of was Jake. Something was happening out there and it wasn't good.

When the two men *did* finally come bounding back through the General Store door, Terry felt a new rush of energy. She ran up in a flash, fingers digging and clutching at Jake's jacket.

"What happened out there? Are you okay? Let me see."

Jake set both of his bags on the ground and held her back from him a little.

"I'm fine," he said. "Something attacked Colin. I shot it, but I don't think I killed it."

"Maybe if your fucking aim was a little better you would

have," Colin sneered.

Terry glanced at Colin and saw the spray of blood on his coat, but she still couldn't hide her look of revulsion. He was a little creep and something about him made the hairs on her arms stand tall.

Nick, Rudy, and Ramp had all circled around her now and were talking excitedly. The men were cataloguing the plunder and all seemed quite pleased.

Colin let his sleeping bag of goodies clank to the floor and headed off in the direction of the restrooms in back.

"Was it one of those *things*?" Terry asked Jake. "Whatever it was that attacked him?"

Jake nodded.

"I couldn't get a good look, but it was definitely human. Or at least it used to be."

"If it was waiting out there, don't you think there might be more?" Nick asked.

"I don't know. If it was waiting, then why didn't it attack until we were headed back, and armed?"

"Maybe it isn't such a good idea to head out just yet," Nick said. "I mean, if there was one, there might be more. We'd be sitting ducks out there."

"Well, boys, we're back at it again," Terry said "What's it going to be, sitting ducks out there, or fish in a barrel here?"

She had meant it to be a little funny but as the old arguments came back fresh to mind, no one seemed filled with much mirth. The reality of it was that the situation was bad either way. They had all drawn straws and the whole lot of them, it seemed, had ended up with the short one.

Either course of action was a gamble. On one hand nothing might happen on the way to the tavern and they would be locked away safe inside. On the other hand nothing might happen at the store and they wouldn't have to take the risk of another trek outside.

"We've gathered provisions already, I think we should stick

with the plan. If something's out there and it wants to get us, then being cooped up in here isn't any safer than walking out there," Rudy said.

Terry looked at the others and nodded firmly. Slowly, one by one, the others did the same. It was a silent assent that passed between the group. Unity. They were in agreement, and they were getting ready to move on.

3

Nick felt the wave of conflicting emotions and doubt come back as he knelt over the slumbering form of his wife. A choice had been made and it was all or none, he only wondered if it was the right choice. Rebecca and Emily were the two things most dear to him and his protective instinct was stronger now than ever.

The store might not be safe forever but it *was* safe for now, and the deserted wind-blown streets of Rockwell had already proven to be otherwise. If it had been only himself whom he had to worry about, the course of action would be clear as day; he would go with the others and fight if he must. But it wasn't that simple. He had to look after them, *and* look after himself. If he didn't make it alive, what would become of Rebecca and Emily?

Nick started as a hand fell on his shoulder. He looked up and saw Jake Blacktree standing beside him, his eyes gleaming dark like coals in the flickering glow. Those eyes almost seemed like they could see inside him, could read his very thoughts.

"Everything will be okay, I promise," Jake said.

"You can't promise something like that."

"No, you're right. I can promise that as long as I'm still drawing breath I'll make sure that no harm comes to your family."

Jake Blacktree was strong, noble, and resourceful and he couldn't think of another man he could ever have faith in as much as him.

"We should get her loaded up," Jake said, pointing at Rebecca.

As the two men unrolled the spare sleeping bag, Terry and Ramp were busy locking Mabel's body in the General Store office. They would be burdened enough as it was without another body to carry along.

A little farther away, Rudy and Tracy were packing away the last of the provisions and off in the corner Colin Green was loading the guns.

As carefully as they could, Nick and Jake moved Rebecca onto the makeshift stretcher. She didn't wake up and the only sound that escaped her lips was a dull groan. Nick wasn't sure if this was a good sign or not. Deep down his instinct raised its alarms.

He still hadn't decided what to do with Emily. If he carried her it would leave him unarmed and the group would have one less gun to its battery, but if she walked their pace might be slowed and *she* would be more vulnerable.

Terry and Ramp had come back from the office. Nick could see how tired and old Ramp suddenly looked. It was if the man had aged twenty years in just one night. He realized then that for some of them, living through this ordeal meant getting spit out on the other side with a life that might not be worth living. Even *he* wasn't exempt from this fate yet.

As the group made their final preparations to go, it was decided that Jake would lead and Colin would bring up the rear. Rudy and Nick would carry Rebecca, while Ramp, Terry, and Tracy would walk on all sides of Emily.

Emily was standing in front with the others but she had a vague and faraway look on her face that went deeper than having just been roused from sleep.

Everyone was armed and with the exception of Rudy and

Nick, all were laden with cargo. *His* cargo was bundled tightly in the sprawled out sleeping bag. Two shotguns rested, one on either side of Rebecca's body.

The group checked their gear one more time. Jake opened the front door and the fury of the wind rushed at them screaming. Nick and Rudy each lifted their ends of the sleeping bag and seconds later the entire caravan was out in the cold.

4

As the procession started off down Main, it wasn't the driving wind or the biting cold that bothered Tracy. It wasn't even the fear of what might be lurking in it or how her parents were doing that occupied her thoughts. It was the gun in her hand.

She'd never held a gun before in her entire life; in fact, she couldn't recall having even seen one up close. She didn't like it, not one bit.

The cold and heavy piece of metal in her hand smelled greasy like oil and somehow just the size and heft of it almost seemed obscene.

They had barely gone ten feet before her arms began to shake a little and weaken. She tried hard to keep the barrel from dipping into the snow stacked by her feet but it wasn't easy. The whole endeavor took so much of her focus that she barely noticed where they were going.

Even more than the revulsion she felt for the weapon at hand was the thought of actually having to use it. She didn't know if she'd even be able to raise it up when the time came to fire it and if she somehow managed past that obstacle there was still another. Would she be able to pull the trigger?

She didn't know.

The gun had dipped into the blanket of white while she

thought. It dug a little trench that stretched out behind her. She watched it for a moment then lifted the gun higher and turned around to catch a glimpse of the little path.

Behind her the dark shape of Colin Green was following. She faced forward quickly but could still feel his eyes burning into the back of her head. Now she shivered, only it had nothing to do with the cold. She didn't like him at all. She didn't like the way he looked at her, or the way her skin crawled whenever he was near.

As much as she hated to admit it she hoped that something *would* come along, if only to snatch up Colin Green.

Tracy was so caught up in her own thoughts that she hadn't noticed the group come to a halt until she had walked right smack into the back of Nick Anderson. The gun slipped from her fingers and dropped to the ground with a soft thud.

From beside her there was a sharp gasp from Terry. They had made it all the way to the corner of First and Main she saw. The sign had been missing there for months but even in the darkness she still knew her town.

The tavern was close, really close, so why weren't they moving? In front of her Rudy and Nick were setting the sleeping bag on the ground and picking the guns up off the tarp. As they bent down to retrieve their weapons Tracy got a glimpse of the street ahead.

There were two shadowy figures crouching on the sidewalk before them. She thought that one of them made a hissing sound but it might have been the wind.

For a second it reminded her of one of those standoffs in the westerns her Dad liked to watch. No one on either side moved a muscle. Then there was a terrible yell that cut through the night as one of the shapes got up and sprinted for them.

In the next instant there was a whirlwind of activity. Jake leveled the barrel of his gun at the thing that was closing fast on them. She saw almost in slow motion as his finger pulled back on the trigger. Nothing happened. The attacker flew through the air now aiming right for him. Rudy's gun went off with a deafening roar and a blast of light but went wide and missed.

The bright flash from the muzzle revealed something glinting like steel in Jake's hand. His gun was now lying in the snow but he spun a half-turn with one arm outstretched, whistling through the air.

Just as the thing was about to slam into Jake it seemed to go a little crooked in the air. He managed to sidestep it and the body came smashing down into the snow next to him. She saw with wide-eyed horror that it no longer had a head.

The other thing had taken off for them during the first melee, and Jake was yelling for the rest of them to make a break for the bar as he moved up to intercept.

Nick and Rudy had picked up Rebecca again and were trying to hurry away from the new assailant. Tracy stood rooted to the ground as Ramp and Emily rushed past her.

Now there was another blast but this time it was from Terry's gun. The recoil of it knocked her off-balance and she dropped into the snow as the thing that looked like a person and sounded like an animal connected with Jake and pulled him down. The two fell flat on the headless corpse and the machete Jake had been holding slipped from his grasp.

Tracy finally found her feet again and took off after the others leaving Terry, Jake, and Colin behind. She was almost to the bank vault door when she realized that her own gun was back there as well.

5

Colin had seen Regina White and Myra Ellington crouching in front of the tavern long before the others did. His eyes were getting sharper by the minute and the darkness held fewer surprises now. *He,* however, still had a few. Even if he hadn't seen the two women he would have smelled them. His nostrils seemed to pick up a little bit of everything around him. There was the cashier girl's shampoo, Terry's sweet syrupy flavor, something old and dry coming off Ramp. There was also the smell of fear. His nose pricked to it and the scent made him feel good inside

Even better than fear was the smell of hurt, pain and the rich coppery scent of blood. It ignited a feeling in him that he was only just beginning to understand.

The whisper voice of the wind was louder now in his ears and so were the heartbeats of his companions. When the group stopped, all of them started pounding faster as if he were in the center of a drum circle. Well, almost all of them. Jake Blacktree still seemed calm, cool, and collected. *We'll just see for how long, Blackie Boy,* he thought.

When the gun he had given to Jake didn't fire a wicked grin spread over his thin lips, pulling them even tighter.

He hadn't counted on the blade, however. That had taken him by surprise.

As his night-bright eyes watched Regina White's head fly off her body and roll into the snow, Colin realized he might have to rethink his strategy.

A glimmer of awe and admiration actually passed over him as he watched the big Indian move. The guy was quick as a cat.

Terry fired off a shot next to Colin and the stench of gunpowder stung his overly sensitive nose, bringing tears to his eyes. There was a small bit of satisfaction though as she dropped to the ground with a cry.

Now it looked like the others had made it to the safety of the tavern. Jake was trying to fight off the strong arms and snapping jaws of the former Myra Ellington, and Terry crawled around blindly, searching for her gun.

With a slow and deliberate stride Colin approached the two wrestling on the ground. Jake wasn't faring so well in the hand-to-hand combat it seemed. Myra didn't notice as Colin lowered the shotgun even with her head. He watched for a minute and then listened. Jake's heartbeat was up now.

Colin adjusted his aim so that some of the spread would hit Jake, too. But just a little.

"Say goodnight, you fat bitch," he said grinning.

He pulled the trigger and fire leapt from the barrel. Myra's head exploded in a spray of pulpy matter. From the stump of her neck a thick, dark, half-dead blood pumped out onto Jake. A little of the shot *had* torn into the man's shoulder, eliciting a brief cry of pain. The big bastard might be bad, but not bulletproof.

"I guess that makes us even steven," Colin said then headed for the bar.

Behind him he could hear Terry struggling to get the bloated corpse off of Jake and help him to his feet.

Colin whistled a little tune to himself as he walked through the door to the Rockwell Tavern. His time was coming. He would wait for it patiently.

6

As soon as Terry and Jake were safe inside, Rudy spun the great big wheel on the back of the door muttering under his breath as he did so.

"Dixie Dew, two ounces bourbon, teaspoon crème de menthe, teaspoon triple sec."

As the heavy steel pins clanked into place he finally let loose the breath he'd been saving away. From the inside, the Rockwell Tavern locked up tighter than a nun on Easter, a fact which he had known but never had the occasion to test until now. The outside lock, the one which he engaged every night before going home, was just a regular deadbolt he'd installed for ease of use. From the inside though the big metal guts of the beast could really go to work.

Despite all of the crazy shit going on he finally felt himself ease up a bit, like a king safe in his own castle. Nothing was getting in unless he wanted it to and *that* you could take to the bank.

Jake moved to a booth back over by the wall with Terry clinging to him like she was trying to hold up a tower.

"Christ man, are you alright?" Rudy asked.

"Fine. Just got to catch my breath," he said and plunked onto the vinyl seat.

From across the room there was a rustling in the darkness and the light chiming sound of broken glass. Ramp's voice boomed in the darkness.

"Two of them are broken but I think this one feels okay."

Then the whole place emerged in an orange glow as one of the gas lanterns flamed to life. Ramp moved the light over to the bar making the shadows dance around the room like thick, black phantoms. For a second Rudy's head swam and his stomach did a little flip, then the brightness settled into place and everything was still again.

Nick was over where they had lain Rebecca down and was bundling Emily in his coat. Even with more layers than anyone else the girl still shivered. There was something about the look on her that seemed out of place. She didn't have that dumb, shell-shocked, look of fear. No, her expression reminded Rudy more of the way kids get when they've been caught doing something bad, it was guilty, even sorry.

Tracy on the other hand *did* have the appearance of a kid who'd just been through hell and back. She sat cross-legged only a few feet from Emily and maybe that was why he noticed it. There was a deep contrast between the two and judging by faces alone you would have pegged Emily for the older.

Rudy checked the door one more time then went along the wall where his window had been and pressed against the bricks feeling for any signs of give. There were none.

With that done, everything seemed to be in perfect order. Everything except- He looked around the bar quickly and didn't see him. *Where the hell was Colin Green?* He had opened his mouth to ask that same question out loud when a hint of movement far off in the corner caught his eye.

Colin was sitting in the farthest, blackest corner of the room. Only the toe of one of his boots made it into the circle of lamplight. Rudy looked away quickly not wanting to stare, but in that moment he was sure that he could feel Colin's eyes digging into him. Digging yes. That wasn't the worst part, though. Even hidden away behind his veil of shadow, Rudy had been certain that Colin was smiling.

7

Nick had been a little more than surprised at how well Emily was holding up. Things had been worse earlier for sure, only now the girl seemed to have settled into a sort of complacency. He wondered if this were a good sign or not. Good or bad, for the moment it was what it was.

When he had finally reassured himself that she'd be fine on her own, Nick crawled off the floor and stretched his stiff legs. Rudy was standing behind the long stretch of lacquered wood bartop and Ramp was sitting on one of the stools on the other side. The scene struck him as funny. Just another regular night in Rockwell with the good old boys at the bar. He realized then that Rudy was probably in the place he was most familiar and comfortable with. After all, how much time does the barkeep really spend on the other side of the log?

Nick walked over and stood next to Ramp. As soon as that huge vault door had sealed them in, the nervous checking over your shoulder feeling began to drain away. Now it was a bit of fatigue that he finally felt swimming in his eyes and head.

Fatigue, and a dull aching throb that asserted itself in his temples and ran hidden along his scalp. He hadn't had a smoke in ages, it seemed, and the tell tale signs were screaming *it's time!*

"Is there someplace I can light up?" he asked Rudy.

"Hell, man, this ain't the Ritz."

Rudy produced an ashtray from under the bar and set it in front of him. Nick had scarcely pulled the pack of Luckies from his pocket before Jake Blacktree was there, too.

Nick lit one and slid the pack on over. Jake fished one out and did the same. Jake, he noticed, had his black and red flannel shirt unbuttoned half-way down his chest. A small white patch of gauze stuck out a ways under it, up and around his shoulder.

"Did one of those things get you?" Nick asked.

"Colin," Jake replied quietly.

None of the four at the bar said another word on the matter. It was as if some unspoken agreement had passed between them, an agreement and an understanding.

Nick had wanted to choke Colin Green ever since the realization had come that it had been *he* who was driving that truck. Although in the time he'd spent in the man's company since then, Nick was pretty sure he would still harbor the same dislike had things played out differently. It was damn near impossible to find anything to like about the guy.

When they had first gotten inside the tavern and Colin, Jake, and Terry were slow to come, he had actually caught himself wishing that one of those things had grabbed him and torn him to bits. It wasn't a nice thought, he supposed, even for a scumbag like Colin Green.

Having him locked in there with them was the only thing that still kept the hackles up a bit. You couldn't quite put your guard down when you wondered about what might be going on in that shifty little brain.

"Anyone get a look at how we fare on supplies?" Rudy asked.

"We're short a couple guns," Jake said. "Mine's still out there and I think Tracy left hers, too."

Nick craned his head around and saw that Tracy *and* Emily were stretched out on the floor. Over in one of the booths Terry seemed to be doing the same.

"So, what now?" Ramp asked.

Nick turned back to the bar and stubbed out his cigarette.

"Couldn't we just hold up in here until the storm passes?" Rudy asked. "I mean, someone's bound to come check on us."

Jake shook his head solemnly.

"Won't do. This storm might take a few days before it blows itself out and even then it'll be at least a day or two before the county guys get up here to clear the roads. We aren't fixed *that* well on supplies."

"What about the people right here in Rockwell?" Rudy asked.

"We don't even know if there are any more *people* in Rockwell," Nick said.

Rudy let out a long frustrated sigh.

"So what do you propose?" he asked Jake.

"Colin says Crosscreek is a no-go on the Devon side and even though I have strong doubts, there's a chance that the way to Bedford Falls might be clear. I think that come morning we should head down there to check."

"Whoa!" Nick butted in. "I agree that I don't think we'll be able to last this out in here, but what you're talking about is more than just a jaunt across the street."

"I know."

"How are all of us supposed to make it?"

"All of us aren't," Jake said and stole another Lucky from the pack. "We'll have to send out a small party again just like tonight. If the road is clear then we'll come back, load everyone up, and get the hell out of here."

"I don't think I like it," Ramp said.

"Neither do I," Jake finally replied. "What else can we do, though?"

The four of them decided to put off the big decisions until morning. Each was feeling haggard and worn, their minds slowly spinning down like the fans in the coolers back at the General Store. They would try and get a little sleep and face the new day with fresher thoughts.

As Nick settled in next to his wife and daughter, Rudy turned off the lantern on the bar. They would need to conserve as much of the gas as possible until they knew for certain where they actually stood. Slowly the place faded back out of sight, at first in golds, then orange, and finally a deep red rust before it vanished completely.

Nick closed his eyes and tried to let sleep overtake him but found that he couldn't. As weary as he was the breakers just wouldn't shut off. The guard was still up. He felt like a kid at a sleepover trying his damndest to outlast everyone else. If you weren't the last one out, God only knows what might happen while you dozed. A hand in warm water. Peanut butter in your hair. Or worse.

It was this last category that kept him blinking in the darkness. As long as he knew Colin Green was still awake he wouldn't be able to slumber, and he *knew* the man was bright eyed as ever. He could just feel that gaze moving around in the darkness.

Off by one of the booths came the sound of Jake shifting. Nick wondered if the same thoughts were going through his head. He suspected they probably were.

8

When Jake first opened his eyes he blinked them rapidly not fully understanding the darkness. He'd never intended to fall asleep but the soft touch of Terry's jeans and the warmth of her body had finally lulled him away.

Now as he sat up in the inky black he listened instead of looking. The low and steady sounds of sleep echoed back to him with a soft whooshing. To his right Ramp snored loudly, providing the tempo for the others.

Jake got up and moved silently to where the sleeping bag of supplies had lain. He could still see the layout of the room in his mind but walked carefully just the same. Taking a candle from the bag he lit it and shielded the flame with his hand.

Jake moved around toward the back corner taking even more pains to let only a sliver of light peek out. There he saw with great relief that Colin appeared to be sleeping, too. When he turned back around a little shock of surprise ran up his spine. Emily Anderson was sitting up and looking at him.

"I'm hungry," she whispered.

With his usual stealth Jake went over to her and took her hand. Emily pulled herself up using his long strong arm for support. As the two headed for the supply bag, Jake was amazed to see how easily she navigated in the gloom. The girl didn't even need to look around her checking for obstacles as Jake still found himself doing. It was almost as if she *knew* what was there.

Not wanting to wake the others they had taken a couple tins of Vienna Sausages and a box of Saltines, and headed back for the little hall leading to the bathrooms. There they sat and quietly munched on what had to have been one of the worst breakfasts in history. The thought of breakfast, however, made Jake realize he'd never checked his watch.

It was seven-fifteen in the morning. With the tavern bricked up there was no real way of knowing whether it was day or night, or whether the storm still raged outside.

Emily had finished eating and scooted the rest of the food closer to Jake.

"Hardly seems edible does it?" He laughed.

She shook her head in a resounding no.

As he finished taking his own fill he looked over her carefully. She had seemed to fare better than he expected but still there was a deep set worry running across her face.

"Your Momma will be fine," he said to her.

"I know. It's not that."

"Well, what's bothering you?"

She took a deep breath and her bottom lip trembled. For a moment Jake thought she'd burst into tears. She didn't though.

"I did something," she said. "I did something and all of this is my fault."

"How could you think that?" he asked.

When she had finished telling her story, Jake sat back and thought it over. It seemed hard to believe that the little doe-eyed girl before him had been the catalyst for all of this but at the same time it made sense. If something had awakened, it very well may have been her that did the waking.

"Do you hate me now?" she asked.

"No, of course I don't. Don't ever think that again. This isn't your fault and *nobody* hates you."

"I heard you say they took your Momma."

A little chink appeared in the barrier he had thrown up. Some of the sadness he held at bay washed over him.

"That's true," he replied. "But I don't blame *you* for that. Some things maybe should never have been, but they were. If you hadn't come along and brought all this back, someone else would have in time. You can't keep something buried forever."

"But maybe it would've stayed buried until we were long gone already," she said.

"Yes, maybe, but the answer isn't to hide from a problem and pretend it doesn't exist. The answer is to face it and take care of it because you can."

"We can't, though. We can't take care of it," she whispered breathlessly.

"You know what I believe?" he asked. "I believe we're here because we *can* do something about it. There are no accidents in this universe. It isn't by chance that all of us are under this roof. Together I think that we have the power to put an end to all of this. Do you believe that?"

"I believe it if you do," she answered.

"Good," he said and ruffled her hair. "Can you go back to sleep for a while until the others wake up or do you want to talk some more?"

"No. I think I can sleep."

Jake watched her as she traveled back through the almost complete darkness never glancing down at her own footfalls. As she left there was a new lightness about her and he figured it must have been good to get that off her chest. Jake put out the candle between his thumb and forefinger, then smiled.

He sat there just like that and waited for the others to begin stirring. The time would come soon when he may have to give his life to keep just one or all of them safe. As he pictured the deep amber pools of Emily Anderson's eyes, the prospect seemed a good and noble end.

He had told Nick that as long as he drew breath no harm would come to the man's family. Now he meant it more than ever.

CHAPTER EIGHT

Rudy stood by the heavy steel door shaking in spite of the myriad layers that bundled him. The cold wind-whipped world was still held at bay by the walls of the Rockwell Tavern, but for how long now?

"Cape Cod, two ounces Vodka, five ounces cranberry. Rocky Mountain Shooter, one ounce bourbon, one ounce amaretto, half-ounce lime."

In just a few moments he and Jake Blacktree would be stepping out into the world they had wanted to hide from. It had been decided after almost an hour of debate that the two of them, and only the two of them, would set out to see if the road to Bedford Falls was clear.

It wouldn't have been right for Nick Anderson to go, what with his daughter and wife needing looked after. And Ramp, well good old Ramp was just a little on the wrong side of the hill for a trip like this. Terry had fought like mad to not be left behind but in the end Jake had won out. That pretty well only left Colin. None of them were quite sure what to do with him. The question of him leaving with Jake had never really been a question at all, but on the same hand no one really wanted to leave him behind either.

In the end though, things had been settled and now Rudy only half-realized he was turning the wheel to the vault door.

"Frisky Witch, two ounces vodka, half-ounce Sambuca."

The heavy steel pins slid back into their hiding spots with a sharp clang. The door groaned deeply on its hinges and moved open just a fraction. All at once icy fingers of air stole their way in through the small crack and seemed to draw out the warmth inside.

Jake stood to one side with his gun leveled at the door as Rudy finally gave it the push that shoved it wide.

Outside, the snow was still falling and the skies were a relentless wall of clouds, but the fury of the storm seemed to have abated for the time being. The town was covered in a thick blanket of white that almost seemed to glow brightly as it reflected what little light made it to the ground.

"I-I don't see anything," Rudy said.

Jake lowered his gun and turned back toward Terry who stood vigilant behind him. She reached up a hand and pressed it to the side of his face.

"Please be careful, Jake," she said.

Rudy noticed the wet sheen in her eyes as Jake nodded solemnly then turned away once more.

"Come on," he said.

He took a long stride away from the safety of the tavern and Rudy followed him tentatively. Behind them there was the loud slam of the vault door closing, followed by the pins sliding back into place.

Rudy turned and stared at it for a moment and wondered if he'd ever see the inside again. When he faced back forward, Jake had already moved up ahead. He shifted the weight of his pack then jogged up to Jake's side.

They had moved along several more feet when Jake stopped. It took Rudy a few seconds to realize what exactly was lying in front of their feet.

The corpses of Regina White and Myra Ellington were just a couple of shapes in the snow. It had piled on top of them thick and soft in the night until there were only two vague humanlike mounds rising from the white.

"Jesus Jake. We killed them. Last night I was so scared that it never sank in. But they're dead.

Jake nodded in reply.

A few feet away was the head of Regina White. The two walked over to it and saw her features pushing out, ghostlike from their frozen shroud.

Her lips were still pulled back in a tight snarl which contorted the rest of her features.

Rudy wondered why her head wasn't completely covered by the snow like the bodies had been. Then he saw that nearby there were footprints circling where they stood. It was like someone had come up and fetched the head out, then put it back down.

"What if they could have gotten better?" Rudy asked. "I mean, how do we know they wouldn't go back to normal?"

"Let's move on," Jake said.

As they moved down from First and out on to Main, the two men had held dim hopes that perhaps they would see some life back on the street. It had only been the day before that people had gone about their usual business up and down the road. Now it was deserted. Could everyone really be gone? All in one night? It seemed fairly unlikely but then again both Jake and Rudy had an advantage over the rest of the town. They had known what was coming.

Rudy could picture them, sitting bundled up in their homes while the storm whipped and ravaged outside. Then there would come a knock perhaps, and a plea for help. The unwitting good Samaritan would open up and that would be the end of it.

Further down Main they paused beside the wrecked hulks of Ramp's station wagon, and Colin's truck. The snow had piled up deeply around them, giving the whole scene the appearance of something old and half-unearthed.

Up ahead on the left, the windows of the General Store stood broken like jagged open mouths.

"Christ!" Rudy muttered, and shivered beneath his layers of clothes.

He was still walking and staring at those cavernous holes

when Jake put a hand on his chest to stop him.

Rudy looked up the street and saw a woman kneeling in the snow.

Her clothes were old and drab. She wore a long heavy dress that fell all the way down to her ankles, with sleeves that partially covered her hands. The entire outfit was unsuited for the weather.

As they stood motionless and stared, she raised her head and looked toward them. Her eyes were deep, dark circles and her face was impossibly gaunt. When she saw the two of them, she began to get back on her feet.

Rudy lowered his rifle and took a bead on her head. Jake grasped the barrel and pulled it down.

"It's okay," he said. "She isn't one of them."

The woman was on her feet now and taking shambling steps toward them. Her face seemed to be a terrible mask of hunger and pain.

Rudy felt himself instinctively raising the rifle once more but suddenly she was gone.

"What in the name of-"

"A spirit, a hungry ghost," Jake said. "They're trapped up in all of this. They're a part of it."

Rudy shouldered the rifle again and took a deep breath. Ghost or not, he didn't like any of it. They were too vulnerable just strolling down the road. At the rate they were moving, it would take them the better part of the day to make it out to Crosscreek and check for a blowdown.

"Dwight Rexell's got a pretty heavy duty four by four doesn't he?" Jake asked.

"Sure as shit he does," Rudy exclaimed. "Tom was working on it before he turned up dead. Wonder if he got it fixed?"

"I don't know, but it's worth checking out."

The two changed their course, cutting across Main and heading for Seventh. As they walked, Rudy couldn't help but think how strange it was that the big bastard seemed to know what was going on inside your head sometimes. It was strange, yes, but somehow a little comforting, too.

When they got to the aging hell hole that had been Tom Parson's garage, Rudy felt some of his spirits waver. The place was sealed up tight. He hadn't necessarily expected it to be sitting wide open, but maybe he'd hoped it would be.

The rusty, metal roll-down door was resting against the concrete slab secured in place with several solid looking Fortress padlocks. There was only one window on the outside of the building, the one that led into the small cramped office, but it would be a smidge too tight for either of them to crawl through.

Rudy had been there often enough to know that the only other way in was a door around back, but Tom kept mounds of shit stacked up in front of it most of the time.

"Stand back," Jake said, and held his shotgun close to the garage bay door.

The blast was deafening and Rudy's hands flew up to his ears at once. When he opened his eyes there was a hole torn in the rusted-out metal. Jake set down his gun and took off the pack he'd been wearing. From the side of the pack he untied a hatchet and set to work about the hole.

Rudy stared in awe as the blade connected time and time again, throwing off little orange sparks into the snow. The opening was beginning to widen now. Jake stopped, threw down the axe, and began to wrench the metal with his hands. It groaned in protest at first, but then began to tear like paper.

When Jake was finished his hands were torn and bloody.

"Jesus, Jake, why didn't you just shoot the locks?"

Without saying a word the Indian picked up the shotgun and aimed it at the two padlocks. The roar was terrible again and made the ringing ten times as bad. When Rudy looked down at the locks he was stunned to see them twisted and misshapen, but still firmly in place.

"I always thought that was just shit they said in the

commercials, you know, to sell more," Rudy said.

Jake grinned at him and spoke, but the reply was lost in that God awful ringing.

As they climbed through the hole Rudy cried out in pain as one of the jagged slivers of the door caught on his pants and tore a groove in his flesh. Jake helped him the rest of the way through.

Inside the garage was dark, dimly lit by the pale light leaking in through the punched up metal. They both took off their packs and pulled out a couple of flashlights.

In the glow of their beams Rudy could see Dwight Rexell's pickup sitting in the farthest bay. It was huge and gleamed brightly, all chrome and shiny black. The hood was closed and everything appeared to be in good shape from the outside.

"Looks like that old sonofabitch might have got her fixed up after all," he said.

Jake moved over to the driver's side door and tried the handle. It opened. Soon he was up sitting in the cab and searching around the seat for something. When he came back up again there was a little click, then the truck roared to life. The headlights came on and Rudy yelled. "Hot damn!"

He grabbed their gear and hopped into the passenger side.

"One thing though," he said. "Just how the hell are we gonna get back out?"

"Same way we came in," Jake answered. "We'll just punch a bigger hole."

The truck shifted into reverse and hit the stack of boxes behind them. Cardboard crates came tumbling down like an avalanche and thudded into the bed of the truck. The whole frame shook and shimmied for a second.

Jake shifted into neutral and revved the engine. Rudy put on his seatbelt quickly and tried to brace himself as best he could. The truck shot into drive, the tires spinning and screaming before finally grabbing the concrete and catapulting them forward.

Rudy let out a brief yell as they slammed into the roll-up door and ripped through it like it was gauze. Jake slammed on the brakes as soon as they were out of the shop, throwing both of them hard against their belts. He engaged the four wheel drive and cautiously rolled out onto the road.

Ten minutes later they were cruising back down Main once more, still going slowly, but at a better pace than before.

Even though the truck lost its footing occasionally and seemed to bog down in the deeper drifts, the two of them felt a little more jubilant. Maybe there was a little light at the end of the tunnel.

They cut off of Main and over to Wendover, still crawling. Along both sides of the street stood some of Rockwell's nicer houses. All of the windows stared back at them black, and empty, some of them even stood open. So did some of the doors.

"Jesus."

Rudy felt a little admonished for his happier thoughts only minutes before. Here and there a splash of red would glare at them from banks of bright white.

"It really *is* the whole town, isn't it? I mean, we might be the only ones left," he said.

Jake just grunted and pushed down on the accelerator slightly. As the truck pressed on for Crosscreek Rudy thought he saw movement in windows from time to time. He didn't mention it, though. He didn't even want to think about it.

They had actually made it a good ways out of town heading for Bedford when the snowy barricade of fallen lumber rose up to greet them.

"Shit," Jake muttered.

For awhile it had almost seemed like they might make it out. Just as the fears had begun to dissipate, this ugly thing had to rear its head.

"I guess we go back," Jake said. The defeat in his voice was unmistakable.

Rudy couldn't think of a single thing to say and now it was he who simply shook his head.

They carefully turned the truck around and got it pointed north again on Crosscreek.

All of their hopes had been hanging on this one thing, and now that they were heading back he realized how shortsighted their plans actually were. What would they do now?

These thoughts were still racing through his head as they began to leave the encroaching woods behind. The road was opening up again and before long they'd be back on that nasty cemetery stretch of Wendover. From somewhere in the cab a dinging sound started up. It took Rudy a bit to even take notice of it, he was so far up in his own head.

"Shit," Jake was muttering.

Then it dawned on him. He strained to lean over and get a good look at the instrument panel. The gas gauge was buried deep below empty and a little yellow warning light blinked on and off. The engine sputtered once and the truck coasted to a stop.

In their haste, neither had bothered to check the fuel.

Farther ahead the houses of Wendover loomed in the distance like the vague grey shapes of mausoleums, hidden under colonial facades.

2

Colin Green had spent most of the previous night and mid-morning hours feigning sleep. He sat there motionless in his corner and carefully sized up the others.

Sometime around eleven that morning his head felt like it split wide open. He shivered for moment and a small gasp escaped his lips as sharp pain spread from his ribs down the length of each arm. None of his companions seemed to notice.

Since then the feeling of change was stronger. Things were speeding up now. The whispering voices of wind that had echoed through the halls of his mind were louder now, and clearer. Now it was a single voice, terrible and ancient, speaking in a primal tongue that he could only understand on an instinctual level. His own thoughts were suffocated by it. If he was going to act, it would have to be soon. Very soon.

He was fairly confident about overtaking the others. The only one who would have given him pause was Jake Blacktree, but Jake was gone. Ramp was old and slow, Nick's weakness was his family, Emily was just a small girl, Tracy had a dumb half-catatonic look about her, and Terry, well Terry might still be a bitch but no real match.

Colin curled up in his corner and listened to the rest of them milling about. He needed an opportunity and needed it soon or else he'd have to make one of his own. He kept his eyes pressed closed and waited.

3

"Ramp, Terry, can you two give me a hand?"

Ramp had been sitting in a bar stool, flexing his swollen joints when Nick called to him. Terry was positioned on the stool closest to the door. She'd been sitting there holding vigil ever since Rudy and Jake had left.

Slowly, Ramp eased himself onto his feet and followed Terry over to where Nick sat on the floor.

Rebecca's eyes were open and seemed a little more lucid with her fever dropping away. Emily was holding one of her hands and Nick was brushing the hair off of her face.

"I need to unwrap her leg," Nick said. "It needs sterilized if we're going to be trapped in here for a while."

"Hey there, pumpkin," Rebecca said, rolling her eyes to look at Emily.

Ramp settled on his haunches and smiled.

"I don't think we brought any alcohol or peroxide, or anything like that. Terry, why don't you go see what's the strongest thing Rudy's got behind the bar."

Terry left and came back holding a mostly full, clear bottle.

"It's Everclear," she said.

"That'll do it. How about maybe bringing us something to loosen up our throats, too," Ramp said.

This time Terry returned with a bottle of brandy. They each passed it around and took a deep drink. Nick held the open mouth down to Rebecca's lips and poured a little in. She coughed and sputtered for a second, her eyes watering. Ramp took a second swig before he and Nick began unwrapping the dark sticky bandages.

"I don't know if this looks good or not," Nick said.

The bandages had been completely pulled away now and Rebecca's leg trembled slightly as the air hit it. She drew in a sharp intake of breath and Ramp saw that her bottom lip was clamped tight between her teeth.

Terry picked up a flashlight and pointed it down toward the wound. Nick planted both of his hands firmly on his wife's shoulders as Ramp opened the bottle of Everclear.

"Hold tight, pretty thing. This might sting a bit," Ramp said, beginning to pour.

As the alcohol hit her flesh Rebecca pinched her eyes closed and her whole upper body lifted from the floor like a cat arching its back. A tiny trickle of blood appeared where her teeth bit into her lip, but she made no sound.

He set the bottle down and off to the side, then with a clean rag began to wipe away the dried blood and gore. Nick let go of her shoulders and tore open a new package of bandages.

Tracy had come out of her daze for a moment, and now held the flashlight as Terry put the makeshift splints back in place. Emily squeezed her mother's hand tightly while Nick and Ramp began to encircle the battered leg with gauze.

Ramp had never noticed Colin leave the room during all of this. In fact, none of them had. By the time they finished with Rebecca, he was tucked back in his corner as if he'd never left.

Rebecca Anderson had closed her eyes again. Tiny beads of sweat dotted her forehead. Terry took the bottle of brandy and raised it to her lips before passing it on.

"You think she'll be okay, Ramp?" Nick asked.

"I figure she will. Looks like the bleeding got stopped last night pretty good, and the booze should hold off infection."

He didn't need to say any more. All of them knew that unless they could find some way out of Rockwell, there was a chance Rebecca might never walk on two legs again.

"Daddy, there's smoke!" Emily cried out with alarm.

All at once they looked to where her small white finger pointed. Great billowing clouds of thick, dark smoke poured down the hallway leading to the bathrooms.

Nick and Terry were on their feet in an instant and running for the hall. Ramp hauled himself back up with a great deal of trouble as Emily shot by him and ran for the bar.

Bright orange-red flames licked in and out of the open door to the men's room, curling the paint along the frame.

"Doesn't Rudy have a goddamn fire extinguisher somewhere?" Nick yelled.

Ramp moved to the side as Terry tried to head past him, but then she stopped in mid-stride. He looked behind and saw Emily standing there with the red canister already in hand. Terry took it from her and plunged back for the door.

The four of them were coughing something terrible but the flames appeared to be dying out. The extinguisher gave its last just as the bathroom sank back into smoky blackness.

Nick went into another bad fit of hacking and stumbled backwards against the wall. His foot connected with something and sent it sliding along the floor. Terry stooped to pick it up. A look of disbelief clouded her face as she held the thing out for the others to see.

It was the bottle of Everclear, charred and empty.

"Colin!" Nick growled and ran back down the hall.

Emily matched her father stride for stride, and Terry kept right on their heels. When they reached the end of the hall the trio stopped, and as Ramp caught up with them he heard Terry gasp.

4

When the engine died, Jake didn't try to juice it one last time. There was a chance that it might spark back to life and carry them just a little farther but not far enough. Listening to the sudden silence in the cab, he began to think that perhaps it was a good thing the truck stopped where it did. Had it gone even a minute longer they would've stalled in the middle of Wendover Street, and there was something about those dark and empty houses that he didn't like. Not one bit.

"Christ! I can't believe we didn't check the gas," Rudy was saying in a frustrated and whiney voice. "What a dumbshit thing to do. I even thought about it, too, but when she fired right up-"

Jake opened the door and coldness rushed in, washing over the two men. He stepped down onto the ground and took a quick look about them.

The wind seemed to have picked up some and the snow was falling stronger than when they first left the tavern.

"Look at all this shit," Rudy said from the other side of the truck.

Jake turned and leaned over the bed expecting to see a couple of gas cans perhaps. Instead there were three cardboard boxes lying haphazardly across the liner. He pulled one of them closer. All contained cans of Wurth Brake Cleaner. They had landed in back when he gunned the truck in reverse and started the avalanche of Tom's supply stack.

He had just started to slide the box away again when the diamond-shaped sign on the bottom caught his eye. It was a warning sign and inside the diamond was a little flame with the words FLAMMABLE LIQUID printed underneath.

"So what do you think?" Rudy asked.

Jake was about to tell him just what had crossed his mind when he realized that Rudy was looking up the road and no longer gazing at the boxes in back. It *was* probably a dumbshit idea as Rudy had put it and he let it pass from mind.

"I'm not sure," he replied. "I don't think we should go down Wendover, though. The first time we drove it I got a bad feeling."

"I thought I saw stuff moving around in a couple of the houses," Rudy added. "Course there isn't any other way *to* go, is there?"

Jake thought about it for a moment then nodded in agreement. Crosscreek ran along the very outskirts of town and the only two roads that connected with it were Wendover on the south side and Hawthorne on the north. They *could* follow Crosscreek all the way up to Hawthorne but the trip would likely be a longer trek than they could make before nightfall and both the thinner patch of woods to the west and the endless ones to the east were far more than he wanted to brave going down the middle of.

The only choice was pretty clear cut. They would have to take their chances passing in front of the deserted houses of Rockwell's upper-middle class.

"See how many of these cans you can fit in your pack," he said to Rudy.

"What the fuck for?"

"Monster repellant," he tried to joke, but the sound of it wasn't funny at all.

Between the two of them they had managed to square away

about a case of the stuff before finally heading off. As they started away from the pickup, Rudy kicked its side hard enough to leave a dent.

They walked on, the wind picking up even harder now and driving fat flakes of snow into their eyes. By the time they reached the first house Jake could already feel a slight ache in his legs. Ahead the street seemed to stretch on forever and in the thickets of falling snow it was impossible to see far enough to catch it bending its way back toward Main.

Beside him Rudy was muttering under his breath. The voice was faint but he could still make it out.

"Raging Indian, quarter shot Everclear, quarter shot Kahlua, quarter shot orange, one quarter mango."

Jake couldn't help but laugh. Rudy looked up at him with wide uncomprehending eyes.

"When we get back, you just may have to fix me one of those," Jake said.

Now Rudy couldn't help but laugh too. Both of them marched on through the steadily falling snow occasionally laughing again.

Jake couldn't help but wonder how they might look if there *were* someone still alive in those houses. A great big Indian and a scrawny bartender tramping down the street like two drunken soldiers in the middle of a snow storm, and laughing on top of it. Somehow it seemed right in line with all of the other weirdness.

Rudy's arm shot out and grabbed him by the back of his coat before Jake had even realized he was standing stone still behind him.

Up ahead Jake saw the movement next to one of the houses. At first he thought it was just his imagination pulling people and shapes out of the falling swirl of snow. But then he saw it again. There was someone kneeling almost out of sight beside a house five doors down from them. The movement he saw was a person's arms as they flew high into the air, then pummeled down against the ground.

"Over there, too!" Rudy said pointing.

On the opposite side of the street a figure was silhouetted in a doorway and looking right at them.

"A-Are those some more, what did you call them, angry ghosts?"

"No, I don't think so," Jake replied.

He quickly stole a glance to either side of him. On the right was a large red-brick house with dark green shutters. The front door was standing wide open. As his eyes scanned up and down the visible length of Wendover more and more half-glimpsed movement drew his attention.

"Get ready to run. The house on the right," he whispered.

Rudy was already panting heavily behind him. The figure that had stood in the doorway was now slowly moving down the drive. Jake raised his shotgun and fired without even aiming, then took off for the open door.

He didn't look back as his boots pulverized the ground underfoot. He prayed Rudy was close behind. As soon as he stamped up the steps to the threshold he stopped and whirled around as Rudy rushed past him inside.

Their pursuers were fast and had almost made it to the front walk. The barely human looking things that sped toward them uttered an awful choked cry that sounded like a dog trying to howl with its throat torn out.

"See if there's a cellar," Jake screamed over his shoulder as he backed up and slammed the door. Rudy's feet pounded over the hardwood floors as Jake threw his pack to the ground in front of him.

"Back here!" Rudy called out.

Jake took two giant strides backwards, his hip crashing into a small table and sending ceramic knick knacks crashing to the ground.

There was a thunderous blow on the outside that made the wood groan on its hinges. A small click came from the latch as the handle depressed and the door flew open. Jake fired his remaining shell at the discarded pack just as the first two attackers swarmed the threshold.

The explosion was bigger than he could've imagined. A ball of fire engulfed the entryway and sent him flying through the air as those guttural cries became screams of pain.

Jake landed hard on his back as what might have been a leg rushed past his head. The impact knocked the wind right out of him and his eyes flew open, wide with panic as he realized he couldn't breathe enough to get up.

Something else came bounding out of the flames for him but this time it wasn't just a limb. The warped and fire-singed body of Molly Carter hit him square on the chest and forced the little air he had gained back out.

Through the ringing in his ears he was vaguely aware of Rudy yelling before Molly lunged for his throat, teeth gnashing. Jake managed to dig his hands into her shoulders and shoved her back.

The hair on her head was burnt and still smoking. Her jaw worked furiously, snapping at the air from behind blood-rimmed lips as hard fingers dug into his arms. The shirt beneath his fingers ripped away and slid off of the girl like a snake shedding its skin.

She was back on him in an instant. This time he managed to get a foot between himself and her, kicking out with all of his might. Molly flew back and struck the ground hard, giving him just enough time to reach the barrel of the shotgun. As she flew through the air at him, he swung the gun like a bat. The stock connected with her face and knocked her into a chair. The wail was unearthly.

Jake scrambled backwards until he hit the wall. Molly got to her knees and snarled at him. Her mouth was a dark and bloody hole now with only a few teeth clinging loosely to the gums. An eyelid fluttered for a second over the liquefied right eye.

He had just managed to suck down enough air that the

blackness around his vision began fading. In the small moment before she rushed him again, Jake saw that the first two through the door were a mess of severed limbs and pulp. There was never a chance to wonder about the fourth before those bony, claw-like hands were encircling his wrists once more.

From the corner of his eye he could now see Rudy on his back down the hall. The fourth thing was on *him*. Rudy's arms shot up like pistons using the body of his rifle to leverage the fiend off.

Molly Carter clamped her open wound of a mouth on Jake's shoulder, gumming at his coat with a horrible ferocity.

Suddenly there was the report of a gunshot and the girl's head exploded all over him. Jake shoved the bleeding thing off of him and looked down the hall. Rudy was still on his back and fighting for dear life. Jake managed to get to his knees, still bewildered, when the second gunshot rang out and the monster clawing for Rudy convulsed then fell limp.

Jake felt his head spinning as he did a slow motion turn toward the front door. His long, blood-spattered hair stuck to the sides of his face and made a streaky wall before his eyes.

In the doorway stood a man.

Pulling the dark slimy tangles away he could see clearly again. Sheriff Rawley stood large as ever, silhouetted by the whiteness outside. The pistol hanging by his thigh let out a thin stream of smoke as the man offered his hand to Jake.

"Just part of the job Jake," he said. "Comes with the badge."

As Jake got back to his feet Rudy came over, shaking and head down. He was looking at the corpse of Molly Carter and trembling. Jake reached out and put a hand on his shoulder but he shook it off.

"You okay Rudy?" Rawley asked.

"No, I'm not okay, Sheriff. I'm pretty fucking far from okay. Just what the hell are we doing here?" he shouted. "That's Molly, isn't it?" Suddenly the anger and frustration in his voice were gone.

Jake nodded in reply.

Rudy moved over to the couch nearest him and sat down, burying his face in his hands. When he spoke again he sounded on the verge of tears.

"This just isn't right. Not any of it. I've watched her grow up, known her since she was just a baby. Now look at her. If the only way I'm going to live through this is by killing everyone I've ever known, then you just go ahead and shoot me now. I won't do it. This is just crazy! We're all insane!"

"Look, Rudy," Rawley began. "This is my town, too. Half of my life has been spent trying to protect it and nobody wants to see things go back to normal more than I do. If someone comes at me intending to kill, I'm going to defend myself even if that means their death. None of this changes any of that."

As Rudy spoke Jake was busy looking at the blood and pulpy matter covering him. He didn't like it, but for more reasons than just the obvious.

"Rudy, go wash that blood off. Now," Jake said.

Not questioning the command, Rudy slowly walked into the kitchen almost as if in a trance. Jake went in and stood beside him, waiting for his own turn to get clean.

The question had been running over and over in his mind all last night. *How was she spreading out? Why weren't they changed?*

He looked at his sticky red hands again. It might be a stretch but he wasn't willing to take any chances.

5

The massive, steel tavern door stood wide open. Light spilled across onto the floor, making the pale lantern glow fade away. Snow poured in as they stood there unblinking. Nick felt something shove past him as Terry cried out in alarm.

"The girl! He's got the girl!"

In that blind moment of panic Nick spun around thinking she must mean Emily, but then his daughter's voice screamed at him from across the room.

"Mommmmmmmy!"

Nick felt a wrenching sensation tighten in his chest as he flew over to his daughter and wife.

Emily had thrown herself on top of Rebecca and as he tried to pull her off she swung madly with her fists. Terry was there in an instant and helped drag the girl, kicking and screaming, from off her mother.

"Rebec-" the words died on his lips.

Rebecca Anderson stared at the ceiling with wide, glassy eyes. Her throat was torn open in a dark bleeding gash that still poured onto the floor.

At first he thought his *own* heart had stopped as a wave of grief, terror, and anger surged up from his chest. It crested and broke in a yell that made the insides of his throat go numb and raw instantly. His temples pounded and white flashes erupted behind his eyes.

Nick grabbed a gun from the floor and took off, still howling, for the world outside. Tears of rage stung the corners of his eyes as he bolted headlong into the snow, teeth now clenched tight. Outside of the door his foot caught something and for a second he faltered, then regaining his balance he flew through the bitter cold, heart hammering against his ribs.

With adrenaline surging and eyes narrowed to slits he watched as every step of his own smashed down on top of the other set of prints already etched in the snow.

He'd made it all the way past the corner of First and Main when something charged him and smashed hard into his side. In those bare seconds after the shape dislodged itself from the side of a building, Nick caught a glimpse of it from the corner of his eye. His grip tightened around the shotgun and he prepared for the blow.

Nick was knocked clean off his feet, his shoulder finally

biting hard into the sidewalk as he came down. The gun remained tight in his hands, though.

In the blink of an eye there were fingers digging into his scalp and a knee connected with his shin. He shoved the muzzle of the gun against the body pressing down on him and fired. His attacker flew backwards in a spray of blood and burning flesh.

Nick screamed again in a hoarse and monstrous voice and jumped to his feet. He took the gun by the barrel and yelled even louder as the burning hot metal scalded his hands.

On the sidewalk in front of him, the half-gutted shell was struggling to rise as he brought the gun down on its head with every ounce of strength he could muster. There was a sharp crack as blood and brain sprayed out and painted the snow.

6

By the time Terry reached the corner of Main, Nick had pulverized the upper torso of the body he was sitting on. With harsh and ragged grunts he continued to bring the stock of the shotgun down onto the cement.

In all of the emotions she'd felt for him in the run between the tavern and there, fear hadn't been one of them.

As she stopped on the corner gasping for breath a sheer terror of the man welled up inside as she watched him bring the splintered weapon down again and again.

"Nick!" she yelled with a wavering voice.

He didn't seem to notice.

Terry ran over, grabbed him by the shoulders and pulled back. He swung out and connected with her knee, sending her sprawling to the ground. Tears poured out of her eyes as she screamed between huge, convulsive sobs.

"Stop it! It isn't him, Nick!"

Her fingers latched onto his shirt and she threw herself back with all of her weight, still screaming.

"It isn't him!"

Nick tumbled back onto her and he finally let loose of the gun. It fell to the ground and broke off the cracked and painted fingernails of the corpse he'd been hammering.

Terry pulled him close to her and hugged him tight against her chest as his body went limp and shuddered with tears to match her own.

"It wasn't him," she said again, but this time in a whisper.

7

Ramp's first instinct had been to take off after Nick and Terry. In those seconds of frenzy Emily Anderson was all but forgotten in his mind, despite the shrill voice calling for her mother behind him.

He'd only gotten three feet out of the door before he stopped.

Lying there in the snow like a child's cast-off rag doll was the body of Tracy. Her head was twisted around on her neck at an impossible angle as she lay on her back with arms and legs outstretched. If it hadn't been for that, and those cold dead eyes, she would've looked like a girl making angels in the snow.

Ramp dropped to his knees next to the lifeless body and buried his face in his hands. It was all too much. He didn't know now why he'd bothered struggling this far. They had all been fools to ever think there was a chance.

From far off Nick's cries finally ended and Ramp reached out a trembling hand to close Tracy's eyes.

He wished that he'd never made it out of that wreck. Wished that he'd died there with Mabel. *Wouldn't that have been better?* To never know the horrors that awaited the still living.

Every single bone in his body ached so goddamn bad that he wanted to just lie down next to the girl and give up.

He didn't, though.

In a movement that seemed to take ages he got back to his feet and tried to carry her inside. If Nick hadn't already killed him, Ramp vowed that he would personally tear Colin Green limb from limb if he ever got the chance.

Even if it was all that he lived for, it would be enough.

8

With the last human thoughts he would ever have, Colin had watched the spectacle go off from atop White's Dry Cleaning.

It had played out even better than he had hoped as Eileen Wilcox sprung on Nick. At first it looked like she might actually get the job done, but that idea didn't hold long.

Still, he sat there on his rooftop perch and licked the blood from his hands, looking on with animal fascination as Nick had turned Eileen's face into hamburger.

All of the blood and screaming brought a powerful lust and hunger back into his head. He felt a stiffening in his groin and licked up Rebecca Anderson's blood more feverishly.

Terry had come bounding onto Main then and ruined the rest of the show. As he watched her far below, the pain and desire became almost unbearable.

He decided that he'd get her before the whole thing was done with. He would feast upon her slowly and make that fucking Indian watch as he lapped up every last bit of juice before breaking all of her bones and sucking out the marrow. That would be a good start.

Colin scampered across the roof and dropped to the ground in back of the building. As he ran through the wind and snow, the voice in his head became almost all-consuming.

The *very* last thought that actually belonged to Colin was how much he hated them all. How much he'd always hated them. The whole town.

Then Colin Green was gone and the cold ancient sound in his head was the only thing left. Consumed with a blinding rage and hate, he moved off in the storm like an animal. He would kill whatever crossed his path. Not just kill, though. He would punish it.

9

Rawley might have been just a small-time cop, but when it came to his sleepy little town he was no slouch. He knew Rockwell like the back of his hand and always felt in tune with the hum and throb of its peaceful streets.

When things had begun to sour, he noticed it. Hell yeah he did. But what could he have done? Everything had snowballed out of control so quickly he never realized just *how* ugly it really was. If he had sharpened up a little quicker could any of this have been avoided?

You should've called in the state boys, you dumb fuck. Should've called them in with Tom Parsons. Even though he knew this to be true, Rockwell was *his* town, and there was a deep sense of pride and protectiveness he felt for it. Maybe that was why he delayed.

All hindsight aside, he'd been glad as hell when the front of 323 Wendover exploded in the glare of his windshield. He had been even more glad when he found Jake Blacktree and Rudy Vitters alive inside.

Now as the big diesel truck, which served as Rockwell's winter-time cruiser, pulled up and stopped in front of the tavern, some of the brief lived joviality the men had felt faded away fast.

The reality of the situation came hammering back at them,

and as Rawley now understood it they were still trapped, alive but trapped. And God only knew how many of those goddamn things were out there.

As the three got out of the truck they stood for a moment and stared at each other silently. Their news wasn't good and now they would have to share it.

Jake lowered his eyes to the ground and Rawley saw his expression change.

"There's been trouble here," he said and spun toward the tavern door.

Rawley glanced down and saw the deep and heavy mess of tracks that led away from the bar, still not quite buried by the freshly fallen snow.

Now all three of them ran. Jake reached the steel beast first and began hammering away on it.

"It's us! Open up, it's us," he yelled.

Rawley eased back the hammer on his pistol. Then a voice small and wary called out in reply, "J-Jake?"

Jake stopped pounding.

"Yes, we're back."

The metal pins groaned and squealed. Seconds later the door was opening and a warm, foul odor rushed out to greet them. It was the smell of fresh blood, burnt wood, sweat, and fear. Rawley pinched his eyes shut and turned his head to the side, already knowing that the sight awaiting him wouldn't be the cozy, warm little scene he'd imagined.

When he did look back Terry was standing there, just a pale shade of the girl she'd been the last time he saw her. She didn't rush forward for Jake as he would have expected, but instead took a small and unsure step backwards.

The three men entered, Rawley shutting the door behind them. They stood there motionless and silent, eyes adjusting to the pale illumination of the lantern.

As best as he could make out there were only four of them settled about in the gloom of the bar. Nowhere did he see the cashier from the General Store or a woman who might have been Nick's wife. And he sure as shit didn't see Colin Green.

"Where-" Jake began but Terry shook her head *no*.

She pointed to a bundle on the floor, something lumpy hidden under what looked like curtains.

Even without the missing folks, Rawley would have known them for what they were. He hadn't seen a lot of bodies wrapped in their shapeless grey bags, but he'd seen enough in his years.

"What happened?" Rudy asked.

Terry answered with one word. Colin.

Suddenly Rawley didn't feel so much like the Great Protector, the valiant keeper of the peace. Instead he felt like a piece of shit, a small-time, worthless, piece of shit.

Even while most of his mind agreed that he'd done the best he could, there was another part that picked away all of the little snafus he'd made up that point.

Yeah, it *had* been his town, but now what was left? *Six of you, that's what.* Maybe there were more, maybe not. What mattered, he decided, was that there were still five people, Rockwell people, that needed his help, and by God if he had it to give, he would. So maybe his watch wasn't over just yet.

Out of all of the faces surrounding him, only Rudy and Jake still had a small glimmer of fight, but he could see it fading quickly, even in those two. Especially in Rudy.

Nick Anderson sat on the floor not too far from the covered-up bodies, chin resting against his chest, and eyes staring at his lap. The little girl, Nick's daughter, was curled in a corner with her nose all but buried in an open book. It was a strange sight, to be sure, but hadn't most of the sights been damn strange lately?

At the end of the bar and leaning like a broken man was good old Ramp. There was a glass of something sitting before him untouched.

Terry had finally gone to Jake but it still wasn't a strong, welcoming embrace. Her head was tucked in the crook of his arm and from the way she shook in her small helpless way she could've only been crying.

The Rockwell Tavern was like looking in on the catatonic ward in the state mental lockup. No, it was more like seeing the terminally ill. There was one thing all of those faces had in common. Each of them had given up. There was about enough hope left in that room to fill a thimble.

Rawley strode away from the door and walked through the bar. His boots made a heavy, dull, clumping noise as his considerable build pressed them to the ground. Around his waist the official accessories of the job jingled and rattled.

He moved down the hall to the restrooms, following that nasty fire-bombed smell as it got thicker and more pungent.

The door to the men's room was charred and warped in the frame. The frame, too, was twisted and had that cold gleam of coal in places. From inside there was a tiny shaft of light that shone down from the ceiling where a small hole had burned itself all the way through the roof. Water dripped down in a steady plink from the snow that had been melted up there.

There was a grimness about the whole place that actually did start to knock the spirit out of you. Rawley took a deep breath and headed back toward the others. The clomping of his boots and the tiny plink of water were the only sounds.

If any of them wanted to live they would all have to snap out this funk and get their brains going again. Even more important than their brains, he reckoned, were their instincts. If they didn't at least try they might as well just open that big goddamn door of Rudy's and wait like sheep for the slaughter.

The main room of the bar was just as somber as he'd left it. The only things that had changed were Terry and Jake now sitting off in a booth, and Rudy behind the bar pouring himself a drink.

"I think you'd better maybe fix me one, too," Rawley said. His voiced seemed to boom in the silence and Rudy jumped a little as it rang out.

He went over to the bar, picked up the glass of scotch, and sent it on home, already wincing in anticipation of the burn. There wasn't any, though. It went down warm and smooth with just a bare tingle.

"Thought I might as well break out the good stuff," Rudy said. "Seeing as how we're probably the only ones who'll ever be drinking it."

Rawley put the glass back on the bar and turned to face the rest of them. He waited until Jake looked up, then fixed him with a stare. Jake was the one he was counting on now. He was the one strong enough to bring the rest of them around. If there was ever a time for a pep talk it was now.

"Look now," Rawley began. His voice was loud and commanding like Ramp's had once been. "All of us in this room have just been through hell and back. Some of you have lost a lot, too, and I don't aim to belittle none of it. The fact is, if we plan to just sit here and give up, then each of you might as well grab one of those guns off the floor and make quick work of it. From what I've seen that'll be a much faster and more painless way to go."

That got their attention.

"If that isn't quite what you're looking for then I suggest we all sit down and figure out just what the hell it is we *do* want. Things aren't getting any better out there and the longer we do nothing, the less chance we've got. Do all of you hear me, or am I just talking for my own sake?"

There was a low murmur now. No one spoke to each other but all seemed to be mumbling to themselves. This was good, he thought. Maybe he hadn't lit a fire under their asses, but at least he'd made a spark.

In the back of the room Jake Blacktree rose to his feet.

"I want to get out of here," he said. "And more than that, I want to put an end to all of this. The only way I'll roll over and die is if I give it my best shot first."

"Me, too," Terry chimed in.

Next to Rawley at the bar, Ramp was nodding. From behind him came Rudy's voice. "He's right. We made it this far. I guess that's something."

Finally, from farther off came the soft voice of Nick Anderson. "Yeah," was all he said.

CHAPTER NINE

Jake had done his best to fill Rawley in on everything that had been happening. From time to time someone would burst in and cover pieces that he missed. The little round of story time bore an eerie resemblance to the one they had shared the night before, and when it was all over no one said a word. For a moment.

"So what now?" Rudy finally asked.

"Well, why don't we start with the facts as we know them," Rawley said. "Something's happened to everyone but if Jake's line of thinking holds true then there has to be a source. We can't just go on killing every person we come across because Rudy might be right and if we put a stop to this then maybe they'll change back. So where's the source? How do we stop it?"

The silence didn't surprise Jake in the least. It wasn't as if each of them hadn't already asked the same questions hundreds of times. They just didn't know enough to answer.

Nick walked over to Jake and held out his pack of Luckies.

He had held little hope for Nick after returning from the trip out to Crosscreek. What he'd seen was the look of a man who didn't care anymore, a man who had given up. Even Emily Anderson hadn't looked like *that*.

Thinking of the little girl made him decide he should see how she was faring. He stubbed out his half-finished cigarette and headed over to the corner where she sat.

"What are you doing?" he asked, crouching beside her.

"I'm reading," she stated flatly. "If I can keep my head busy all of those other things seem to stay away."

Jake nodded in understanding.

"What are you reading?" he asked.

She held the book out to him and he took it, carefully marking her place as he turned it to the cover.

"The Bartender's Bible," he said out loud and couldn't help but smile.

As he handed the book back to her something slipped from between its pages and struck the floor with a metallic *ping*.

He reached for it, but Emily was quicker. She snatched it in her little hand, looked at it, then dropped it back to the floor.

"It's just a penny," she said with an air of disappointment.

Jake picked it off the ground and held it between his thumb and forefinger.

"You should always keep a penny when you find it," he said. "Did you know that some people will even nail a penny over their door for good luck?"

She reached out and touched the copper disc once more, then shot Jake a look of incredulity.

"Honest," he added.

2

Rudy had been on his way over to offer Emily a glass of water when those three magic words caught his attention.

The Bartender's Bible.

That had been enough to shake him loose from his own thoughts, but what *really* grabbed him were the words Jake spoke next.

All at once he had the missing piece to his little puzzle and everything fell into place.

The glass of water fell from his hand and shattered with a deafening crack on the floor. Suddenly everyone froze in mid-motion, the way people sometimes do in plays.

"Holy shit!" he yelled.

In the silence that followed you could have heard a pin drop. Rudy whirled around, not quite sure who to address first.

"T-The penny," he stammered. "The penny is what brought it back. The penny nailed over the door."

All eyes remained glued to him but he could see the uncomprehending looks, only frustrating him more as he tried to get it out.

"Every night when I heard that thing coming up my basement stairs I'd close my eyes or try and drown it out with the television. Every night I kept thinking *this is it, it'll get you tonight*. It would make it to the top steps and scratch at the door. Christ, that scratching would go on for hours, but then it'd stop. It never did come through. I've thought about it ever since. I've kept asking myself why? Why didn't it come through that door? The penny is what brought it back."

"I'm afraid I don't follow," Rawley said.

"Jake, you said how sometimes people will nail a penny up over a door for good luck. I did that. Right over my basement door. Except it wasn't a penny.

"Gosh I must've found that thing when I was fifteen or so, back in the woods, you know? Guess I hung it there over the door as kind of a throwback to being a kid. Ward off the monster in the cellar and all."

"Slow down a sec," Ramp hollered. "You nailed *what* over the door?"

"I don't know what it is. Just something I found back there in the woods. It's flat and round, feels like maybe it's made out of bone. There's a little hole through it and one of those symbols, you know, like what's on those big damn rocks. I always just thought it was a pretty cool find, so I kept it all these years. Except now I wonder if maybe that was what kept *It* from coming up."

He stopped to catch his breath finally. Jake and Emily were

talking rapidly to each other in whispers, but everyone else remained silent.

"Do you think I'm right?" Rudy asked Jake directly. "You think this might mean something?"

"I'm sure it does," he replied. "I don't know just what. Do you remember what was on it? The symbol?"

"Christ! That thing's been up there for ages now, I wouldn't have a clue."

Jake let out a sigh that made Rudy feel a little low. He thought maybe they were disappointed in him for not remembering. Then Jake spoke up again.

"There's a little part of this story that has been omitted. Emily I think you should tell them now."

By the time the little girl had finished recounting her role in the whole thing, tears were welling out of her eyes.

Nick Anderson had placed a comforting arm around his daughter and brushed her hair with loving strokes.

"It's okay, honey," he said in a soothing tone. "You didn't do anything wrong."

Things had progressed quickly after that. Rudy had as much of a clue about the thing over his door as anyone did. The one thing they all felt certain of was that it was something important.

The group had decided quite unanimously that they would head over to Rudy's house in Sheriff Rawley's truck, and fetch his lucky charm. This time everyone would be going.

They took little in the way of provisions, most of the attention going to weapons and ammunition. The plan was to make a quick run and be back at the tavern before dark.

Half an hour after they'd started getting ready, the six of them stood shoulder to shoulder in the snow out on First. Rudy engaged the deadbolt from outside, then they hurried over to the truck.

The wind had driven piles of snow all around it but by no means did it look stuck. That hefty diesel truck had been bred for weather like this.

"Unless there's any objection, I think Emily and Ramp should ride up front in the cab," Rawley hollered. "Ordinarily I'd say it should be the two ladies, and no offense, Ramp, but you're not quite a spring chicken anymore."

There was a moment of nervous laughter but everyone agreed. Emily, Rawley, and Ramp all climbed inside the truck, while the rest piled in back.

The little window in back of the cab slid open.

"Just holler if you see anything," Rawley said, and fired up the engine.

As the truck lurched forward, the back wheels still trying to find their grip, Rudy started into his old routine.

"Winter Tropic, two ounces vod-"

A little voice cut him off from inside the truck.

"Vodka, two ounces cranberry, two ounces strawberry margarita mix," Emily chimed.

He tried again.

"Winter Breeze, one ounce-"

"Crème de Cacao, one ounce vanilla schnapps, one ounce Irish cream, add milk."

She read the whole goddamn thing, he thought. Or at least the W's.

3

As the pickup headed away from the Rockwell Tavern, Terry could feel a warmth inside of her again despite the fact that her skin was bitterly cold and she sat exposed in the open bed of the truck. She was kneeling and facing out, shotgun held at ready. The black plastic liner had begun to press hard into her shins and knees making a small throbbing pain, but she hardly noticed.

Instead, Terry leaned in closer to Jake and closed her eyes, finding a sudden comfort in her thoughts. For the first time since the whole ugly mess had begun she could actually sense a resolution. She could see herself emerging somewhere on the other side, changed yes, but not necessarily for the worse.

As the tavern faded into a swirling white mist behind them, she thought she could see shadows gathering around it. Lots of them. They shifted and cajoled, growing thicker and darker, like black flames in a fire. That was the past however, and everything in front of the truck was the future. A future they were cruising headlong into.

Rudy Vitter's place was a modest, two-story, country charmer. It wasn't spectacular by any means, probably not half as nice as Nick Anderson's even, but still it was a damn sight better than *The Reservation* on the other side of the tracks. Rawley pulled up past it just a bit, then backed the truck up into the driveway.

Terry felt the pickup rise on its shocks as Rawley got out of the front. He stood there, providing cover for the others as they hopped out of the back.

As the group moved up the walkway toward the front door, they settled into an almost instinctual formation with Emily buried deep in the center. Nick and Jake brought up the rear.

Rudy fumbled with his keys for a minute, then finally the door opened and carefully they shuffled into the freezing blackness. Almost at once and almost in unison, a volley of flashlights clicked on and sliced into the darkness.

The procession stopped dead in their tracks, all except for Rudy.

"It's right up here," Rudy said.

Moving on down the front hall as it shot back for the kitchen, they crept silently, alert and on-guard. Terry still had her happy thoughts somewhere, but they had been stashed away safely for the time being. Good vibrations, after all, weren't going to keep them alive.

When the party halted they were stretched two by two down the hall.

"There it is," she heard Rudy say up ahead.

Jake began threading his way up from the rear guard and for a moment Terry made to follow him, then decided better of it. She had her place for now and the two of them could have all the time together they wanted once all of this was over.

At the front of the line, Jake was reaching up and pulling the little white disc down from the nail driven into the top of the door frame.

"Emily," he called out. "Come up here."

The little girl wriggled her way through the adults until she was standing next to Jake. The sight of the two of them standing like that had almost made her want to laugh. One so little, the other a giant.

"Do you recognize this?" he asked.

"No," she replied.

"Are you sure? This marking wasn't anywhere on the stone? Think hard."

"She doesn't have to," Nick said from behind. "If she says it wasn't there, you can bet your life it's true. She's got a special memory. It's flawless."

Jake didn't say a word, but Rudy made a funny sound that made it seem as if this one statement had explained the whole world to him.

"We should probably be getting out of here," Rawley said with a hint of uneasiness. "We can take this back to the bar and figure out what it means there."

The bar. Somehow Terry, in her childish fantasy had never actually thought they would have to go back there. She wasn't truly sure what she *had* thought they would do, but had a pretty good feeling it involved brandishing their talisman and vanquishing their foes into puffs of smoke. End of story.

"There might be a problem there," she said sheepishly.

4

Jake felt more than a little worry as Terry told them what she'd seen while leaving the tavern.

"I don't know that I've got enough faith in our little good luck wheel to try and drive off a whole horde of those things with it," Ramp said.

"If we're expected, maybe it'd be best if we held up here for a bit," Rawley added.

Nick fumbled with something back by the door, then made his way up closer to the others.

"We didn't really bring much in the way of supplies," he said. "How are you fixed for food, Rudy?"

"Not too well, but probably well enough long as we don't make a vacation out of this.

While Ramp, the Sheriff, and Terry headed down into the basement, the other four remained upstairs. Rudy and Nick were gathering what scant supplies they could from the kitchen and bathroom, while Jake and Emily talked.

"If we're staying here, I think I should put this back," Jake said to her. "Before I do, though, I want you to take one last good look."

Emily nodded then stared at the artifact while Jake positioned the flashlight above it.

"Got it?" he asked.

"Got it."

Jake hung the circle over the door just as the other two came back from the kitchen.

Together they descended the staircase into the near darkness that awaited them. The occasional pass of a flashlight down below would streak across the wall like a brilliant ghost. As they moved deeper Jake's nose pricked to the stale and cloying mustiness that rose to them.

With the arc of four flashlights swinging to and fro, cutting across each other's paths, it was at first hard to make out the basement clearly.

"Hold tight a sec," Rudy called out.

Seconds later the black dissolved into the steady orange glow cast out from a kerosene lantern. Jake's instincts carried his eyes crawling all over the cellar, taking in every detail.

For the most part it was pretty spare. There was a table in the middle on which the lantern sat along with some scattered papers and what looked like magazines. Next to the table was a chair. Other than that there was nothing else in the way of furnishings or even clutter for that matter. Except, of course, for the boxes.

Stacked at least chest high around three of the walls were long rectangular cardboard boxes. Each one had writing across the side in a neat and precise script.

Rudy caught Jake's narrowed and inquiring eyes as they passed over the boxes again.

"Comic books," Rudy said. "Well, not like Superman or anything. Mostly old EC stuff, Tales from the Crypt, Weird Fantasy, things like that."

Jake really only had a vague idea of what he was talking about. In *his* house growing up, there had been plenty of tales but all of these had come straight from Momma Blacktree. There had never been books and definitely not comic books.

Emily had moved over to the table and picked up what Jake had first mistaken for a magazine. Nick followed her closely. In that one instant the similarities between the girl and her father were impossible to miss. Both had the kind of childish glaze over their eyes that you find on Christmas mornings, when the tots have discovered what's beneath the tree.

"Wow," Nick said.

"I never really bought them to collect. Mostly I just read them down here when I was a boy. My Ma used to call them penny dreadfuls. She said they were nothing but trash. It's kind of funny, but even after she passed on I'd still come down here to read them. Habit, I guess."

"Look," Rawley boomed from across the room. "I don't mean to spoil this little trip down memory lane, God knows we could all use some happy thoughts right about now, but the fact is shouldn't we be trying to figure out just what the hell we aim to do?"

5

Emily tucked herself away in a corner amidst the damp smelling walls and coating of dust that streaked beneath her legs. In her hands were a small and fading flashlight and a copy of Weird Tales number thirty-seven. On the cover was a zombie sitting high on a throne of bodies. In his hand he held a stone that gleamed with power. Beneath that and in the foreground was a pretty woman in a tattered dress being drawn before him by two more zombies. Tears streamed out of the corners of her eyes and spilled down her cheeks in half-tone blue.

Pressing her back into the chill of the basement wall, Emily drew her knees toward her chest, spreading the comic over them. She clicked on the flashlight and its thin amber glow pooled out over the open pages.

The voices of the others began to fade out as she fell into the world of the Zombie King.

When the flashlight finally died she still had two pages to go. She strained to make out the last panels through the flickering light of the kerosene lantern across the room.

As she closed the comic on her lap and stretched and her aching and dead legs beneath her some of the conversations began echoing back as she reflected on the story just finished.

"What if we just burn the place?" Terry asked.

"What place?" Her father now.

"The town, all of it."

Someone else muttered, "Jesus," but Emily couldn't tell who.

Suddenly there was the sound of a door banging open overhead. Everyone stopped talking. The glow of the lantern dimmed until it was almost extinguished.

There were slow and heavy footsteps now moving up the hall toward the cellar door. They thudded loudly over the floor boards above. Much closer to her came the slightly muffled sound of several guns chambering their rounds.

The steps seemed to stop at the top of the stairs. For a moment the house was dead silent, then there came a faint scrabbling sound like fingernails running over wood. In the near darkness, Emily could see the barrels of three guns leveled at the door above them. From farther off there came another set of feet, these moving a bit faster. She hadn't realized that she was holding her breath until she heard the scream from out in the street. It was the shrill, piercing yell of a woman. Emily had to stop herself from taking up the cry, too.

The footsteps upstairs retreated and moments later the front door banged shut.

"Christ almighty!" Rudy said. "I don't think that was one of *them*."

"She sounds like she's in trouble," Terry began. "Do you think we ought to-"

Terry's voice trailed off as the sound of feet once again echoed throughout the basement. Emily didn't need to see very well to recognize the heavy tread of Jake ascending the wooden stairs.

"Jake, no!" Terry cried out in the darkness.

He ignored her and pushed on. Now there was another set of feet following him. It was the rapid and slightly awkward gait of her father.

Way up in the blackness the cellar door creaked on its hinges. First it opened, then it closed. It seemed suddenly as if everyone must now be holding their breath because the basement was quiet and eerily tomblike.

Emily listened to the sounds of Jake and her father making their way to the front door. There the footsteps stopped and waited. There was never the report of gunfire, just that empty, breathless silence. A few minutes later the cellar door opened and closed again as the two men returned.

"What did you see?" Rudy asked.

"Nothing. Whoever it was, they're gone now," her father replied.

"Yeah. Gone," Rudy echoed.

"How about the truck?" Rawley boomed out of the darkness. "They didn't do anything to the truck, did they?"

"Truck's fine." Jake answered.

"Now I know that little lucky charm up there is supposed to keep us safe and all," Rawley continued. "But I don't imagine I'm the only one thinks we should maybe be heading back someplace a little safer."

"Sheriff's right," Jake said. "We got what we came for and now it's time to head back. Being holed up in the basement is like shooting fish in a barrel. The tavern is the safest place still. We'll load up, head back, then put together a plan of action."

All nodded in somber agreement.

Emily didn't like the idea of another drive, but she *did* like the idea of going back to the bar. It felt much safer there.

As the others began gathering things up again, Emily took one more long hard look at the Zombie King and his poor captive before setting the comic back on the table.

6

As the others began getting ready for their journey back, Rudy paced back and forth in the cellar. He realized it had been almost a full day now since he'd taken a piss and somehow sitting on that cold cellar floor had turned the works back on.

He couldn't wait until they got back.

"I've got to go upstairs," he announced suddenly. "Bathroom break," he added when the uncomprehending gazes turned to him.

"I don't think you should go up alone," Jake said.

"I'm pretty sure I can handle it. Just give me a gun and a flashlight. I'll meet you by the front door," Rudy replied.

The truth of the matter was that he *didn't* want to go up there alone, not really. And even though he was about to burst, he knew that even the presence of someone outside the door would shut the system down in a heartbeat. It was just one of his idiosyncrasies; he could never piss with an audience.

Grabbing a flashlight and Ramp's revolver he rushed up the basement steps, taking them two at a time. Upstairs the house was dark and silent. He kept the flashlight turned off and made his way toward the other stairs leading to the second floor. He had spent his entire life in that house and could navigate it blindfolded if he had to.

Taking care to avoid the creaky third, and fifth step, Rudy hurried to the landing. The second floor seemed colder and all of a sudden the distance from his companions felt all the greater. Fortunately the bathroom was right next to the stairs. He went in, clicked on the flashlight, then fought madly with his zipper, barely getting it undone in time.

After he had finished and zipped back up, Rudy turned to the sink to retrieve the flashlight and revolver. All at once the temperature dropped. Every breath he took puffed out like a fog in front of his face. The beam of the flashlight dimmed to the point that he was sure it was going to blink off any second. The shower curtain to his left rustled softly.

Nervous and jumpy now, he spun in the direction of the noise. His right hand hit the barrel of the pistol and knocked it off the sink, dropping it to the darkness at his feet. There was another rustle and this time he was sure he could see something push against the curtain.

He was so scared he couldn't move. The bathroom was tiny and the door opened inward. If he tried to make clearance for it to swing he'd have to get right next to shower.

The gun. The flashlight still sat on the rim of the sink, throwing its dull amber glow across the ceiling and walls. From the waist down, however, it was total darkness. The gun was down there somewhere.

Not taking his eyes off the curtain he began to move his foot around, searching for the pistol. After one pass he still hadn't found it. The gun had dropped off the edge of the counter top so the only place it could go was the floor. *Unless it went in the cabinet.*

The two doors to the empty space under the sink had been missing for years. He'd never kept anything down there and had always figured even if he did, not having doors was easier access. *Maybe the gun fell in there.*

Rudy began to crouch down ever so slowly. His hand groped about the face of the cabinet until he felt the opening. Now he was crouched completely and his hand finally hit something. But it wasn't metal.

There was a gurgling sound that issued from the cabinet the instant he'd felt It. Rudy sprang to his feet, leaping as far from the sink as he could. His leg smacked into the toilet and sent him toppling. He fell straight back, his body at first sinking into the shower curtain, then through it, until he finally hit the tile wall of the shower.

His whole body went into the tub. The curtain rod popped out of place and came clattering down. One end struck the side of Rudy's head hard enough to leave a gash while the other swatted the flashlight onto the floor.

Now the bottom half of the bathroom was bathed in the waning glow. The gun lay on the floor where it should have been, but he didn't notice. His eyes were locked on the space under the sink.

The space was big enough perhaps for a child to hide in, but the thing crammed up in there was no child.

Still sounding like it was choking, the person under the sink began to unfold itself from the tight quarters. A dead and milky eye suddenly peered out from behind the ratty, coppery hair as she pulled herself out onto the floor and toward him with a jerkiness like stop motion animation.

Even before Rudy screamed he could hear feet thundering up the stairs. By the time the first knock came upon the door she was already on him. The gnarled muscle that had once been tongue flicked around uselessly inside her mouth as those hard bony fingers dug at him, pulling her closer and closer.

The butt of a rifle splinted through the door but it still didn't open.

Now her face was right in his. Tears sprang from his eyes and mixed with the blood running down his face. Her expression was beyond hate. The breath from her mouth was sour and sharp.

He squeezed his eyes shut and screamed even louder, trying to turn his face away. There was a loud crash as the door gave in and fell into the bathroom. Rudy could taste the salty tears and blood in his mouth now as he shoved his face tight into his chest.

Two hands gripped him hard, pulling him up from the bottom of the tub. Rudy's eyes snapped wide open with terror.

It was Jake, not her. It was Jake dragging him to his feet.

He wanted to say something but found that he couldn't. Jake seemed to be taking a quick inventory of his injuries.

"Can you make it downstairs?" Jake asked.

Rudy simply nodded.

Jake bent down and grabbed the revolver then led him to the steps.

Downstairs was empty. The front door stood wide open and Rudy could hear the sound of Rawley's diesel engine idling in the cold.

The others were standing next to the truck with their

weapons at ready as he and Jake went out.

"Rudy, my God, what happened?" Terry asked.

He held up his hand and squeezed his eyes shut for a second.

"Just give me a bit," he said, then climbed in the back of the truck.

Their progress was slowed by the wind and the snow which had picked up again.

Rudy tried to shove the image of her far into the back of his mind but that awful face seemed to be burned in.

"She was there," he said weakly. "She was right on me."

When he looked up Jake and Nick were both eyeing him in a way he didn't like. He hated that look because he already knew what lay behind it. The question was in his mind, too. *Was he still the same?*

"I'm fine," he said loudly and with as much conviction as he could muster.

Nick looked away, but Jake held his gaze for a moment.

Later that night after settling back into the relative safety of the Rockwell Tavern, Rudy was the last to drift off into a fitful sleep.

The images that he thought would haunt his slumber never came, instead he dreamt. In his dream he was frightened and cold. He was deep within the woods, the drifts of winter snow freezing his poorly clothed body.

Ramp, Nick, Jake, Terry, and Sheriff Rawley were all there but they were different now. The people that had been his friends before sleep had now become his enemies. Rudy realized he was being shackled to a long stone wall, forced to watch as the others slaughtered his friends and family.

He knew now that he was the last. All of his people were dead and he was the last. Screaming at the top of his lungs, he writhed and fought against his bindings.

Nick Anderson walked over smiling savagely and hit him. The blow left him dazed and he fell limp against the stone. Nick grabbed him by the jaw and lifted his face up. Rudy tried to scream again but before he could there was another hand digging into his mouth. Gagging and choking on his own blood Rudy vomited as his tongue was torn from his mouth.

The others stood around him pointing and laughing, their shapes becoming vague and shimmering as the pain and tears blinded him.

Rudy prayed for it to be over. He wished they would just kill him and be done with it, but they didn't. Instead, Terry came to him and undid his bindings telling him he could go. The others were still laughing.

Scrabbling forward on his hands and knees he had only made it a couple of feet before the terrible fear took hold of him again. Getting to his feet he tried to run but his head was a twirling mess of confusion. From behind him there was a sharp yell then something clubbed his right ankle. The bone made a loud crack as it splintered, dropping him. Rawley stood over him with a large club which he brought down on his other ankle.

The scenes that came after played out in a blur of time passing. When the images slowed again he felt empty, frozen, and stabbed by the acute pains of hunger. There was an iron shackle around his wrist tethering him to the wall once more. Unable to stand or walk he crawled slowly back and forth at the base of the stone, watching, and listening to the others as they sat around a great fire.

As he watched them a feeling stronger than the pain and loss washed over him. It was hate. Pure unadulterated anger.

When Rudy awoke from his dream he was back in the darkness of the tavern. His clothes were soaked with a thin layer of sweat and his body trembled.

In the gloom he could see his companions sleeping. As he watched them, the feeling of hatred surged. It was something more than just a carryover from the dream. He knew that as time passed this feeling wouldn't fade. It was growing inside of him.

He wanted to kill them all. He wanted to make them pay.

Shaking and cold in the blackness, with murderous intent consuming him, Rudy knew what he must do.

7

Jake awoke with a start. His mind quickly tugged at the veil of sleep and tried to pull away the fog. Something was wrong.

The sound of the rushing wind and tiny flakes of snow hit the side of his head. There was a pale grey light creeping into the tavern, washing its walls with a dead, icy, glow.

Jake rose to his feet and looked around. The heavy, steel, bank vault door stood open, making a small illuminated passage to the outside world.

Turning frantically where he stood, Jake did a quick head count of the others who were just beginning to stir. Rudy wasn't among them.

He made it to the threshold in three giant strides. With one hand on the door and the other on the frame he stopped, bracing himself.

Out in the swirling snow and early morning light sat Rudy. He was about thirty feet away with his back to the tavern. The man's head hung down as if he were staring into his lap.

Something about the scene shook Jake's nerves, sending cold prickles of fear all over him. He took one step forward. There was a soft squish as his heavy boot compacted the snow underfoot.

Suddenly Rudy raised his head.

"Stay where you are, Jake," he said.

His voice was thin. It sounded as if he were struggling just to get anything out.

"Rudy? What's happening?"

For a second Rudy's entire body convulsed. Jake still couldn't see the man's face. Watching as the tremors subsided, Jake took another step forward.

"Goddamn it, Jake! I said keep back!"

"Okay, Rudy. I won't come out there. Just tell me what's going on."

Jake could hear sounds behind him now. The others were gathering and pressing into the doorframe.

"Remember how I said all of this was crazy?" Rudy began. "Remember how I said we didn't even know if the people might change back? How we can't kill them; it'd be murder?"

"I remember," Jake said.

"Well, it's all a load of shit. There isn't any coming back. Once she gets you it's over."

"We don't know that, Rudy," Jake said taking another couple of steps forward.

"I do," Rudy replied.

Jake cautiously stole another couple steps before Rudy shivered again.

"Stop!" Rudy screamed, his voice choked with tears. "Goddamn it, Jake, keep back! I don't want it to get on you!"

"You don't want *what* to get on me?"

"The blood."

With those words Rudy's head exploded, spraying a deep dark scarlet all over the pristine white. Behind Jake, Terry and Emily screamed.

Almost in slow motion, Rudy's body fell backwards. The place where his head had been pumped a thick bloody pool into the drift of snow. For the first time they could see the shotgun still clasped between his hands.

Jake closed his eyes and lowered his head. When he opened them again he saw the bright red splatter that streaked the ground before him. It reached almost to his feet. He took an instinctive step back. Then another.

As Jake swung the steel door back in place and bolted it, the soft empty sobs of Emily and Terry filled his ears. For a moment he stood there in front of the door, his eyes staring ahead into the blackness. For a moment he wanted to cry, too.

A rich orange glow sprang up and shoved the darkness off into the corners of the room. Rawley was carrying the lantern over to the bar.

The faces of his companions echoed his own feelings within. Rudy's suicide had meant much more than just the passing of a friend. It chipped away at the hope they had held on to. There were still some things that they had no protection against, things that couldn't be held at bay with bricks and steel.

Even beyond all of that, Rudy's death marked their time running out. Little by little they were falling and still no one knew what to do, or how to find a way out.

CHAPTER TEN

"It sounds like the storm's finally blown itself out," Rawley said.

Nick looked over toward the door where the Sheriff stood with his ear placed against the cold steel. He wanted to say something like "Who gives a shit?" but didn't.

He was still waiting for the nightmare to be over, holding out hope that any second he'd wake up back in Palmdale, sweating and scared, but otherwise okay.

"If the storm's over then we shouldn't have long to wait before help gets here," Terry said.

"I wouldn't count on it. You know as well as I do that it could take a week still before they get Crosscreek cleared and move on in here," Rawley replied.

Nick pushed his back up against a wall and stuffed his hands into his pockets. He felt the crinkle of cellophane against his fingers. Pulling his hand back out, he discovered the smashed remnant of his pack of Lucky's. There was still one left, bent but unbroken. Nick lit it and drew in deeply, feeling the sore tightness in his chest as the smoke filled his lungs.

"We can't wait that long," came Jake's answer. "We don't have enough food for more than two days and that's being generous. There are only two ways out of this. We have to put an end to whatever is out there."

"You said two ways. What's the other?" Ramp asked.

"We die."

"I was afraid you might say that."

Nick took another deep drag and watched the way his fingers glowed bright orange as he drew in. There was already a long ash dangling from the end of the cigarette. He gave a quick tap and the ash went scattering to the ground next to him.

"And just how the hell are we supposed to put an end to this? We don't have a goddamn clue what's going on," Rawley said.

Next to Nick Emily shifted and sat upright, brushing the hair from in front of her face.

"Maybe we have to destroy the stones," she said softly.

"Emily, honey, what do you mean?" Terry asked.

"It's like the Zombie King. All of his power was held up in a rock. When they destroyed it, they destroyed him too."

"Zombie King?" Rawley asked.

"It was the comic I read back in the basement," Emily answered.

"Christ almighty! A comic book. Is this where we're at now? Trying to save ourselves with the funny pages?"

Rawley walked across the room and dropped into a booth that groaned in protest beneath him.

"She might have a point," Jake said.

"Christ Almighty!"

"No. Listen. We don't have anything else to try and it isn't as half-cocked as it sounds."

Nick watched as Ramp got up and shuffled in closer to the others. He moved much slower than when the two had first met. He looked much older now.

"Do you mean the standing stones?" Ramp asked. "We destroy those and it's all over?"

"I'm not sure," Jake replied. "Before I had said that I thought the energy of this spirit, of all these spirits had been trapped and held onto by the land. Maybe it isn't the land but it's the rocks, like Emily said."

Nick stubbed out his cigarette on the floor next to him and shook his head. He'd never been sure what the solution to this problem might be but he *had* been sure that once they hit upon it everything would click. Suddenly all of it would make sense and their action would be clear cut. What his daughter and Jake were proposing didn't set off any bells. It didn't feel any more right than if they had said a ritual sacrifice was the only way to stop it.

"It's too dodgy," Nick finally spoke up. "I don't have any better idea but this-" He waved his arms in the air.

"I'm afraid I have to agree, Jake," Rawley said. "I mean, we're not talking about an easy task here. The risk is too great for something that seems like we're just grasping at straws."

Jake got up and paced the room for a second.

"No, I don't think we're grasping here, I think Emily's right. Those stones were put there for a reason. There are eight of them encircling the town. If you consider megaliths around the world, most were constructed with a relation to the stars or natural paths of energy. Almost all of the rock in this region is loaded with quartz and quartz conducts and stores energy. I don't think it's a stretch at all."

"Even saying we all agree," Rawley began. "how in the hell do you propose we destroy them?"

"We could blow them up," Nick said. "Does the town keep any sort of explosives, like for building or demolition?"

Rawley shook his head.

"I know Gene Gantry did a lot of the demo work for the new bridge they built in Devon a few years back but I don't imagine he would have anything like that himself," Rawley said.

"I know who would." Ramp spoke with the air of a child finally confessing a secret that he wished he never knew.

2

After his death, Ramp had tried harder than usual to push

Tom Parsons and some of his more unsavory aspects from his mind. Even once things had started going far south there had never been too much time to really reflect on him. They had been going from one jolt to the next so quickly that he barely had time to recover before some new horror had filled his head. Then there was yet one more undeniable fact. Ramp was just too damn old and no longer the sharpest tack in the pile.

Even though Tom Parsons had considered Ramp a friend, he couldn't really say the feeling was mutual. They would sit on his porch drinking beer and shooting the shit, but he had never *liked* Tom. Tom was just one of the old-timers in town, and though he wasn't as far in his age as Ramp, the two shared a common ground in things they had lived through, the ways of the past.

All the same, Ramp had been privy to more of Tom's secrets and philosophies than he would have liked.

"If anyone in town has something we can use it'd be Tom Parsons," Ramp replied, finally giving in to the expectant faces all around him.

Though Tom had never donned the white hood he had pretty well spent his life hating all of what he called the "inferior races," which covered pretty much anyone who wasn't a white American.

Ramp knew only too well that back on his property out behind Shady Acres he'd spent years fortifying his place and preparing for the day when "the cleansing" would come.

Tom had had his own warped concept of a judgment day where God would make the earth cleanse itself of all inferior races. He had reasoned that when the disasters began happening only the whites would have the skills and the wits to outlast.

"Ramp, are you okay?" Nick asked.

He blinked a couple of times, then looked back up at his companions. The expectant faces had turned to masks of concern. He waved his hand and forced a smile.

"I'm fine. You start to get lost in your thoughts too easy

when you get to be my age."

"You were saying, about Tom?" Jake asked.

"Yeah. I've got an idea that we might find what we need up there. Maybe even more than we need. If nothing else there's food."

3

Terry had wanted to fight the decision tooth and nail, but she never uttered a word. Her motives were selfish, she knew, and ultimately the decision wasn't hers. It was Jake's.

Only Jake would be going to Tom's place. It was too risky to move everyone until they knew if the trip was even worthwhile. Jake would go alone.

There had been no debate this time. Out of the group there was only one man cut out for the task; she just wished it wasn't hers.

When Rawley, Ramp and Nick had begun getting Jake's gear, she pulled him aside off in the corner. The tears had come then. She lowered her head and tried to hide them, but he took her chin and raised her eyes until they met his.

"I have to do this," he said.

"I know," she whispered softly. "I just wish you could stay here. We don't even know if any of us will make it out alive and I don't want to spend my last hours alone."

"I'll come back, and we *will* get out of here. All of us. Then we can leave this place and never look back if that's what you want. But now, we have to try."

"What makes you think they won't get you, that she won't get you? You'll be vulnerable and alone, just like Rudy was."

Jake pulled at a thin leather cord around his neck producing the little white disc they had retrieved from Rudy's. He had strung the cord through it and now wore the piece like a necklace. *Or a talisman.*

She shook her head and cast her eyes back toward the ground. The sinking feeling in the pit of her stomach said he was never coming back. He pulled her head against his chest and said, "Trust me."

When the heavy steel door had been opened again and Jake stood upon its threshold, Terry wanted to hide. She didn't think she could watch him go. Steeling her nerves, and freezing the feelings inside, she stood by his side, strong if only on the outside.

Jake turned back toward the tavern and gave the others a smile before heading out into the world.

They stood there as a group and watched him as he marched onto the street and over to Rawley's pickup. Terry's heart was pounding away fast inside her chest.

Before she even realized what was happening, her feet were already carrying her through the snow as she yelled Jake's name. The overdressed giant of a man stopped and turned back toward her as she plowed into him. He didn't go down, though.

Jake dropped the gun and bag he was holding and wrapped his arms around her before momentum could carry her off.

That was when she kissed him. It was the first time ever in front of others, and somehow that one simple act alone pulled all of the heaviness and darkness away from her heart.

"You come back, Jake," was all she said before turning and running back through the tavern door.

Inside as the minutes ticked away like endless hours, Terry found herself wishing she had a watch and yet thankful all the same that she didn't. It was a waiting game now. There was a stony silence in the room. For what seemed like ages no one spoke a word.

Terry had been sitting in one of the booths with her knees drawn into her chest and her mind far from the present when the hushed voices of Ramp and the sheriff brought her back.

"Do you think he can do it?" Ramp asked.

"If anyone can find a way it'll be Jake. If he has to go out there with a hammer and do it one chip at a time he will," Rawley replied.

"What are you talking about?"

Terry was out of her booth and over to them in a flash.

"Shit," Rawley said, getting to his feet.

"What is this?" Terry asked again with disbelief.

"Look," Rawley began. "We didn't want to upset you. Jake's going out to Tom's to look for something to use on the rocks."

"And?" Terry demanded.

"And then he's going to take care of them," Rawley replied.

Before reason could stop her, Terry hauled off and punched Rawley square in the jaw. As the big man wobbled and faltered, she spun around to face Nick.

"Did you know about this, too?" she asked.

Nick cast his eyes to the ground and looked away.

"This is bullshit!" she yelled. "I'm not one of the women folk who needs protecting, you know! I'm as much a part of this group as any of you!'

"Jake wanted it this way," Ramp spoke, but softly.

"It's not Jake's call," she said and stormed off to the hall that led to the restrooms.

Terry sank to her knees and pressed her fists into her temples. A hand fell upon her shoulder. She shook it off and spun around, ready to launch into another volley, but then she stopped. It was Emily.

The main room of the tavern was silent again as Emily dropped onto the floor next to her. She didn't say a word but the look in her eyes spoke volumes. Terry reached her arms around the girl and cried.

Even through the bitter tears and wracking sobs she managed to worry. She worried about Jake, the snow, the woman, and the dead. But most of all she worried about Colin Green.

He was still out there and though she knew he had become

something else, she also knew deep inside that whatever he was now, he'd still be looking for Jake.

4

With the wind slowed to a breeze and the snow barely falling, Jake had made good time out to Shady Acres. The trip through town had been uneventful, allowing his thoughts to linger on Terry and their kiss. It was this alone that he drew warmth and hope from as the pickup made its way down the little road sandwiched between those towering walls of forest.

The gate to Tom Parson's place was massive and solid. A thick, serpent-looking coil of chain wound through the iron bars and terminated in not one, but five locks. The gate itself was set back into a block wall that stretched all the way around the property and stood easily seven feet high from the ground.

There was no way he could ram it without the risk of disabling the truck. He would have to go in on foot.

Jake shut off the engine and got out of the cab, making sure he'd gathered everything he might need before stepping out. Cold little phantoms of breath curled out of his mouth as he exhaled and stared at the wall.

The top of the gate had been ringed with barb wire and there were shimmering pieces of what looked like shattered bottles set into the cement atop the wall. The crazy son of a bitch had done a good job sealing himself in.

He got back into the truck and fired up the engine once more, then pulled forward slowly until the front grille came to rest against the cement blocks.

Jake got back out and slid his two shotguns through the open bars of the gate. Climbing on the hood of the truck, he took one more look around before letting his machete follow the guns to the other side. The cold rushed in and stung his skin as he pulled off Rawley's thick, oversized jacket and draped it over the glass bottles stabbing into the air.

Getting in might be no problem but getting out would be another matter. Placing his hands as carefully as possible onto the fabric of the jacket he pushed down a bit and tested their positions. Vague points and ridges pushed into his palms but it seemed like the jacket might hold back the worst.

Taking a deep breath and closing his eyes, he hoisted all of his weight up onto his hands as quickly as possible. Sharp slivers of glass broke through the jacket and sank into his palms in several places but Jake didn't cry out or stop moving. Getting one foot up then the other, he jerked his hands off of the wall and crouched there trying to maintain his balance.

Blood ran out from the stinging gashes as he surveyed the damage. Nothing had gone too deep; it was mostly just surface wounds. Jake jumped forward from his perch and landed with both feet touching down at almost the same time. In a flash he put all of his weight onto the right leg and hurled his body into the drive as his left foot seemed to break through the surface of the ground beneath it.

He landed flat on his stomach with a thud that kicked the wind out of him and made his teeth smack together. When Jake was able to breathe again he pushed himself up from the snow, leaving two pinkish-red splotches where his hands had been. He walked over to the wall where he landed and saw that his foot *had* broken the surface.

A trench had been dug out a couple feet from the wall and covered over with dirt. Even without the snow he'd never have seen it. In the bottom of this ditch were more broken bottles and rebar spikes that had been sunk into the ground. Jake had been lucky enough to get at least one foot on solid ground even as the other had slipped away.

A wave of disgust took him as the vision of being hobbled so early in his quest played though his head. Tom Parsons had been more than mean; he had been sick.

Picking up the two guns and machete, Jake started down the drive. The house now seemed to loom as something menacing and malicious. He felt like he was walking into a maze of razor blades. One wrong turn and you'd get cut.

Jake took the front steps with extreme caution, expecting one of the boards to break away at any second. None did.

Standing before the front door, he tried to get into Tom Parson's head. There was no room for any more mistakes. He would have to keep one step ahead of the crazy bastard from here on out.

Tom wouldn't have been foolish enough to think the wall could keep everyone out. There might be more traps inside, and these far deadlier. He was going into the belly of the beast.

There was no real way for him to think like Tom Parsons, he realized. What might pass for logic in the real world could end up being entirely foreign to a mind like that.

Jake tried, though. He tried thinking his way through it but only ran around in circles like a dog chasing its tail. Minutes dragged out and the biting cold sank deep beneath his flesh.

Tom had been on his way home when he'd been killed which stood to reason that there had to be a safe way in. It wasn't like he had been holed up inside with all mechanisms in place. If there were pitfalls waiting then they either had to be disengaged easily or entirely nonexistent.

The thought crossed his mind that perhaps being the logical point of entry, the front door might be the worst choice. Maybe Tom came in through the back. But what if he was wrong, and the front were safe? Would he go blundering into his own death around back merely by trying to outthink the crazy old drunk?

Jake grunted in frustration, dropped his weapons to the porch below, and in one quick and easy movement picked up a weather-beaten rocking chair and hurled it through the window. The glass shattered with a sound not unlike wind chimes, sending pieces of the window and rotten wood rocker all over the porch in a dizzying array.

The sound had seemed loud to him but he knew that by the time it reached the back of Shady Acres there would be nothing left. Blowing the locks with the shotgun however would've been like sending up smoke signals that spelled out in big grey letters, *come get me, I'm here.*

Using the stock of one of the guns, Jake cleared away most of the jagged pieces of glass that remained along the edge of the frame. He tossed both guns in through the opening but kept the machete tight in hand as he hauled his body inside. He would have to trust his instinct from here on out and hope that any lurking danger would set off alarms before he stumbled into it.

The front of the house opened right into the living room, he saw as he climbed off the couch which had sat under the window. That was good. There was a chance still that he could get right in and out without having to venture deeper into the dark corridors of the house.

Wasting no time and abandoning stealth Jake was over to the coffee table and sliding it away in a flash. Next he grabbed the rug with both hands and flung it to the far side of the room where it knocked over a small table, sending its contents crashing to the ground.

In the pale light that washed in through the windows he could see the large metal square set into the wood, just as Ramp had said. There was a large metal latch, the kind you have to pull up then turn clockwise to disengage. The metal squealed loudly and there was a hollow bang from the underside as the bolts slid out of place. Jake raised the door until it settled back on its hinges standing at an angle from the floor.

From the dark hole at his feet a cold stale air seemed to rush, not so much blown, but more like it had been sucked into the room above. He reached into his pocket and pulled out the small metal flashlight that had been digging into his side.

The tiny beam cut a short and narrow path into the blackness down below, just barely illuminating the first couple steps leading down. He wished then that he had brought along the larger heavy duty light that was still sitting on the seat of Rawley's truck.

Jake bent down and crouched at the mouth of the hole trying to probe farther into the darkness with the small weak beam. To get down he'd have to climb the ladder, leaving himself open and vulnerable until he reached the ground, unless of course he just dropped. The thought of his last plunge off of the wall made the latter option seem like a bad idea.

Taking both guns by their straps, he slung each over a shoulder and around his chest until they formed a metal and X across his back. With the flashlight clenched between his teeth and the machete in his hand he put a foot on the first rung of the ladder and began his descent.

5

Nick and the other four were lined up against one of the tavern walls, sitting close and shoulder to shoulder when the banging startled them from their silence. Everyone seemed to jump as one, a tiny shudder passing from one body to the next.

The pounding was coming from the other side of the bank vault door. Someone was out there hammering away with their fists.

"Jake!" Terry cried out and sprang to her feet.

Emily grabbed her arm as she was about to run for the door. Had it been anyone other than his daughter, Nick thought that Terry might have gone swinging again.

"We don't know it's him," Emily said with a grim seriousness.

This at least made Terry stop and think before running off and throwing the bolts open.

"Jake? Is that you?" she called out.

The voice that answered was a woman's. It was borderline

hysterical and punctuated with the panicked gasps of sobbing.

"Oh, thank God! Thank Jesus! Hello? Please let me in! Oh, thank God!" the woman yelled.

Everyone was on their feet now but no one made a move for the door.

"What do you think?" Ramp asked.

Nick looked down at his daughter who was shaking her head in an emphatic No.

"Please, goddamn it, let me in! I know you're there. Why won't you let me in?" the woman screamed again.

Had their visitor come just an hour before she would already be inside, shaking off the snow and perhaps settling her nerves with a shot of bourbon. But things were different now. *The game was changing.*

They knew now that they had been naïve before. Whatever it was that moved against them wasn't just some single-minded thing bent solely on killing, like the maniac in a teenage slasher movie. There was intelligence and cunning here. Deception and misdirection. No matter how you chose to look at it, they were being herded, hunted, forced into an ever-closing circle that could shut at any time.

"Please! They'll be here soon!" the woman shouted.

Her voice had grown hoarse and the words were harder to understand as the crying began to muddy and wash them out entirely.

"What if she really does need our help?" Terry asked.

"Yeah but what if she just wants us to open that door and get overrun by a horde of those *people*?" Nick replied.

"I can't place the voice myself," Ramp added.

It was Rawley who broke the standoff and walked toward the door, his feet thundering over the ground.

"Who are you?" his voice boomed.

"Please just open the door! They're coming! Please!"

"Give me a name," Rawley demanded.

"Goddamnit, open the fucking door!"

This last yell was so piercing and loud that it almost seemed to come from inside. The voice broke off at the end as if she had screamed all that she could.

Rawley was looking back at them now, posing the question with his eyes. From the other side came another hoarse scream and then suddenly something smacked into the door so hard that it made a hollow boom like a canon going off.

Nick jumped and smacked his head against the wall. Rawley sidestepped so quickly that he almost lost his footing.

There was silence after that, but even the silence left them hanging. *Was it good? Or did it signify the aftermath of something terrible?*

Rawley moved away from the door and settled back against the wall. Terry followed suit. No one said another word as they sat there and waited. Either way, the implications of what had just happened were bad, and each of them knew it. They didn't need to discuss it.

The quiet didn't last. There was a single sharp rap from above, punctuated by several more in quick succession.

Nick craned his head up and followed the noises with his eyes as they crossed the roof above them and moved away from the front, seeming to head for the area of the restrooms in back.

Two more sets of scrabbling crossed the roof now and followed the first.

Nick opened his mouth to say something but a hand fell over it before he had managed to make a sound. It was his daughter, reaching up with wide eyes.

For a second there was total silence, then it was shattered by the sound of something crashing into the roof, the sound reverberating out of the dim hall. It was repeated again and again until it became a steady thunder that shook dust and white flecks of foam down from the drop ceiling.

Springing to his feet almost in unison with Rawley, Nick took off for the hallway.

He stood in front of the charred doorway and looked up through the hole in the blackened ceiling. Above, was the little shaft of light shining down from outside, but even as he caught sight of it the light vanished and another blow came crashing into the roof. This time when the light returned there was more off it; the hole was larger.

Rawley was just coming up as Nick took a step back, tiny pieces of debris settling into his eye.

"What is it?" Rawley asked in a whisper.

"They're breaking through the fucking roof," Nick said, taking another step back and waving Rawley on.

Still rubbing a sore and watery eye with his fist, Nick spun around at the sound of Terry's voice.

"What do we do?" she asked.

Ramp and Emily stood beside her, all three faces upturned toward the ceiling.

"Christ!" Rawley muttered.

The five of them scurried back into the main room of the bar. As they spoke in still whispered voices the frantic drumming on the roof almost drowned them out.

"We can't stay here," Rawley said. "If they get through we might be able to take them out but the gunshots could draw others to us and we don't have enough ammo for a standoff. If they surround the place with us inside that'll be the end of it."

"If we go outside we're sitting ducks, too," Nick replied.

Rawley grunted and shook his head.

"I'd rather take my chances somewhere we can at least run if we have to. In here we don't know what's coming and we have no way out," Rawley said.

Ramp moved up between the two of them as if he were afraid their debate might come to blows. He raised both hands in the air then looked from Rawley to Nick, then back again.

"Hold on just a sec," he said. "I'm afraid Rawley's right. We can't take the chance that others won't come. Not now. I'll grant you there isn't another place as secure as this but if we can get out of here unseen then we might be able to hole up someplace long enough for Jake to do his thing."

"What if Jake comes back?" Terry asked. "We don't even know that destroying the rocks will *do* anything. We don't even know he'll be able to. What if he comes back here for us and we're gone. He'll be walking into his own death!"

Ramp took the floor again. Nick couldn't help but notice the calm way he was handling the situation, like a man with a plan.

"Okay, here's what we do," Ramp said. "If we can get out of here then we go over to the Pump n' Pay. We can hide out in there and still see the tavern and the street. When Jake comes back we'll know it. If things aren't any better by then we'll hop in the truck and head out to Tom's place. At least we can regroup in his cellar and figure out another course of action."

"What if they come for us at the gas station?" Nick asked.

"Let's pray that they don't. No matter where we go after here our only choices are to run or stay and fight. At least the Pump n' Pay's got three exits, all on different sides," Ramp replied.

Nick didn't like it. He looked down at Emily and balled his hands into fists, clutching them tightly at his sides. Even though he knew the others were right he still couldn't handle the idea of taking her out there into the unknown. The tavern wouldn't be safe for long but at the moment it still *felt* safe, even with the ever widening hole above.

He felt a small hand wriggle its way into his own, breaking the bonds he'd made with his fingers. Looking down he saw Emily staring back up at him. Her eyes were still large but they weren't filled with fear. There was a depth and understanding in them that he hated. He longed to see that carefree and childish gleam in them again but he knew it was gone. She'd seen too much to ever be that same little girl again.

"We have to go," she said softly.

Nick simply nodded, unable to speak as the warmth of tears filled his eyes. There was so much he wanted to say just then that everything seemed to stick in his throat with a great choking lump. All he could do was nod again.

Terry put a reassuring hand on his shoulder while Rawley and Ramp did what men were best at. They pretended not to notice. And he was grateful to all three.

"We can't load ourselves down if we're going to get out of here fast," Rawley said. "I vote we bring the guns and ammo and leave everything else behind except for maybe a couple of flashlights. It'll still be light enough to see for a while so we don't want to use any of our own light, even more so once it gets dark. There'll be food inside the station. Can't be any worse than the shit we've been eating."

"What's the plan for busting out of here?" Ramp asked.

While Rawley scratched his head mulling the idea over, Nick wiped his eyes with the back of his hands. His episode only moments before was over now, leaving in its wake a strange calm and strength he hadn't expected.

The idea came to him at once.

"Here's what we do," Nick began. "Terry, Emily, and Ramp are first out the door if everything's clear. The three of you take off running. Rawley, you follow them until you've got enough distance to turn around and cover the bar. I'll wait here in the doorway until you give me the all clear. As soon as those things come down from the roof we should be able to take them out fast and get across the road before anything else heads our way."

The plan wasn't foolproof by any means but no one objected. Given their circumstances it was probably the best they could do.

The clamor of the roof being rent and torn seemed louder now as everyone scattered to load up.

6

Ramp stood huddled next to Terry and Emily in front of the steel door. As soon as Nick opened the place up Rawley would be the first out in case there was already trouble waiting. If the coast was clear he'd hold back and then the trio would be off.

Terry and Emily were to lead. Ramp had played it off as male bravado, bringing up the rear to keep the other two safe, but the truth was he didn't want to slow them down. He was going to give it all he could but when you got to be his age there was a certain distrust you held for your own body. Things didn't always work like they were supposed to. At least if he went down they might not know, they might not stop to help.

"Is everyone ready?" Nick asked.

There were solemn nods all around. Ramp could feel his heart rate climbing fast and already draining his reserves before the door was even open.

"Come on. Let's do this," he said.

The next instant was a mess of adrenaline fueled confusion. At first he didn't know what was happening but he knew it was all going wrong.

Nick threw back the bolts and pulled the door inward, the cords in his neck standing out strained as he tried to heave it in one quick arc.

Rawley pushed off with one foot as he prepared to take off running, then all of a sudden the big man was going down. As his body slammed into the snow the shotgun he was holding went off with a deafening roar. Bits of icy dirt flew into the air, spraying out in all directions.

Terry, caught up in her own momentum and not expecting Rawley to stop, got tangled in the Sheriff's outstretched legs and went crashing down beside him.

There was panic and shouting as Terry scrambled onto her back and Rawley struggled to lift himself to his knees.

Nick was yelling something, too, but Ramp couldn't make it out. He was frozen in the moment unsure of what had happened or what he should do.

Without even realizing it Ramp bent over and struggled to help Terry get Rawley back on his feet. His legs suddenly felt rubbery and sweat dotted his brow as he pulled with everything he had.

He saw then what had happened. The bloody and battered corpse of a woman lay stretched out in front of the door. Her face was set in a mask of terror and her jaw hung broken at a funny angle. *What have we done?*

Ramp felt two hands seize his shoulders. It was Nick, and he was yelling.

"Go! Go! Go!" he screamed.

As if in answer there was another terrible scream from the rooftop.

Snapping out of it, Ramp realized that Terry and Emily were already running ahead of him. Rawley had recovered and was already on point with his shotgun. Ramp began to run.

Before he had even taken five steps it already felt like his lungs couldn't keep up. The cold grabbed his chest like pincers and just kept on squeezing.

From behind there was a gunshot, then another. Someone or something was crying out in pain. He didn't stop to look back.

The Pump n' Pay was growing closer and closer with each footfall but still he didn't know if he could make it. His chest hurt, a sharp needling pain ran through it. His knees felt like they might shatter at any second.

Up ahead Emily and Terry were disappearing through the front glass doors.

Ramp pushed himself on and on until the scenery going past him no longer registered. He fixed his vision on that one point and nothing else existed. Either he was going to make it or he was going to die in mid-stride, but at least it would be a good clean death. A *natural* death.

Two sets of hands were pulling at him before he even realized he had made it. Emily and Terry were ushering him in.

A thick blackness swam before his eyes as he struggled to fill his lungs. Beneath him his legs gave out and he went down. As his head grew light the girls' voices began to sound metallic and hollow, distant and senseless.

The blackness overtook him and their voices were gone altogether.

7

In the bottom of the basement room the temperature felt almost ten degrees colder than above and Jake found himself wishing for Rawley's jacket again.

The room wasn't large, perhaps only spanning half of the house above it, but in the intervening years between Ramp's visit it seemed that Tom had been busy.

Jake panned the light around the room, trying to get his bearings. In one corner a heap of furniture had been shoved against the wall and out of the way. Farthest from him a small room jutted out, fully framed but lacking a door.

Everywhere he looked there were boxes filled with tools and materials. Two by fours, screws, and nails littered most of the floor.

Jake saw a propane camping lantern sitting on one of the shelves lining the wall. Gripping the flashlight between his teeth again, he turned the knob on the canister the gave it a sniff. The thick nauseating smell of propane filled his nose, almost making him gag. It had only taken a second then to fish out his lighter from a myriad of pockets before the cold steady glow of the lantern reached out and washed over the concrete walls. Jake clicked off the flashlight and stuck it in his pants.

Now that everything was in plain view the room didn't look quite like the hazardous mess it had moments before. The furniture in the corner was stacked away neatly. He guessed that it had already been in position but had gotten moved to clear away a work space. With the exception of the stacks of wood on the floor most of the mess seemed to come from a collapsed shelf that had strewn its contents about.

Walking to the room in back Jake peered through the open door frame. There was a mattress resting on the floor with a small table next to it. Higher up on the wall above the makeshift bed was a painting depicting ducks in formation over a summer lake.

As he returned to the main room again Jake found himself wondering if that had been meant for Ramp and Mabel. Somehow the thought of them living and sleeping in that little space gave him the chills. It would be like living in a mausoleum.

Against the wall adjacent to the stairs sat the generator with coils of extensions cords plugged in and resting by its side. Above, a hole had been busted through the concrete and dark brown earth spilled through, falling to the floor. That must have been where the exhaust vent had gone. Tom had torn it back out for some reason.

Jake went over and put his hand into the hole. There was a sharp, chilly draft coming through it. Apparently some of the shaft remained clear and open to the world above.

Turning back to the shelves again his eyes picked out two cardboard boxes. For a second his heart did a small leap in his chest as the word scrawled in black marker hit home. P-DEF it said. *Perimeter defense.*

He crossed the room in a flash and grabbed one of the boxes, handling it as if it might contain hundreds of angry snakes ready to strike. Placing it carefully on the floor he pulled back the cardboard flaps slowly and gingerly.

There was a mess of metal, wire, and black electrical tape inside, but on top of the pile was what looked like a prototype or working model of something nasty.

The contraption consisted of three steel pipes capped at each end. Wires ran into the pipes from a set of nine volt batteries, which were in turn connected to a metal plate fixed atop a small plunger. *Mines. The crazy bastard was making mines.*

Jake thought of his walk up to the house again and

shuddered. Had he gotten lucky? Was there already a whole array of these things hidden just below the surface? There was no way of knowing for sure but he was suddenly glad that he had stuck to the drive and hadn't ventured to the back of the house looking for a way in.

He left the box where it lay and pulled the other down from the shelf, taking even more care with this one. Inside were more of the cut lengths of pipe, each end fitted tight with a cap. These, however, weren't wired like those in the prototype, these each had a waxy green length of fuse jutting from small holes drilled in the ends. *What were these for?* Jake didn't want to know, or even venture a guess.

He had found exactly what he had come for.

Just then the air around him grew even colder. Now the smoky white phantoms of breath escaping his lips became more substantial as the temperature dropped. The light from the propane lantern seemed to dim but it didn't go out.

Hurriedly Jake shook loose one of his guns, chambered a round, and leveled the barrel in front of him. There were footsteps now overhead. They stopped just short of the opening leading from the basement to the living room above.

Cautiously Jake raised his weapon and moved slowly around the base of the metal ladder trying to catch a glimpse of whomever waited there. He couldn't see anyone. There was enough light spilling from that hole in the floor to illuminate part of the room above, but if someone *were* standing up there they had been careful to stay just out of his line of sight.

There was a groan of metal and Jake's finger tensed on the trigger before he'd realized what was happening. The steel door was coming down. It had slammed in place with an ear-splitting crack before he could reach the ladder to stop it. There were more sounds from overhead but these weren't the light taps of footsteps.

Furniture was sliding across the wood floor in the room above. The couches and tables all made a terrible screech as they left the wood and settled on top of the steel.

Dropping the shotgun to the ground, Jake was up the ladder and pushing against the door with everything he had but it wouldn't budge. He was trapped.

As his mind reeled with thoughts of escape, a sour raspy voice seemed to whisper in his own head. *Goddamn redskin savage.* For a second the smell of whiskey clogged his nose and the inside of his mouth puckered with the dry taste of booze. But then it was gone. The house was silent again. And he was still trapped.

CHAPTER ELEVEN

When Rawley moved through the doors of the Pump n' Pay close on the heels of Nick Anderson, the first thing he saw were the girls *and* Ramp.

Nick rushed over and dropped to his knees next to the old man. Ramp's eyes were shut and Terry was shaking him by the collar of his jacket.

Rawley didn't rush over to the others. He remained standing just inside the closed door and let his eyelids drop, shutting out the scene. They weren't going to make it, not like this. All of their eggs were now in one basket, Jake's basket. If he couldn't do what he'd set out to, or if they were wrong, then that was it. Game over.

There was a short, raspy, intake of breath and Rawley braced himself for the sobs that would follow, except they didn't come. Slowly he reopened his eyes to see Ramp blinking rapidly and looking around.

Rawley felt some of the heaviness lift, but not much. Ramp was alive, though not quite kicking, but it still didn't change the situation.

The old man pulled himself up onto his elbows and chuckled slightly. The sound came out thin and dry, turning into a cough almost as soon as it had escaped. Terry growled in frustration and slapped a hand across his shoulder.

"It's not funny," she said without real anger. "We thought you were gone."

"Guess I've still got a little left in me," Ramp said with a smile. "Though I don't think another move will be in my future. At least not on foot."

Rawley turned and looked out the door behind him, scanning the whitewashed landscape for any sign of movement. Satisfied that they hadn't been followed, he began scouting around the store for something to block the windows.

Nick Anderson rose to his feet and ran a hand through sweat-dampened hair. He fiddled with something in the pocket of his coat, something that made a muffled click over and over. Rawley stopped for a minute and watched as he walked around behind the register and looked up, searching. Nick pulled down a pack of cigarettes, started to open it, then looked around sheepishly.

"It's okay," Rawley said. "I think given the circumstances they won't miss them."

Nick's face flushed slightly with embarrassment, then he pulled a smoke out of the pack and produced a chrome lighter from his jacket. *The clicking.*

Rawley continued his search into the small back office where he found a stack of cardboard boxes neatly flattened and sitting in a pile. Grabbing several of them he made his way back into the store. He stopped off in the little miscellaneous aisle and grabbed a roll of packing tape from a shelf where it was sandwiched between playing cards and car air fresheners.

With Nick helping, covering the storefront windows had been quick work. They had left several slits open to look out from and it was through these that the scant light now came in. The new gloom inside the station gave the impression that half the day had passed since Jake left, a thought that brought even more questions to mind.

"You don't think that seeing the windows closed up will tip them off to us do you?" Terry asked.

"Not as much as seeing us moving around in here," Rawley snapped back.

His tone just then had been short and coarse, but even as the words came out he knew it wasn't Terry's second guessing that upset him. It was his own. *Should've called in the state boys,* the voice inside his head nagged on.

On some level he felt that it was second guessing which had gotten them all into this mess to begin with. If he hadn't kept on with the stubborn, macho track of wanting to handle things himself might they not have gone so far?

Doesn't matter now. Keep them alive and consider it redemption.

Nick was behind the register again, this time producing a well-used yellow plastic ashtray. He stubbed out his cigarette in it, then scooted it away along the counter. He then took the pack of smokes and the little chrome lighter and slid them alongside it.

From the corner of his eye, Rawley saw Ramp leaning forward and sitting full up. Turning to face him, he saw a shine in Ramp's eyes which was fixed on the counter by Nick.

"Terry, why don't you take Emily in back there and have a look around. Scout for some supplies," Ramp said.

The look she gave him was immediately contemptuous. Her eyes narrowed and the corners of her mouth turned down.

"What did I say before?" she asked.

"Right. Sorry. Old habits, that's all. You know, there's a lot of women would swoon having a man trying to protect them."

"Yeah, well, I'm not one of them. At least not now. Don't keep me out of things."

"Fair enough," he replied. "What I was going to say is that we need to have a plan. We need to think about what we're going to do if they come for us in here, or what we'll do if Jake doesn't make it back."

Terry froze like a statue as these last words came out. Rawley could see all of her features lock up, but it was her eyes where the real action happened. All of the emotions she tried to keep from busting out shone clear and true in her eyes.

"I've got an idea," Ramp began again. "None of you will like it, but just set your emotions aside for a sec and hear me out."

2

Jake had managed to get control of himself before the panic *really* dug in and took hold. He needed to be focused now more than ever.

The feeling of imminent danger had passed. Old Tom Parsons had done his worst for now. *Had it been Tom?* He thought again of the sour taste of whiskey and the cold outraged voice in his head. There was no doubt.

In the forefront of his mind he held onto the image of his friends locked away in the Rockwell Tavern as he set about his work. They were waiting for him, and it was that knowledge which drove him on.

Jake moved quickly into the makeshift bedroom at the back of the basement. He pulled the top sheet from the mattress on the ground and carried it back into the main room, spreading it open over the concrete floor.

Next he emptied the box of homemade pipe bombs into the center of the square, then went about searching some more.

It hadn't taken long to find what he was looking for once he spied the batteries. Sitting cradled in their chargers were three battery packs, the kind he hoped belonged to a cordless drill. Not far off from that was a milk crate piled with tools.

Jake turned the crate upside-down and scattered its contents across the floor, eyeing every piece as it fell out. The drill landed hard on its side, splintering off a small chip of blue plastic. He seized it quickly and popped in one of the batteries, letting out a huge sigh of relief when the bit on the end began to spin.

The drill was already fitted with a one-inch diamond bit that had white streaks of concrete embedded in its grooves. This is what Tom had been using on the wall.

From the mess on the floor Jake selected a long steel spike

and short handle sledge then placed everything in the center of his tarp next to the pipes.

He folded in the corners of the sheet, then wound a length of twine around the top to secure it. Now that he had his bag of goodies he just needed to get out.

The exhaust vent for the generator had been the first thing that came to mind when he surveyed the room again. The hole in the concrete wall was only about a foot in diameter, but the concrete itself was thin enough to widen.

Moving the generator and its coils of cords out of the way, Jake grabbed the larger, heavier sledge resting behind it.

The wooden handle was cold and stuck to the drying blood on his wounded hands as he tested the heft and found his grip. Jake took a deep breath and swung at the perimeter of the opening with everything he had. There was a loud thud that echoed through the basement as the vibration flew up the shaft, digging deep into his wounds.

Concrete broke away and was chased to the floor by dirt spilling in. It was going to work.

What seemed like an eternity later, the hole still wasn't large enough for him to fit through. His arms were shaky and weak. The sharp sting of sweat mixed with the blood on his hands creating a slick painful layer between his fingers and the wooden handle.

At the point when he wasn't sure if he could go on, Jake forced himself to think of Terry. He found the image of her in his mind shifty and hard to hold on to. The more he tried, the more it evaded him. Another face pushed its way up from his subconscious. It was the face of Emily Anderson. And he had made a promise.

Jake wiped his hands off on the sack he'd made from the bedsheet, then picked up his hammer once more. As he brought the head down again and again on the wall, a whole parade of faces marched through his mind. There was Emily, and Terry, and Mabel Rampart, Rudy, Tracy, and Ramp. The most haunting he discovered wasn't Emily but the face of his own Momma.

Like a machine now, he brought the hammer down but barely realized he was doing so. His eyes felt burning and wet and a few small tears cascaded down the dark skin of his cheek. *I'm sorry, Momma.*

When the hole in the wall was large enough to crawl into, Jake began pulling armfuls of dirt into the basement. He widened as much as he could but the rest would have to be done as he ascended.

Taking the length of twine still hanging loose from the knot on the bag, Jake tied it tight around his ankle then took a step forward. He had to pull hard with his right leg to drag the bundle along behind him as he climbed into the hole.

Jake closed his mouth and eyes, then began digging his way up through the ground. The deep smell of the earth washed into his nostrils, filling them with a scent that was old and dank.

His fingers finally touching the cold wetness of snow above, Jake fought desperately to pull himself out of the ground with everything he had left. As his arms strained to lift him from the ground his right foot began to numb from the dead weight of the sack.

Finally emerging in an effort that must have looked like the living dead crawling from a grave, Jake stood upright and stretched the muscles of his legs which were threatening to cramp.

His hair and clothes were damp and clotted with dirt. Taking one of his sore and mangled hands, he tried to wipe the earth from his face but stopped when he felt the blood from his hands turning the soil to a streaky mud across his skin.

He bent down and untied the cord which had bound his makeshift sack to his ankle. The skin underneath his sock felt sore and grooved where the twine had dug in. As he set the bag down in the snow beside him a voice called out freezing him in place.

"Jake."

In that instant his heart had gone from an exhausted calm to full speed ahead. The voice was soft and seemed almost to float over across the expanse of yard to him but he recognized it without looking.

She was standing there on the other side of the open yard where the empty stretch of white stopped sharply at the base of the woods. She wasn't dressed for the cold, wearing only an old faded housedress and a shawl draped over her shoulders.

"Momma?" he said in a whisper.

His feet had begun to move on impulse alone but the toe of a boot became ensnared in the bedsheet stopping him suddenly.

He looked at the yard again buried under its shroud of snow. This one long open stretch was the only thing that separated the two of them but he couldn't move. If his foot hadn't gotten tangled in the bag he might have rushed out there without thinking. But it *had* gotten caught and that was what stopped him. Not the bag, but what was inside it. *P-DEF. Perimeter defense.*

"Why do you leave me cold, Jake?" she asked, her voice still distant and soft.

He knew with every rational bone in his body that it couldn't really be her, not the Momma that he knew. She couldn't have survived the woods and snow. She was a spirit, or if not a spirit then still somehow changed.

It didn't matter, though. He couldn't take the chance. He couldn't turn his back on her and just hope he was right. Jake rolled his fingers into tight fists that he drummed hard into the sides of his legs as hot tears swam down his cheeks, cutting paths through the grime. He would never be able to go on unless he was sure, not into the near future, nor even the far and distant one.

"Stay there, Momma! Don't move, I'm coming to get you," he yelled.

Jake bent down, grabbed the bag at his feet, then hurled it through the air several feet in front of him. It landed with a clank as the contents inside rattled against each other. There was no explosion, though.

He jumped across the blanket of snow and landed on the damp sheet. His feet rolled over the top of the pipes inside almost making him lose balance.

In the distance his mother was turning away from him and moving back into the cover of trees.

"Momma!" he yelled.

Jake grabbed the bag again and hoisted it up, ready to throw when the sound of snapping branches halted him. He looked up and saw her still standing at the edge of the forest, her back to him now. The snapping of branches continued even though she remained still.

His heart was beating wildly now as he expected something to come bounding out of the trees to snatch her. And something *did* come bounding out of the trees.

It was a rabbit, almost the color of the snow itself that came dancing its way out of the underbrush and into the wide open yard. He watched it come speeding in his direction with great, long, effortless leaps.

When the rabbit had made half the distance to him it stopped, its little nose working the air furiously. In the next instant it was off again, but this time when those small padded feet landed there was a muffled click. Jake could hardly blink before the ground erupted in a gigantic boom scattering a dark spray of earth and bright bits of red across the yard.

The blast knocked Jake backwards and in that moment of flailing uselessly at the air, he was sure there would be a small, soft click when he landed, too. There wasn't.

His back was sore from the impact but he was still able to breathe. He struggled onto his elbows, his eyes immediately moving to where his mother had stood. She was gone. There was no movement in the treeline. For a second he tried to listen for footfalls or the gentle breaking of twigs, but the explosion had left his ears ringing. *Momma.*

The rabbit had forced him to stop much the same way as

snagging his foot on the bag had. It forced him to stop and to reason. Twice in the blind panic to reach his Momma he had lost his grip and gone leaping feet-first into certain death.

It had never occurred to him what would have happened if the bed linen bag had actually landed on a mine. It wouldn't have been his feet tripping the switch but it might as well have been.

Jake looked at the gaping muddy crater in the yard and felt his throat tighten. His foolhardy mine sweeping attempt would still have put him in range of the blast. *And if the other bombs had gone off too? The ones in the bag?*

Bloody pieces of fur dotted the once pristine white of the yard, their deep scarlet fading into pink as the snow absorbed the fluid like syrup on a snow-cone.

"White Rabbit, three ounces Stoli vanilla, three ounces vanilla liqueur, one ounce milk, ice."

The words were out of his mouth and gone before he even realized they had been spoken. He had felt disconnected from them just then. The words had been in his head, but at the same time they didn't belong to him. *Rudy. The rabbit.*

Everything hit home in a clear and pure flash of insight. His Momma had been bait. He was sure of it. She had been there lined up against the trees like a pawn in a chess match, confused and not acting out a will of her own, but the will of something else entirely. But not everything seemed to be under the power of this influence. Hadn't Rudy just proved that?

Jake got back on his feet and turned to face the side of the house and the hole he'd crawled out of. His escape tunnel was almost within jumping distance to the front porch. If he could just make it there, then he could follow the safety of the drive back out to the wall.

This time he threw the bag as hard as he could, hoping to make it over the weather-beaten rail of the front porch. The sheet was heavier now, completely soaked through from the snow. It caught the wooden beam and hung there half on and half off the porch, dripping water down with a steady rhythmic splat.

Jake stretched his legs then leaped toward the open mouth of the exhaust vent hole. As his left foot hit the edge of it, the loose dirt along the rim began to avalanche almost sucking him down with it. He managed to regain his balance, taking a deep breath as he tried to size up the distance to the porch.

He was so close to the house that reason said Tom wouldn't have planted explosives close enough to do damage to it. Of course he didn't have much faith that Tom even knew what reason was. He couldn't take the chance.

Shifting all of his body weight onto his right leg, Jake bent low and sprang forward with all of his might. A hot burning tear rippled along the muscle of his thigh as it strained too hard. His hands were outstretched and ready to clamp on to the wood.

Instead of coming up short as he had feared, Jake overshot his mark and crashed through the rotted railing. He landed hard on top of the wet sheet, metal pipes pushing against his ribs. He had made it, though, and he wasn't hurt. Nothing serious at least.

A thin smile stretched across his lips even as the pain of getting up made him wince. *You just might do it,* he thought.

There was still the matter of getting back over the wall. He had used Rawley's truck for a boost the first time but now he needed a way to scale it from this side. Turning, he faced not his intended target, but the worn front door to Tom Parson's house. He didn't want to go back inside, but there didn't seem to be any choice. He had to find something to climb up the-

The wall.

Even as he turned to face it the movement along its top grabbed his attention. A pale and dirty man wearing nothing but blood-streaked jeans was clambering over the top. He landed in the trench on the inside, a rebar spike piercing his shoulder and popping out the other side. The man cried out in pain but struggled to get back up and tear himself loose.

There were more of them at the gate. At least twenty. Dead white arms and hollow angry faces pressed through the open sections of the metal. Some of the thinner ones were trying to wedge their bodies into the tiny openings, but it was impossible to get through.

How didn't he notice them? The answer was immediately clear as their screams and shouts disappeared when he closed his eyes. The only thing that remained loud and constant was the ringing. His brain just filled in the rest. The man with the impaled shoulder had gotten free and was now running across the yard, running straight for Jake.

Before he could even unsling one of the shotguns there was another huge eruption of earth and snow and body parts. Jake winced as a section of arm, from the elbow down, came flying and landing not five feet from the front steps.

The others stood silent for a second like animals dazzled by something strange and new, then continued their assault on the gate. So far none had followed the first man's lead and clambered up on the truck, but it wouldn't take them long to figure it out.

Jake grabbed his bag and took off running down the front steps. Half-way up the drive he stopped.

The writhing mass of bodies on the other side of the wall went into a frenzy. They fought and clawed against the concrete blocks, the metal barrier, and each other. Two women were making their way onto the hood of the pickup now. One was completely naked, her body covered in dark purple bruises and bright red scratches. The other wore a muddy night gown.

Dropping to his knees he undid the twine binding the sheet together and pulled out two of the pipe bombs. Then he fished in his pocket, found his lighter, and flicked open the lid.

Even as he got ready to light one of the waxy fuses he realized the truck would be history if he followed through.

Four hands appeared on top of the wall, flailing and grasping at the broken glass. They were growing redder by the second but not deterred. *The truck won't do you any good if they get in.*

Jake spun the flint wheel of his lighter with his thumb and watched in dismay as it sparked but didn't catch flame. Frantically he tried again and again. On the sixth spin of the wheel he finally felt the heat of the almost transparent fire. He held the end of a fuse over the wind guard and it jumped to life, sending a shower of hot sparks onto his hand.

He pulled back his arm and threw, not taking the time to get a good aim.

The metal canister spun through the air, spraying its orange shower out like fireworks. There was only a second as it landed in the tangled mess of bodies before it exploded.

Jake didn't see the first blast because he was busy with the second fuse. There was a muffled rumble underneath the ringing and he could feel the percussion move through the air in a wave, but he didn't see the carnage until the second bomb was spinning through the air on the heels of the first.

The gate hadn't fallen completely but hung lopsided, still attached at the bottom on one side. There was a brilliant flash as the second explosion went off.

When the smoke cleared this time the gate *was* lying flat on the ground and most of the wall to either side had crumbled. The mass of bodies no longer resembled people in any way. The smell of gunpowder and the sharp metallic scent of blood mixed in the air and hit him hard.

Jake leaned over and threw up in the snow. His entire body hurt as the muscles in his chest and abdomen were wracked by spasm after spasm.

When the heaving subsided he remained on his hands and knees, raising only his head to look at the opening again.

The pickup was lying on its side and thick black clouds of smoke poured out of it. Bright hungry flames licked at it and the body pieces nearby.

In addition to the blood and gunpowder, the heavy, greasy

smell of burning flesh pooled in the air around him. Jake wanted to heave again but didn't.

The explosions and smoke will draw others. He had to get out of there now, and the rest of his journey would be on foot.

3

The sound of the first explosion greeted them with the roar of distant thunder. Terry felt a sudden rush of mixed and conflicting emotions overwhelm her. At first there was an anxious panic, followed quickly by a sense of elation. She had to clasp a hand over her mouth to keep from crying out.

In the near darkness of the Pump n' Pay she watched similar expressions play out on the faces of the others.

"Well, I'll be damned," Rawley said in a gruff whisper.

They listened in silence for a while until the second two blasts came in quick succession.

"Two down, six to go," Ramp said smiling.

"Two? You really think so?" Nick asked. "I'm not sure if there was enough time after the first one for him to have gotten to another stone."

"You're probably right. But that had to have been one gone for sure," Ramp replied.

The five of them waited expectantly but heard nothing else. Terry felt her initial sense of elation go slipping away as time pressed on.

The explosions had been the first and only sign they had gotten that Jake was all right, and now in their absence she began to worry again.

Outside, several loud and feral cries pierced the quiet. Rawley and Nick scrambled over low to the ground and grabbed two of the guns off the floor.

The screams were close and filled with a bitter rage. They

seemed to be right out in front of the station.

"The lighter!" Ramp said. "Get the goddamn lighter!"

Nick scurried back across the floor, gun in hand, popping up only for a second behind the register. Appearing again next to the counter and still in a crouch, he slid the lighter across the floor to Ramp, with a look of shame.

The yelling and guttural sounds were moving in fast. Terry could hear the heavy pounding of feet hammering into the ground. She reached over and took hold of Emily by the shoulders, readying the girl to take off running.

Outside, the noises came right up to the building and swept past as quickly as they had come, rapidly fading into the distance.

Everyone remained at ready for another five minutes then finally relaxed, albeit uneasily.

"Must've heard the blasts," Rawley said.

Terry thought he seemed on the verge of saying more but his eyes locked with hers and he pressed his lips together tightly, until they were little more than a thin line.

"That was no good," Ramp said. "If they had really been coming for us we would've been cooked. Jake may be a while yet, I think we should put the plan into action."

Across the room Nick nodded, and Rawley grunted in reply. Terry found herself not saying anything and in turn no one looked to her for a response.

She had always thought of herself as a strong woman, maybe not a modern day empowered type, but strong nonetheless. When the cards were down on the table, though, did it really hold true?

She realized then that it was Jake who made her helpless. Until all of this, she had never admitted how deep her feelings for him ran. As soon as he was in the path of danger all of that changed. A little barricade inside her heart was swept out of the way, and it was those feelings now which were so crippling. She *was* strong. But she was also scared.

The fact that she found herself powerless to keep Jake from harm, in turn, made her feel powerless to do anything. *You're not, though. You're as strong as any of them.*

"First things first," Ramp was saying. "We need to lift those covers off of the two tanks. They're heavy and if we have to do it on the fly it'll never happen."

"You want to cover me if I go out?" Nick asked Rawley.

Rawley never got a chance to reply. Terry got up fast and stood between the two men.

"I want to do it," she said.

Rawley began to open his mouth again to protest, but she shot him another look.

"I'm doing it," she said. It was no longer open for discussion.

"Those covers are heavy," Ramp said from the ground beneath her. "Maybe you should let Nick-"

"No offense, boys, but I don't think any of you are in any better shape than I am," Terry said a little mockingly.

Nick was the only one who hadn't issued a challenge and it was to him that she looked now.

"Let me see if I can find a pry bar or something in back," he said and walked from the main room.

Terry bundled up and prepared to go out.

The snow was falling again, but gently like a soft powder from the grey above. Terry gripped the pry bar tightly with both hands then took a tentative step forward. Her senses had gone into overdrive, locking on to any little sight, sound, or smell that might betray the presence of danger.

The two metal discs that covered the gas tanks were larger and more formidable looking than she had remembered. The very sight of them chipped away at some of her bravado as she worried for the first time that they might not open. At least not under *her* power.

Terry looked around again quickly but nothing in her surroundings seemed amiss. She would need to do this quickly *and* quietly.

Kneeling, she pressed the flat end of the pry bar into one of the little notches etched out of the cover. Putting all of her weight behind it, Terry pushed down on the bar and felt the lid lift slightly. It *was* heavy.

Using what little leverage she could muster, Terry tried to slide the edge of the cover out of the hole just enough to where it wouldn't fall back in. Hopefully she could move it by hand after that.

The metal circle groaned against the concrete as it slid several inches out of place. In the total silence of the world around her, the noise seemed enormous and terrifying.

She pulled out the bar, letting the cover drop back down again. It made a hollow boom that echoed in the tank below. Terry then took her fingers and slipped them through the opening she'd made, got a firm grip, then pulled hard. This time it slid about five inches farther as her initial momentum carried it grating across the concrete.

She stopped again and listened. Only the rapid sound of her breathing broke the stillness now. The metal cover had been slid almost half-way open and she reasoned that it was probably enough. Turning back to the glass door behind her, she saw Nick Anderson nodding in affirmation. *One down, one to go.*

There was less hesitation and a little more spring in her step as she got up and moved to the next cover. She felt good actually, and yeah, maybe just a bit empowered. A smile spread across her lips as she knelt by her next target.

Nothing had alerted her to his presence until it was too late. He had come up fast and silent behind her. What *had* caught her attention in the last second was a sound from the door behind her. Terry turned toward it just as the fist came crashing into the side of her face.

The blow took her so off-guard that the innocent and childish smile still played about her lips even as her head went reeling from the impact. Her fingers opened involuntarily and the pry bar flew from her grip and into the snow out of reach.

A body fell hard onto her, crushing the air from her lungs even as fingers closed around her throat like steel. She felt a mouth clamp down on her shoulder, teeth working furiously at the fabric of her jacket, but she didn't fight back. She *couldn't* fight back.

Her body panicked as it tried desperately to suck in air. She could hear a great deal of commotion now, but none if it made any sense.

"Don't! You might hit her!" somebody screamed.

For a second the weight on top of her seemed to lessen as if it were being pulled off, and the fingers around her throat lost some of their purchase.

She gulped in a huge lungful of air, making a sound not unlike a seal as she did so. Burning hot tears filled her eyes, then the weight was on her again.

This time she *did* fight back. Feet kicking and arms flailing, she hammered against her attacker. There was another second of lightness as she felt him being dragged away once more, and this time she saw his face.

That face had reminded her of a dog she once had. The dog had come home one day with rabies, all twitchy and snarling with misplaced rage. This face looked like that. But there was something even more terrible about this visage.

It belonged to Colin Green.

Nick and Rawley had managed to drag him completely off her this time and Terry bolted forward on her hands and knees, still coughing and gasping.

Rawley yelled out in pain, and Terry stopped, turning back to them. Her head moved just in time to see Colin throw Nick through the air at one of the gas pumps. Rawley was on the ground and struggling to get up. Both of their guns lay abandoned in the snow.

Colin whipped around to face her again, pausing only a second before making his charge. Instinct told her to run, but the best she could manage was another burst of frantic crawling. As she moved forward, one hand landed on the metal pry bar she had lost.

Terry dropped and rolled to her back just as the dark silhouette of Colin plummeted down on her. With both hands she thrust upward with the pry bar, feeling it hit something, then after a pause go sliding in farther. Colin screamed, landed on her, then rolled off. He was back on his feet in an instant, bounding away howling.

Nick came rushing past her and there was the thunderous boom of his shotgun going off. It was a sound that wracked her head and made her ear drums throb in pain.

In the next instant Terry felt Nick put his arms around her, lifting her from the ground. He half-dragged, half-carried her back into the shelter of the Pump n' Pay.

"Are you okay? Terry, let me see. Are you all right?" Nick asked.

Rawley came in and shut the door fast, throwing the latch in one fluid motion. Terry looked up into Nick's wide eyes and tried to speak, but found herself launching into a fit of coughing instead.

When she did finally speak, her voice came out cracked and froggy. For a second she didn't even recognize it as her own.

"Okay," she said. "I'll be okay."

Before the last word had fully left her mouth her body began shaking and she burst into tears.

The outburst didn't last long. Even through her own sobbing she listened to the words being said in between all of the *you'll be fines*.

"Shit!" Rawley said stamping his foot. "That was a hell of a lot of noise."

"It's worse than just that," Nick replied. "Colin got away. Terry hurt him but I don't know where or how bad. I took a shot but he was already too far."

Terry felt a queasy, sinking sensation in her belly. It was her fault. If she hadn't needed to prove something then maybe things would've gone off differently.

As it stood, she thought there was as much chance for her making a quick run anytime soon as there was for Ramp. Already her throat seemed to be swelling and thick welts formed where Colin's fingers had been.

In the distance there was another sound like a muffled and faraway thunder clap. *Jake. Two down.*

The five of them looked to each other silently for confirmation, each face asking the same question. *Did you hear that, too?* Terry smiled. It was the only reply she could give.

4

The fuse had been a quick one. Jake felt the blast shove him through the air, both feet lifting off the ground as he flew face-first into the forest floor. Pieces of the rock pelted his back and a fine dust brushed over his skin like sandpaper. It hadn't been a good start.

Drilling the first hole had gone easier than he'd expected. The diamond bit showed little wear, giving him hope that it might last long enough to get the job done, but the bit *was* smaller than the diameter of the pipe.

He had widened the opening with the steel spike and handheld sledge, then twisted and shook one of the pipe bombs into place. After that the only thing left to do was light it and run. In theory.

Jake pushed himself up from the snow and did a quick check for injury. If he lived to see several more days he would most likely be a mess of bruises, but otherwise he found little more than minor scrapes and abrasions.

The stone was still behind him. He hadn't turned to survey the damage just yet. Part of him was loathe to do so. Even though the thought of seeing his lack of success weighed heavily, it was nothing compared to the burning curiosity he felt. Jake turned slowly, drawing the moment out. Just as the rock began creeping into his peripheral vision it issued a low rumble, growing steadily into the sound of stone grating on stone.

Jake turned to face the monolith quickly now, his eyes just getting the full picture as what remained standing toppled to the ground. Even though he watched it happen, the final thud of rock pounding into the earth made him jump. A haze of smoke and dust lingered in the air like a fog.

He walked toward the pile of rubble with hesitant steps, still unable to believe that the entire thing had gone down in one blast. Even as he had drilled the first hole, Jake had figured it would take a least three to bring the beast down.

The winter had helped him. Not just one winter, but every single freeze and thaw that had swept across that land since the stones were first erected. The rock was weakened and fissured. Tiny cracks ran like veins across the surface and through the subsurface.

Taking a fist-sized chunk of stone from the ground Jake held it in his hand and closed his eyes. He thought that if the rocks *were* really responsible for harboring the past then perhaps he would feel something from even the broken bits. He *did* feel something, but it didn't come from the rock.

Jake whirled around to look behind him. He had raised the piece of stone high in the air like a weapon, ready to throw or bludgeon if anyone was there. But there wasn't. At least not that he could see. The hair on his arms and neck still stood on end and the sensation of being watched remained strong.

He realized then how precarious his situation had become. The deafening whine in his ears from all of the explosions made listening for danger impossible. Anything or anyone could come up close behind and he'd never know unless one of his other senses gave the tip-off.

His fingers pulled the leather cord away from his neck and ran down the length of it until they came to rest on the little white disc. It *was* a gamble. He only hoped it would pay off.

The light had already grown a few shades dimmer in the overcast grey above as Jake began threading his way back through the forest for the road. Several times as he walked, the feeling boring into the back of his head grew so strong that he dropped the bedsheet sack and spun around, hoping to catch his pursuer. Wet, leafless trees and snow. Nothing more.

By the time he'd stepped out of the forest and back onto the shoulder of Crosscreek the activities of the day began taking their toll. His body felt ten times heavier than usual. His fingertips were numb, muscles ached, and his head throbbed along with the ringing.

The first stone had been dispatched but there were still seven more to go. He had started with the closest one, hidden away in the trees behind Shady Acres and Tom Parsons' place. There was no way of telling how long his adventure had taken but it felt like forever. Daylight was slowly draining from the sky and the cold wind was picking up speed again. No matter how tough he was or wanted to be, he would never make it. Not on foot.

From the side of the road he could see the thick black pillar of smoke rising from the trailer park and spreading out like ink into the curtain of grey overhead. He didn't want to go back there. Anything that still had eyes and any curiosity would have found the place by now.

Jake did a quick check of the ammo he still carried and realized with a sickening despair that almost all of it had still been in Rawley's truck. Losing the truck had never been part of the plan, but it had been a stupid and shortsighted move to leave so much in it.

He was woefully unprepared for a fight now if things came down to it but if he went on by foot and hit trouble later he'd be even worse off. *Better take your chances now.* Later he might not have any weapons *or* any strength left.

Nearing the carved-out niche of Shady Acres again, Jake felt a small sense of the wonder that the winter season usually held for him. Under its frosting of white the trailer park looked less like a gypsy camp than it did any other time of the year. Somehow the snow always had a way of smoothing the rough edges from things, giving them an almost serene and tranquil look. Appearances could be deceiving.

Jake hurried to the first trailer and crept along the backside of it. The woods were behind him again and he could feel the density of them as they towered over his head. He moved cautiously and slowly, making each step more deliberate than he would have if he could still hear.

Peeking out between the trailers from time to time, he made his way around the outskirts hoping with each new glimpse that he would find a vehicle, any vehicle.

Most of the residents worked over in Devon or Bedford Falls and had probably gotten stuck outside of town when the storm had gotten bad. The few cars he *did* see were either up on blocks or so old that he wasn't willing to chance it. Shady Acres was probably the worst place in Rockwell to go for boosting a ride.

Jake was standing behind what had been the home of David and Earl Turner and getting ready to dash for the next when a thought invaded his mind. *Creeping Death, three ounces vodka, two ounces dry vermouth, pinch of salt, orange juice. Creeping Death?*

The search for a car had been taking longer than hoped, making him press on with less and less caution. Now he froze in place, one foot still hovering above the ground and ready for another step. *Creeping Death?*

Jake moved like he was underwater as he put his foot down and slowly moved to the edge of the rusted-out RV. He put his eye as close to the side of it as possible and inched his head out little by little. There was movement. Someone or something was between the Turner's RV and the trailer next to it. He hadn't gotten a chance for a better look.

Setting the bag down in the snow, he pulled out the machete and stretched his arm, trying to get it limber and the blood flowing again.

5

Ramp stretched out his legs, groaned, then began pulling himself to his feet for the first time since entering the Pump n' Pay. Terry immediately moved to help him, but he waved her off.

"Just got to keep the joints from getting creaky," he said.

Moving over to one of the slits in the boarded up windows, Ramp stooped a little and peered out.

There wasn't a working watch between the five of them, and the winter skies made it hard to guess how late it was. The landscape was beginning to dull and take on the ashen hues of dusk. Night would come fast and hard soon. Too soon.

Turning to face the other four, Ramp cleared his throat then shuffled over to the counter, leaning on it for support.

"We need to reconsider our situation again," he said. "It won't be long before it's dark out there, and there's no way Jake will finish and make it back before then. Once the light goes out we won't be able to see anything here until it's right on top of us, and that's not such a cozy idea if Colin Green is still out there."

"So what are you proposing?" Rawley asked.

"Nothing. I'm just making sure we're on the same page. We can't stay here through the night."

No one made an outright objection to his last statement but there was an immediate buzz of muttering. Ramp could already see the spark ignite in Terry's eyes. It was the little fire of defiance.

"Where can we possibly go?" Nick asked. "The tavern was practically a fortress and look at us now. The last thing I want to do is spend the night running around town looking for hiding places."

"Nick is right," Terry began. "We don't know that Colin will come back. We don't even know that *anyone* will find us before Jake does. I say we lay low until we *have* to move."

"And what if that's too late?" Ramp asked.

No one said another word after that. Ramp knew that moving wasn't the issue. It was the *other* part of the plan that brought forth the opposition and silence.

The last time they had discussed it, before Terry had been attacked, it was more of a last resort option. The idea wasn't a reality then. What he proposed now, however, was immediate. This was real, and he wouldn't be moving on with them.

Ramp moved away from the counter and to the window, turning his back on the others. The ache in his limbs had gone past the dull throb it had once been to something fierce, like a current that cut through him with every heartbeat. Pursing his lips together, his eyes closed with a wince of pain.

His battered body wasn't the only reason to remain behind. He was tired, too. It was a tired that no sleep would cure, a tired that went even deeper and hurt even more than the aches. His time was over and he wanted to be with his wife. He wanted to go home.

Ramp opened his eyes and looked to his right. Rawley was standing there, a big bull of a man, but there was a softness in his features. Their eyes locked for a moment, then Rawley nodded almost imperceptibly. No one else could have caught it because the gesture was only for Ramp.

"There's a place we can go," Rawley said.

All eyes turned toward him. All but Ramp's. His gaze returned to the greying world outside. He didn't see the ground though, or the trees, or the stray flakes of snow cascading from the sky. He saw Mabel. The rest of the world was invisible behind that vision in his mind. *I'll see you soon, May, I'll see you soon.* Everything comes with a price.

6

Jake let the heat of his body melt the snow that covered his hands. He didn't notice the numbness or the cold, only the blood. The thick dark red began to turn watery as he rubbed his palms together.

At his feet lay two bodies, their heads severed. One of the faces still looked up at him from the ground, a snarl forever frozen in its features. Jake took the toe of his boot and rolled the head away from him.

Satisfied that the blood was washed away, Jake picked up his machete from the snow and cleaned it, too, but quickly. From farther off in the trailer park there was the sound of commotion and movement.

With machete in hand and sack in tow, Jake began maneuvering between the trailers once more. He *had* to find a car.

After another ten minutes and several close calls, he had managed to cross almost from one side of Shady Acres to the other. That was when he saw it.

The banged up, purple El Camino was sitting by itself, doors thrown wide. The keys were in the ignition; a white rabbit's foot keychain bobbed from side to side. Jake closed his eyes, took a deep breath and sighed.

"Thank you," he whispered to the wind.

Still quiet and on the defensive, he crept forward and placed his sack in the open back end then crawled into the driver's seat. Leaning over, he grabbed the passenger side door just under the window and slowly began to close it. There was a brief groan that seemed deafening, but was hopefully lost outside. Once he heard the little click of the latch he sat back up and got ready for the moment of truth.

The key turned and suddenly the radio screamed at him full blast. In the distance there was a yell. His heart was beating madly now. Not taking the time to turn off the radio, he pressed the key farther until the engine growled to life. It worked.

Jake threw the car into drive. For a second the wheels spun before finding traction, then the little purple eyesore shot forward as the driver's side door slammed shut.

Before caution could reign him in, Jake yelled and pounded a hand on the steering wheel. He'd done it. But he wasn't in the clear yet.

Speeding down the drive that wound out to Crosscreek he gunned the engine, trying to put distance between himself and the trailers.

From the side of a camper someone lunged out for the car. Their body bounced off the side, tearing the mirror away with it. Farther ahead several more had gathered in the road directly in his path. Jake pushed down on the accelerator and hit them dead on.

A body smashed into the windshield then continued up and over the top of the car. Some of the others scattered, some were sent flying. For a second Jake had to fight to regain control, but then it was open roads again.

Making a sharp turn onto Crosscreek, the El Camino thundered down the road. He felt energized again. The blood was pumping and the adrenaline had begun to flow.

In light of his escape, some of the misgivings he'd held earlier didn't seem to have as much weight. Even though he had only managed to dispatch one of the stones, he at least knew now that it was possible. The question that still remained, was how long it would take to finish the job.

Jake began slowing the car as he approached the sign for Cauffield Street. The stone behind Nick Anderson's house was the next closest on his list, but it was also the closest to the tavern. It took all of his resolve to make the turn and not drive on to see how the others were fairing. Already, so much had happened that it seemed like he'd been gone for days. The real work had just begun.

He eased the car into the Anderson's driveway, grabbed his gear, and got out. Cauffield was quiet and empty up and down its entire length.

The front door of the house stood open, its knob a mess of twisted metal. Holding his machete out Jake took a couple tentative steps inside, then listened. The house was empty.

Even though he'd never set foot in the place once in his whole life, the house felt like a sanctuary, at least temporarily. The floor plan and arrangement of the furniture made it possible to keep an eye on both the front and back doors from the couch so Jake set down his supplies and dropped onto a cushion. He needed a moment to focus, to rest, and prepare.

Lining the top of the buffet on the adjacent wall were family photos. The faces of Nick, Emily, and Rebecca stared back at him like they were peering through a window from another time and place. A better time and place.

It was a single photo of Emily that pushed him back to his feet. It was an older photo than the others. In it she was probably five or six and playing on the beach somewhere. If her face hadn't looked so much the same he might not have recognized her, because *this* Emily had red hair. It was fiery and unmistakable, shining bright in the sun's light.

Picking up the picture, he studied it more closely before setting it down again. His instinct told him that he had stumbled across something important even if he didn't know how it fit just yet.

Jake moved into the dining room with his guns and bedsheet sack. Scattered across the dining room table were all of Emily's school things. There were books, pencils, papers, a calculator, and her book bag. Emptying the contents of the bag out onto the table, he then did the same with his own sack. He transferred everything but the guns and machete into Emily's bag. It was an impossibly tight fit, but being able to carry everything on his back would speed things up considerably.

As he slid the bag off the table, one of the straps got

entangled by the coil binding of Emily's notebook. For a moment it hung in the air before gravity took over and pulled it fluttering toward the ground. Pages fanned out as it landed on the hardwood floor.

Had his reflexes not made him bend over to pick it up, he never would have seen the doodles. Jake snatched the notebook off the floor and held it closer, his eyes wide with disbelief.

Emily had scrawled the same symbol over and over again throughout the entire book. Jake didn't need a photographic memory to recognize it either. Tugging on the leather strap around his neck he pulled out the little bone disc to verify. The symbols were the same. *She lied.*

Leaving the notebook and book bag behind, he was over to the staircase in a flash, taking the steps two at a time. It only took a second to see which room was Emily's before he was off again.

Jake practically slid across the floor as he dropped to his knees at the foot of her bed. Scratched lightly into the floorboards he saw it again. The symbol.

Why did she lie? The question ran through his head over and over as he raced down the stairs, grabbed his bag and flew through the front door. The stones would have to wait. There was a bigger piece of the puzzle still missing.

A single gunshot rang out in the distance just as his fingers grasped the door handle of the El Camino.

7

Ramp was glad there hadn't been time for drawn-out goodbyes. He might have lost his nerve if everyone had gotten all weepy and blubbery on him.

Watching as the other four ran off into the distance, the old man took a deep breath, then whispered.

"Godspeed."

Alerted by the gunshot, he could already hear the cries and yells moving closer to the station. Ramp hurried now.

The body of their attacker still lay in front of the door, its blood flowing around the broken glass, pooling into the snow. Ramp leaned against the door with the little strength he had, but it wouldn't budge. The body was too heavy. He began to panic.

There wasn't time to get out through the back or side door so Ramp got to his knees and frantically tried to clear away the rest of the glass still clinging to the frame. As he crawled out over the body, tiny slivers that he'd missed raked across his back and legs.

They were coming fast now, their outraged cries thundering as they moved in for the kill. From all sides Ramp could see people converging on the station. For a moment their hatred of each other had been forgotten, unified instead by a greater desire.

Ramp dropped into the snow and fumbled around inside his pocket.

There were at least thirty of them, some running, and some crawling. Some clothed, and some naked. All wore streaks of dark crimson blood, like war paint.

Ramp took the lighter out of his pocket and flicked open the lid. They were closer now, but not close enough.

It might have been the Zippo, the blood, or just the numbers of the advancing horde that did it, but something set off a rapid fire chain of thought which toppled over in his head like dominoes. *The War, the memorial! Christ you forgot the memorial!*

The war memorial in the center of town was the largest stone and possibly the oldest. It was a wall, a rock wall. The town's name had even evolved from it. After the revolutionary war, the names of the fallen had been carved on it, and the tradition went on ever since. Over the years it had been reshaped and polished, but under the façade it was the same old stone.

Ramp's heart thundered in his chest as he looked around wild eyed, but there was nothing he could do, no one he could tell.

From behind, something hammered down on his legs, then dropped onto his back, crushing the wind out of him. The lighter fell out of his grasp as blinding white pain coursed through his body. They were descending.

Finally managing to suck in a croaking gulp of air, he fought to crawl forward as more hands grabbed for him. His fingers brushed the polished metal of the lighter twice before he managed to reclaim it.

"I'm coming home, Mabel, I'm coming home," he yelled as his thumb spun the flint wheel.

A blow from above shattered the bones of his wrist. The little silver Zippo slipped out of his fingers, falling down through the darkness of the open gas tank.

Then everything exploded.

8

The four had just reached the courthouse on Main when the explosion roared behind them. Terry screamed but Rawley was faster, clamping his sizeable hand over her mouth before the first sound could issue. Her body went limp, sobbing.

The Sheriff lifted her and pulled her along with him as he ushered Nick and Emily around to the side of the building. He unlocked the front door to the jail then put Terry back on her feet.

"Get her inside and head for the cell block," he yelled to Nick.

Before Nick could say a word, Rawley was on the move again. He took a quick glance back toward the street but it was still empty. Heading across the parking lot he maneuvered for the utility building in back.

Rawley fumbled with his keys but couldn't seem to find the one he needed. Finally the big bear of a man growled and hurled his weight into the door. The hinges groaned then snapped like twigs as everything buckled inward. Carried off by his own momentum, Rawley hit the ground hard, but was up again in a flash.

Snatching a can of orange spray paint from a shelf, he bounded back out the open door, running the best he could for the front steps of the courthouse.

Already a thick black cloud of smoke poured up into the sky over the Pump n' Pay. The winds were grabbing it and pulling it low through the streets of town. Ash drifted down from the sky like dirty snow and the streets began to fade as if a fog were rolling in.

He had to fight for breath as he lowered himself down on his haunches. His lips were flecked with spit as he fought for one wheezing breath after the next.

Rawley shook the can of spray paint then tilted the nozzle down at the white steps and let it go.

Praying to God that their adversaries were no longer the literate type, he stooped and crawled until the single word *jail* was emblazoned across the steps in day-glo orange.

It was the best he could do for Jake. Stealing one more glance around through the choking haze he struggled to his feet then, satisfied, he headed for the jail.

9

The El Camino rattled as the engine strained for top speed. Jake mashed his foot even harder against the accelerator as the car shot down the road toward the swarm around the Pump n' Pay. *They must have left the tavern! But why?*

He didn't have the answers nor the time to fathom the

possibilities. The single gunshot and the advancing horde spelled disaster for his friends if they were trapped inside.

The car was closing fast. With his right hand, Jake fumbled on the passenger seat, drawing the two guns next to him. He didn't have a plan; pure instinct was behind the wheel now.

He smashed into the first two, their bodies breaking and flying off to the side. Jake braced himself as the car closed the last thirty feet, a wall of bodies dead ahead.

Then suddenly the world caught fire and the El Camino left the ground. The car flew through the air, rolling twice as the deafening roar of the fireball exploded all around.

Jake felt his body moving up and outward, passing through the already shattered windshield like it was rice paper as the car tumbled. Something caught on his foot, sailing with him through the air and out of the car.

When he landed there was a terrible crunch as his full weight fell on top of his left arm. The air rushed out of his lungs so fast that the blackness taking its place overwhelmed him. Jake passed out broken and bleeding in the snow. Not far away the El Camino exploded, sending pieces of shrapnel flying through the air and cutting down the remaining few who had escaped the first blast.

CHAPTER TWELVE

Nick stood outside the cell dumbfounded as Rawley unlocked it, opened the steel doors and ushered the girls inside.

"This is it?" he yelled. "This is our safe place? You're going to lock us in a cell?"

Nick never had a chance to react as Rawley's hand grabbed hold of his shirt and reeled him in. The Sheriff closed the door, then reaching his hand through the bars locked the four of them inside.

Still panicked and outraged, Nick paced back and forth like a wild animal. Rawley was leaning against the bars, still trying to catch his breath.

In the windowless dark of the cell it was hard to make out the object he kept bumping into as he moved back and forth. As his eyes adjusted more and more to the gloom Nick saw it looked like the cell had been turned into a storage room. Boxes of office supplies and paperwork were stacked against the walls, and two heavy duty filing cabinets stood back to back in the center.

"This is nuts," Nick yelled again. "We'll be completely trapped."

"They can't get to us at least," Terry replied.

"So what then? We starve to death while they surround us?"

Rawley finally let out an exasperated sigh, stood, and moved over to Nick.

"Settle down, shut up, and help me move these goddamn cabinets," he said in a gruff voice.

Nick immediately sensed that the man was in no mood for

objections, so he backed down and grabbed one end of a cabinet without another word.

The two slid the first up against the wall, then the second.

"What's that?" Terry asked as he turned to face the cell again.

Hidden under the hulking mass of filing cabinets there was a square metal door set into the concrete floor. Rawley wheezed as he got down on his knees and fished the large key ring off his belt. Still not answering anyone he flipped through the keys until he came across a large and old looking one.

There was a hollow click as it turned in the lock. Rawley pulled hard but the door wouldn't budge. He was sweating and his skin had turned a bright red.

"Hang on. Let me help," Nick said.

Together the two of them pulled with everything they had. Finally the door opened with a groan of protest that echoed throughout the entire jail. Nick and Rawley both went falling backwards.

A cold and heavy mustiness poured out of the blackness, filling their lungs with an acrid and old air.

"W-What is this Rawley?" Terry asked.

"I wish I could tell you," he replied. "We're going to need a light. I should've thought of that. Hang on a sec."

Rawley unlocked the cell, walked out, and made his way off somewhere in the jail. Terry, Nick, and Emily stared down into the depths below their feet.

Emily shivered hard once, from head to toe.

Nick went over and put an arm around his daughter but she wriggled out of his embrace. Her eyes were fixed on the opening, unblinking and entranced.

"Ems?"

When she finally looked up at him he felt his throat close for a second as her dark eyes seemed to pierce right through him, but then the second was over.

"I'm afraid," she whispered.

This time when he put his arm around her she didn't try to

shake him off. Nick looked to Terry for reassurance. She offered a small smile.

As Rawley came bounding back into the cell, Nick forgot that scant second when his daughter felt like a stranger. When the glow from the battery-powered lantern spread its soft fingers of light into the hole, Nick found it impossible to think of anything but what lay ahead of them.

A wooden ladder descended fifteen or twenty feet down to the rocky ground below. Beyond that little else could be seen.

"Rawley?" Terry's voice was soft and hesitant.

"It's Rockwell's secret," he replied.

The four climbed down slowly, Rawley first, then Nick, Emily and finally Terry. The wood creaked and groaned with every step until they had all reached the bottom.

Nick tried not to inhale the stale air too deeply. The coldness of it made his chest hurt with every intake.

They were standing in a cave that stretched out away from them farther than the lamplight's throw. It started off narrow by the ladder, only five or six feet, but spread out as it reached off into the darkness until it was probably twenty feet high and wide.

"What is this place?" Nick asked the question again.

"I don't know," Rawley replied. "I've known it was here most of my life but I've never been down. I don't know of anyone who has."

"Who else knows about this?" Terry asked.

"Ramp knew. So did a few of the other old families, the ones that go back a ways. Pete White, Dan Ellington- your father."

"My-My father? Why didn't I ever hear about it?"

"It wasn't allowed. All I know is that going back as far as anyone can remember this place was here and it was up to a handful of us to keep it a secret. No one ever came down. The last time the hole was even open I think was when the courthouse went up. Before that, who knows? When my old man passed on, it became my job. Same with the others."

"But my father- why didn't he tell me before he died?"

Rawley cast his eyes toward the ground.

"Oh. I see," she said. "If I hadn't been Daddy's little *girl?*"

Rawley simply nodded.

With the illusion of safety settling over his mind, Nick began inching his way into the cavern, curiosity overpowering fear. Behind him Rawley and Terry were still talking, but their voices faded into the background as Nick crossed over to one of the walls.

There were carvings and drawings all over the tool-marked surface. The symbols had the same feel to them as the marking he had found scratched into Emily's floor. The drawings were crude and primitive.

"This was their cave," Nick said out loud. "The Tal Teh Thule."

Nick turned back toward Terry and Rawley, their discussion seeming to end as soon as he spoke. For a second he panicked. Emily wasn't beside them. Frantically spinning around to face the dark expanse of the cave he spotted her. She was standing against the wall behind him and just off to his left. The same vacant stare that he thought he'd glimpsed before was back again, clouding her eyes.

"Ems?" he said quietly.

There was no response.

Terry and Rawley were making their way over now. Suddenly Emily shook her head and shivered from head to toe. All at once she seemed normal again.

"I don't like it down here," she said softly, crossing her arms tight across her chest.

In that brief moment, Nick had again felt something chill him deep inside, something far colder than the air around them. He held the lantern out at arms length and tried to brush the feeling off. For a moment as the light swung in his hand, the cave seemed to shift, the shadows dancing about the walls. He took a few steps forward.

Just outside of his vision, the faint outline of something rising from the ground could be seen. He turned and looked to the other three before taking another step.

Terry and Rawley had the same mixed look of anticipation and dread clouding their faces, while Emily seemed truly afraid. Still he pressed on.

Another five steps and the curtain of gloom was pulled aside completely. Behind him there was not one, but three gasps, almost in unison. Nick's heart skipped a beat and the lamp almost fell from his fingers as the sound from behind and the sight from in front caught him completely off-guard.

2

When Jake opened his eyes nothing made sense. The only thing that seemed to ring out loud and clear was that he was dying, or already dead.

The ringing in his head screamed so loudly that he couldn't think, didn't know which way was up or down. His eyes didn't just sting; they felt like they were on fire, and everywhere he looked was a swirling darkness, like a black fog clinging to the ground.

He tried to push himself up but a searing pain raced through his arm. Black and purple spots began creeping in from the edge of his vision as a wave of nausea gripped him. Jake screamed out and dropped back to the ground, his left arm useless. He didn't know where, or how badly, but it was broken. The pain throbbed so deeply it was impossible to pinpoint.

Using only his right arm this time, Jake managed to get up on his knees. Dancing in and out of the thick black smoke were bright red and orange tongues of flame. Everything seemed to be burning.

A fit of coughing shook him so badly that he almost went

back on the ground. The air was thick and hot, impossible to breathe. Smoke filled his lungs, eyes, and mouth.

Jake tore frantically at one of his sleeves until a long piece of material came off. He took the cloth and pressed it into the melting snow below his body, then wrapped the damp and freezing rag around his mouth and nose. It helped, but only a little.

As the disorientation began to fade, thoughts of his friends consumed him. He remembered the gunshot, and the explosion, then panic overtook him.

Rising to his feet, Jake looked around and tried to piece together his surroundings. What was left of the Pump n' Pay burned off to his right. The heat from the fire radiated out and made even the snow near him begin to glisten and melt. The snow was red. All over the ground were corpses or at least pieces of them, all bleeding and burning.

Jake had just started off when something caught his eye. It was Emily's back pack. The bag had fallen not far from where he'd lain only minutes before. He bent over to pick it up, only realizing then that this had been what caught on his foot as he was thrown from the car.

Still struggling to breathe and fighting through the pain that wracked every limb, Jake crawled forward, low to the ground, his body weight balanced on his knees and one good arm. Through the blinding smoke he strained hard to see any signs of his companions.

As he progressed, a twitching caught his eye from time to time but whenever he went toward the movement he would find nothing more than one of the Others in their death throes.

Unable to withstand the choking blackness that invaded his lungs Jake was all but ready to abandon his search when something grasped him by the ankle. Wheeling around he registered the hand clasped tightly to his pants and prepared to lash out, but then he saw the face. It was Ramp.

The old man was pinned under a large piece of concrete slab

that had once covered the underground tanks. His right eye was filled with blood that drained out into the snow, making a small pool where his face pressed against the ground. His left eye still held life, but it was fleeting.

Even as he moved closer, Jake could feel the grip on his leg slacken. Ramp's mouth opened and closed on air, like a fish out of water. Jake scrambled closer, tears of frustration building in his eyes as he realized there was nothing he could do for the man. The slab was more than he could move with just one arm.

Jake leaned in close and said, "I'm sorry."

He wasn't even sure if Ramp truly knew he was there. Other than his mouth slowly opening and closing there was no other sign of consciousness. Jake leaned back to move away when a thought occurred to him.

The ringing in his ears had drowned out almost all of the world around him but as he leaned back down once more he strained and tried to focus for even the slightest whisper from the old man's mouth. It was useless. If Ramp were speaking he couldn't hear it.

Jake sat there until his old friend ceased to move, then with eyes stinging he crawled from the worst of the smoke and struggled to his feet, determined to find the other four.

3

As Wilbur Rampart's brain began shutting down he no longer registered Jake, or anything outside of his own head. In a flash of colors and images, all of his memories seemed to play out in an instant, all the way up to the end. The explosion.

Ramp's body had been saved from the brunt of the blast by the piece of concrete slab underneath him. The same piece of slab that now crushed the life out of him.

Even as the last synapse fired, his mouth tried to push out the word one more time. *Wall.*

4

Terry's mind reeled from the horror in front of her so much that she didn't even register the sharp little cry that escaped her lips. Nick turned back and looked at her and Rawley, his mouth hanging open, dumbfounded as the light stopped swinging and settled back into place. Behind him, she noticed Emily's hands as they balled up into tight fists.

The cave didn't stop as they had first thought but continued on, tunneling off in the distance. Now exposed and even more ghastly under the yellow light were the bodies lining the right wall.

There were skeletons heaped on top of each other almost waist high stretching into the distance. Terry found herself trying to count them but stopped. There had to be a hundred or more. Some were nothing but bones while others were still covered with scraps of decaying clothing, and worse yet were the ones with what looked like dried skin and tissue clinging on here and there.

Her eyes moved to Rawley, looking at the man for answers. His only reply was a feeble shake of the head. He didn't know.

Turning back to the skeletons, she watched as Nick moved closer. Terry's heart raced in her chest and she stretched out her arm, fingers grasping at air as if she could somehow reach him across the distance and pull him back.

He got within a foot of the bodies then leaned over for a closer look.

"They were killed," Nick said, breaking the heavy silence. "There are holes in a lot of these skulls."

"Killed by what?" Rawley's voice boomed a little too loudly, making Terry jump.

"Hang on," Nick said. "I think I see something."

Bending over even farther Nick held the lantern down low. Terry watched in horror as his open hand moved to touch one of the skulls.

"Nick! What the hell are you doing?" she yelled.

He flinched but continued without heeding her.

As he picked up the skull they could all hear something rolling and rattling inside. He turned it over until the object fell out of an eye socket and landed on the ground with a dull thud. He replaced the skull then bent to retrieve what looked like a ball from the rocky ground.

"I think they were shot," he said, rolling the object between his fingers.

Suddenly Rawley moved forward from her right, walking over to where Nick stood. The two men passed the ball back and forth then, leaving it for Rawley to examine, Nick went back to the bones.

"This doesn't make any sense," Nick said. "If the Cansack killed off the Tal Teh Thule, then why do they have musket shot in their heads?"

"How do you know this is them?" Rawley asked.

"Look at the hair," he said pointing to one skull then another. "It's all red. And the markings on the walls, aren't they just like the ones on the stones?"

Terry remained frozen in place, her curiosity still not strong enough to beat out the fear. Or revulsion.

Although her body was still, her mind raced along with the others, trying to jam the awkwardly fitting pieces together.

"Ems, do you recognize any of these markings?" Nick asked.

Terry looked at the girl when she didn't reply. Her fists were still balled up by her sides and her body seemed to be trembling.

"Ems?" Nick said again, still not able to look away from the bones.

Terry finally found the power to move again as she watched the little girl shake. Her arms were already reaching out to comfort her when Emily finally spoke, stopping Terry in her tracks.

"You shouldn't be touching those," she said with a voice both strong and menacing.

This time her father *did* turn, as did Rawley.

Almost as soon as the words escaped her lips Emily stopped trembling and her hands relaxed open again, one of them moving up slowly to tug at her hair.

"Emily, what's wrong?" Nick asked, swinging the light around on his daughter.

She raised a hand to shield her eyes.

"Nothing's wrong. Why does it matter if I remember anything? It's not like it'll make sense. I don't like it down here."

Although there was a hint of defiance in her voice all traces of what Terry had thought she heard before were gone. Tentatively this time she moved closer and put her arm around the girl.

"She's right," Terry said. "What's the point? I'd rather figure out how we're going to stay alive than unravel some old mystery."

"What if unraveling the mystery is the only way we *can* stay alive?" Nick replied.

"I think we should see where this cave goes," Rawley said. "There may be another way out."

"There may be lots of things," Terry added.

"I'd rather take my chances down here than go topside again," Nick said.

Even stronger than the dread of what else might lurk down the road ahead were her thoughts of Jake. Jake coming for them and not being able to find them. Jake thinking they were dead, and losing hope. Jake dying alone up there in the snow.

When she snapped back out of her dark reverie she saw Rawley staring at her.

"I left a sign for him," the Sheriff said as if reading her mind.

"How is he supposed to get inside the cell?"

"How about this?" Nick began stepping between the two. "We know it's safe right here. Nothing's getting in from above. Rawley and I will move ahead a bit and scout things out. You and Emily can wait here for Jake. Sound carries pretty well down here so if there's trouble on either end we can just yell."

Terry waited with her breath held for Emily to object to her father's leaving but she didn't. Finally after a long pause she nodded.

"Fine. But don't go off too far," she said.

"Deal."

Rawley handed over his thick ring of keys, singling out the one for the cell door. Then they turned away.

As the two men began moving off down the tunnel, the soft yellow glow of light trailed with them. Thick black shadows climbed the wall behind the girls' backs.

"Wait!" Terry yelled after them.

Nick and Rawley stopped and turned.

"The light. We only have one light," Terry said.

She heard Rawley swear under his breath as the men began walking back.

"I should have brought more than one," Rawley was mumbling. "Dumbshit thing to do. There's a flashlight up in my desk. I'll only be a minute."

Terry handed over the keys and Rawley lifted his considerable weight back onto the groaning wooden rungs of the ladder.

He had gone about half-way up when he stopped suddenly, head cocked to the side.

"What is it?" Nick asked.

Rawley waved his hand in the air impatiently, motioning them to be quiet.

Slowly and carefully he began making his way back down the ladder. Terry watched as his muscles tensed every time the wood protested his descent.

"What?" Terry asked in a whisper when he reached the

bottom.

"Noises. Someone's moving around up there."

Terry's heart leapt.

"Maybe it's Jake!" she said. Even in a whisper the excitement in her voice was unmistakable.

"I don't think so," Rawley replied. "I think Jake would have seen the light down here and called out or something."

"If it isn't Jake, don't you think *they* would have seen the light, too?"

Suddenly the cave was plunged into darkness as Nick turned off the lantern. Terry had to stifle a yelp.

"Everybody hang on a sec and don't move," Nick whispered. "Once our eyes adjust I'll go up and try to take a peek. If it isn't Jake, we don't want to give ourselves away. All we need is for one of those things to home in on us, then we'll be trapped down here while more and more keep coming."

Terry didn't argue. If they couldn't get back out of the cell, they would die down there, cold and hungry. Their bodies would wither away in the darkness and join the skeletons around them.

Something brushed against her on the left, then seconds later she heard the soft footfall of Nick mounting the first step.

Every so often the wood creaked almost imperceptibly but it seemed to handle Nick's weight far better than Rawley's.

The beating of her heart and the soft swish of her breathing seemed terribly loud inside her head as the three of them waited.

Suddenly from above there was the sharp clang of steel as something hit one of the cell doors.

Now her heart was racing and tears stung her eyes as the panic turned her skin to prickly ice. Instinctively she reached out to grab Emily's hand, but it was no longer there. Almost frantically she waved her arm about trying to locate the girl, but the space next to her was empty. *She moved, that's all.*

All thoughts of what might be going on above vanished as

Terry began turning blindly in a circle, arms outstretched. Her right hand brushed against the side of Rawley's stomach, then she took a step forward, still turning.

Her sense of direction was now completely gone as she moved about in the darkness, taking one step then another. She headed for what she thought should be the ladder, hoping to get Nick's attention.

Now her hand brushed against fabric. Reflexively she grabbed on tight as her fingers curled around the dry smoothness of bone.

Terry scurried backwards. Her foot rolled over a rock and before she knew it, she was going down. In the blackness there was a terrible crash as the pile of skeletons fell right on top of her.

Before reason could stop her, Terry screamed.

From above in the jail there was a yell of fury ringing out in answer as fists began to hammer on the cell door.

Arms flailing, Terry pushed and kicked backwards until her head smacked the rock wall behind her. Suddenly the cave exploded into light as the lantern burned back to life.

"What the fu-"

Nick didn't finish the sentence. Even has he began racing over to her, he stopped. They all did. The *three* of them.

Emily was gone.

5

Moving in the direction of the Tavern, Jake's pulse quickened as the outline of the building swam into view through the smoke-filled dusk.

The massive bank vault door was standing wide open, and something was lying in front of it.

Jake broke into a hobbled run. With every single step bolts of pain ran up and down his body like electricity. He could see the body now, and the long chestnut brown hair fanning out in the snow. *Terry!*

Dropping to his knees next to the girl, he grabbed the body with both hands to roll her over. His shattered left arm screamed at him and bright flashes of white went off in his peripheral like fireworks.

Jake bit his lip so hard to keep from crying out that it bled, warm coppery blood glazing his tongue. It wasn't Terry, though. The body wasn't hers.

Leaning on the door with his good arm, he struggled back to his feet. The task was twice as hard this time.

Jake shook off the back pack, fumbled with the zipper, and pulled out his flashlight. He clicked it on, managed to get the bag back, then stepped inside.

The first thing he saw were the bodies of Rebecca and Tracy. They had been mangled and dragged about the room. Long smears of blood charted their paths. Tracy's body was bent backwards over the back of a booth.

Still off in a corner sat the lantern, unbroken, but cold and dead.

Jake moved about the bar trying to piece together what had happened. Down the hall that led to the bathrooms a pale shaft of light came down from the ceiling. Seeing the hole in the roof he began to understand. *They had to run or be trapped.*

He moved back to the bar and tried to think it out. *What happened at the gas station? Where are they now?*

His eyes roved across the bartop. They lingered on the ashtray, empty glasses, and the book. The book grabbed his attention though he didn't know why. It was the Bartender's Bible, sitting open, spine flat against the counter.

Jake moved over to it and shone the flashlight down on the two open pages, reading the names of the cocktails. *Harvest Moon, Harvey Wallbanger, Hashi Bashi, Hat Trick Havana Coctail, Hawaii Five-o.*

He reread the names three times then sighed. It was nothing more than grasping at straws. Still something tugged inside his head insisting that he pay attention. *What about the white rabbit? And the warning in the trailer park?*

Jake scanned the list one last time, but this time something clicked. In that very instant he saw Ramp again dying out in the snow. He saw his mouth opening and closing over and over again. And then he knew. *Harvey Wallbanger. The wall. The war memorial.*

Jake turned off the light and bolted for the door. He took off for the center of town though his progress had become more of a fast limp than a run.

Pushing on into the black fog and quickly falling twilight, he was focused and intent. So focused, in fact, that he no longer registered the pain in his limbs, the ear-splitting ringing in his head, or the shadow that detached itself from the rear of the tavern.

6

"Emily!" Nick yelled into the darkness ahead of them.

There wasn't a reply.

Overhead, the enraged, hate-choked growls from above had turned into a chorus as other voices joined in. The rattling of the cell door rumbled down to them loud and constant like a never-ending thunder.

Nick yelled his daughter's name one more time but his feet were already moving before the last syllable had found its way out of his mouth. Terry and Rawley took off after him.

As the light swayed and bounced, the cave seemed to shift and change shape as they barreled on. The shadows danced about making it hard to maneuver around obstacles until they were right on top of them.

Nick continued to call for Emily, straining his ears to uncover a response buried within the echoing din of their footfalls. Still there was nothing.

The tunnel kept stretching out and running away straight ahead of them. Along the right wall, the piles of bodies thinned out until it was nothing more than a trickle of random bones.

All of a sudden the lamplight didn't seem to penetrate *all* of the gloom up ahead. Nick instinctively slowed his pace as they approached the new darkness. It was a crossroads. The tunnel they were in branched off four separate ways.

A sick, sinking feeling rose from his gut as he turned to look at Terry and Rawley. No one said a word; the implications were all too obvious. They needed to separate, but there was only one light between them.

"Christ!" Rawley muttered. "Come on."

The trio took off for the leftmost passage.

Fifteen feet in, the passage dead-ended in a small room. It was about three times as wide as the tunnel had been. On the ground were the remnants of several woven mats and a small pile of animal bones. They turned around fast and headed back out. This time they moved off into the next passage over.

Nick called out again and again but there was no sign or sound of his daughter. The sickening feeling had twisted itself, knotting his stomach. He was too worried to think. His body raced on like an automaton, eyes and ears at ready for the slightest hint of Emily's presence.

The new passage dead-ended just like the last.

When they reached the crossroads once more, Nick bounded into the next tunnel. A large strong hand grabbed him from behind and for a second his feet still moved but the force of Rawley's grip held him in place.

"Wait," was all he said.

Nick turned around uncomprehending as Rawley took the lantern out of his hand.

The Sheriff wheezed and groaned as he settled onto his

knees, the light now just inches from the rocky ground. His hand moved over the surface of the floor, never quite touching down.

The interior of the caves was almost completely rock, affording little in the way of dirt to leave a footprint.

Rawley turned his body around once or twice, bent really low, then looked up at the rightmost tunnel.

"There," he said pointing.

Terry and Nick both struggled to help the big man back to his feet, then set off again.

Though they had probably only been running again for a couple of minutes, Nick thought it felt more like an hour. Already the new passage had gone on five times farther than the other two when they came to another choice. This time there were five different branches.

Rawley was already beginning to stoop when Nick heard it. There was a low sound like rock being raked over rock floating out barely audible from the tunnel in the middle.

"I hear her," Nick said, bolting for the opening.

Racing headlong into the darkness he didn't even wait for Terry and Rawley to catch up with the light. The sounds were loud enough now that he could hear them over his own heavy tread.

"Emily!" he yelled.

"Nick wait!" Terry cried out much farther behind.

Rawley still held the lantern, but it was only a faint glow in the background now. Terry had stopped to help him up but Nick hadn't waited. The light grew suddenly fainter, then all at once it was gone. Nick skidded to a stop, then toppled over onto his knees, carried by his own momentum.

Up ahead was the scratching, behind were slow and shuffling footsteps.

"Nick?" Terry called out, her voice quavering.

"I'm up here. What happened?"

A chill pressed into him from behind as if someone had

opened a window.

The shuffling of feet grew louder and more hurried until they were right up on him.

"Slow down," Nick said. "You'll run right over me."

Two cold hands touched him in the darkness making him jump hard.

"Nick?" Terry asked.

"Jesus! Yeah. What happened?"

"Shh. Listen," Rawley replied.

Nick cocked his head and tried to zero in. The grinding sounds had stopped, but from the direction Terry and Rawley had just come from there was a new sound. It was a soft padding, and dragging, and it was getting closer.

"What is it?" Nick whispered.

"It started right after the light died," Terry said.

The air around the three grew even colder. Nick's jaw began to tremble and chatter.

Whatever it was that pursued them was *really* close now, no more than ten feet away. Suddenly it stopped moving.

Nick felt Terry press against him. She seemed to be shifting and squirming frantically. There was a bright flash of light and the thick smell of sulfur as a red orange glow erupted from Terry's hand and spilled into the passage around them.

So caught off-guard by the flame from the book of matches, Nick barely had time to turn his eyes back to the passage before Terry shrieked and dropped them still burning to the ground.

Inching toward them on all fours was the thing they had seen outside the General Store. Two baleful eyes reflected the dying fire like pinpricks set back in black sockets. Her mouth was open and inside a dark scabby mass flicked about as she crawled forward, matted red hair trailing the ground.

Nick didn't have time to react as Terry and Rawley jumped backwards, knocking him to the ground. One last match sputtered to life just as the others in the pack dissolved into wisps of smoke.

From behind Nick felt something moving in fast. A swishing of the air prickled the hairs on his neck. That was when *he* screamed.

7

Jake cut his way off of Main Street as he neared the courthouse and jail. He had never gotten close enough to see Rawley's message through the haze of smoke. The movement had been much clearer, and the figures outside of the courthouse weren't his friends.

Winding a path through the small cemetery behind the Catholic church Jake stumbled back out onto Main, the jail a safe distance behind.

Lack of weapons had never crossed his mind after the explosion, but now with his body threatening to give up on him and the road ahead uncertain, he prayed he wouldn't need them. If he was forced to fight now, all would be lost. He didn't even know if he had enough strength left to finish the task at hand, or even reach it for that matter.

With every step he took Jake felt himself slowing like a clock winding down. Twice as he neared the center of town he had to stop and move into hiding as groups of howling and screaming figures rushed down Main. Each time he restarted his journey his limbs disobeyed. His legs were stiff and unwilling to move but still he managed to press on.

When he finally reached the open expanse nestled under the soft shelter of spread out trees, Jake had ground down to a slow walk.

The Veteran's Park unfolded before him, peaceful and inviting beneath a canopy of white. In all of Rockwell the park was the one place that seemed untouched by the carnage and destruction eating away at the rest of the town. Jake found himself standing still and taking it all in. A sense of peace overtook him and for a moment he wanted nothing more than to lie down and succumb to it.

He couldn't fathom how all of the terrible things that had befallen his family and friends could possibly originate there in the middle of such tranquility. The thought that he was completely wrong was becoming harder and harder to argue with. If so much negative energy were stored in one spot it should be palpable. He expected to taste it.

Slowly and reverently Jake made his way up to the War Memorial. The stone wall rose ten feet from the ground and spread its polished surface fifteen feet across. Even in the day's dying light the crystals that peppered the surface shimmered like chips of ice.

Jake stood in the shadow of the stone and traced the names with his eyes. Only the front side of the wall had been evened out and polished into a fine unbroken surface. The back and the sides were still the same crude and weather-worn rock that had been there since before the town was founded.

The original names had been transposed from the old surface onto the new, many of those belonged to the first colonists. By the time of the Civil War most of the names had dates attached to them.

Moving from one end to the other many surnames popped out at him over and over again. They were familiar. They were the last names of the people he knew. Some went all the way back to the beginning, like White, Ellington, and Smith. One was too familiar, though. Reading Haggert over and over again dissolved some of the peace he'd felt and reopened the hole somewhere deep inside as his thoughts went to Terry. *Where are you now?*

There was another name however that was even more troublesome. It wasn't one of the old town names that he knew, but one he'd only recently become acquainted with. It was Anderson.

The name appeared once or twice around the Civil War then only once sometime before that. Jake continued tracing back through time until he'd reached the earliest names once more but there were no more signs of the Andersons.

In his mind the photo of Emily on the beach with her bright red hair still dug at him. Was it all just coincidence or was there something more to it?

Jake took a couple of steps back hoping somehow that seeing the names in their relation to time would unlock some secret but it didn't. It wasn't until he reread the oldest part of the stone again that his mind made another connection. This time it was McAndirston that caught his eye.

The McAndirston name had shown up with those of the settlers and carried on for a while before disappearing completely. Disappearing around the time that Anderson began. *If they were Scots it could explain the hair,* he thought. Still, there seemed to be an importance hidden just beneath the surface, one final connection that he just couldn't make.

The remaining light in the sky was being choked out quickly by the smoke pouring from the hole in the ground that had once been the Pump n' Pay. Jake abandoned his detective work while he still had strength left.

Moving around to the back of the stone, he began searching its surface for any fissures or cracks that might make the drilling easier. The coppery glow of the sky created shadows on the rock face that made it hard to *really* see the surface.

Stepping back again, this time to study the contours, Jake noticed the hole. It was low and almost hidden by the taller grass around the base of the rock and only as wide as a quarter but it was a place to start.

Jake took off the back pack then eased himself down on his knees to have a closer look. The hole narrowed as it went into the rock almost as if a spike had once been driven there. It would be easy enough to widen, though.

Unzipping his pack and taking out the drill, he placed the bit up next to the opening to size it up. He set the drill down, then leaned in closer trying to see if the hole sunk in straight or angled. That was when he saw the mark.

If the light hadn't been playing tricks with the shadows he may never have noticed it, the grooves were so shallow and worn down. Tracing it with his finger, though, Jake was sure. He wore the same symbol around his neck.

More and more pieces of the puzzle were stacking up quickly but still nothing fit. He found his conviction renewed. The wall had to come down.

Sparks had just begun to fly as the bit wobbled around the hole when the crushing blow hit him from behind. The drill went flying from his grasp, its motor whining as it slowed, and Jake went crashing headfirst into the stone.

He barely had time to roll onto his back before the body was on him, hands grasping like pincers. Jake howled in pain as fingers found their way around his shattered arm.

Looking up, he found himself staring into the face of what had once been Colin Green.

8

Rawley's mind couldn't even process what was happening as it all flew at him in a dizzying matter of seconds.

Nick screamed behind him but not out of terror like Terry. Nick's was a scream of pain. In that same instant the gruesome apparition vanished, the air suddenly grew warmer, and the lantern blazed back to life.

A bolt of pain shot through Rawley's eyes as he recoiled from the sudden illumination. He spun to face Nick, but the scene was playing itself out faster than he could process.

He watched as Nick swung out blindly behind him, his fist connecting with the figure behind his back. Only as the attacker began to go down did Rawley realize it was Emily.

The girl fell backwards, eyes already closed. When her body hit the ground she was out cold.

Nick turned, his other hand already flying to his shoulder as dark blood ran out onto the back of his shirt.

It seemed as if they were all frozen in time for an instant, everyone's brains trying to quickly play catch-up. Nick scrambled forward for his unconscious daughter as Rawley mere steps behind reached out for the piece of sharpened stone jutting from between Nick's shoulder blades.

With one quick tug the rock was out of Nick Anderson's back. Nick yelled again but kept moving forward until Emily's head was resting in his hands.

Terry was frozen like a deer caught in headlights as the Sheriff barreled past her and dropped to his knees. His own weight smashed his legs into the ground painfully but he didn't notice. His focus was all on Emily. Nick, still cradling his daughter's head, looked at him with wide uncomprehending eyes.

"She's okay," Rawley said. "Out cold, but okay."

Nick shook the girl and said her name, but Rawley grabbed him by the arms to hold him still.

"Wait," he said.

"I didn't-" Nick struggled to finish but couldn't.

"She stabbed you." Rawley held out the blood-soaked rock. "With this."

"What the fuck is going on here?" Terry said. "Just what is happening?"

Rawley scarcely noticed as the next several minutes ran by. He tended to Nick's wound, then checked on the girl again before finally collapsing against the wall, exhausted and frazzled.

For really the first time he noticed the new chamber they had found themselves in. It was huge compared to the others. Along the back wall a ledge had been carved out of the rock, reminding him of an altar. Above it were more symbols carved into the stone, but on it was something altogether strange in a completely different way. There was a candle. And a book.

Rawley leaned forward and stared hard before turning to look at the others. Nick was still resting, eyes closed and head back, with Emily draped on his lap. Terry, though, was staring at the book.

"What is it?" she asked.

Nick stirred and opened his eyes but otherwise didn't move. Slowly, Terry began taking steps toward the ledge. Rawley watched her expectantly but couldn't bring himself to get off the ground. His body felt heavier than it ever had as his muscles ached and stiffened.

As Terry opened the cover, a small puff of dust issued from the crackling spine. From his vantage point on the floor Rawley could see that the book wasn't very thick, maybe only an inch or inch and a half, and it looked ancient.

As she turned over the first page, a dry, yellowed corner broke in her fingers and crumbled.

He wanted to ask questions but held off, waiting patiently as she read.

"My God," she whispered finally.

"What does it say?" Nick asked.

Rawley watched as he eased his daughter from his lap and got to his feet. Every time the man moved he seemed to grimace with pain.

"Take it easy or you'll get to bleeding again," Rawley said as he, too, struggled off of the rocky ground.

Together the three of them stood over the ancient text, skimming the pages, and things began to fall into place.

Rockwell's history and dark secret were all there written out by its founders. A chronicle of terrible things that had been hidden away, buried through the years.

The account penned by Jonathan White tarnished the image of noble pioneers making their way through a vast and dark wilderness. It contained a history of struggle, but of bloodshed, too.

The land that would become Rockwell was far from empty when the settlers first arrived. The fair-skinned, red-haired people they encountered lived under the earth in the very caves in which they now stood.

With winter coming on, the group could go no farther so they decided to settle there and utilize what the natives already had. Forced to choose between certain death in the cold months ahead or taking their chances where they had stopped, the settlers chose the latter.

The strange cave dwellers didn't want to share their land, however, and the group was faced with yet another choice, this time between murder or death.

The natives were slaughtered, man, woman and child. Their bodies were piled in the caves. There was one who escaped death, however. She would come in the night and kill, then vanish back into the forests.

By the time the first snows of winter had begun to fall, the settlement had been established, but still many were dying.

It was while out gathering wood one day that they found her. A baby's crying gave her away. She had given birth and was still weak when they set upon her. The child was taken and the woman chained to the wall, hobbled and starved as punishment.

She died there after a week.

The baby was raised by Jonathan White as his own.

"It's horrible," Terry exclaimed.

Nick began to wobble on his feet. All of a sudden he was going down. Rawley managed to catch him, helping him settle to the floor.

"Got dizzy," Nick said.

"It's the blood loss. Take it easy down here for a minute. Get your head straight," Rawley commanded.

After sitting there, eyes closed, for several minutes Nick raised his head and shook it.

"What else does it say?" he asked.

"Not much," Terry replied. "The rest is mostly a chronicle of births, deaths, and marriages. There's a map, too, of the caves. It looks like they go under most of the town. It's really pretty amazing."

"What happened to the baby?" Nick asked.

"Uhm, hang on."

Carefully Terry shuffled back to the beginning of the book.

"She grew up and was married to William McAndirston, the son of Robert McAndirston. It looks like they had six kids, all boys."

Rawley spun toward Nick as the motion caught his eye. He was half-standing, half-falling again as the Sheriff's big hands managed to catch him by the shirt.

"Easy there. You need to take it easy," Rawley said.

Nick managed to squirm out of his grasp almost panting as he stumbled against the ledge.

"Let me see the names," he said frantically.

Terry reached out a tentative finger and pointed to the book as if she were afraid Nick might bite. He flipped through several of the pages, shook his head, then leaned back against the wall. Like a slug crawling along, his body did a slow motion slide until he was sitting on the floor again.

"I can't believe it," he mumbled.

"Can't believe what?" Rawley's voiced boomed with a hint of impatience.

"It can't be just a coincidence," Nick muttered on. "I really think it's Emily. All of this is because of her."

"What?" Rawley boomed again. This time his voice was loud enough to shake Nick out of his trance.

"I can't tell you the names of anyone in my family past my grandparents," Nick began. "Anything farther back and I just don't know. I *do* know that McAndirston is the original family name, though at some point it got Americanized to Anderson."

"Anderson isn't that uncommon of a name," Terry said.

"There's more, though. Look through the book. Look at all

of the birth records for any of the McAndirstons or Andersons. They were all boys.

"My Dad used to say it just showed the strength in our blood, that we could only have males. Of course, I always thought it was just an exaggeration. I mean, no family can have nothing but boys for generations and generations.

"You should have seen the fuss when Emily was born. Every aunt, uncle, and cousin came to visit. Nobody could believe it. There was this amazing little girl with this bright red hair. No one else could remember hair like that in the family. My Dad said it was the Scot coming out." "Red hair?" the Sheriff asked.

"It's colored," Nick said. "Rebecca and I decided the move was going to be tough enough on her. She wanted to fit in, not stand out, so we agreed. We figured once she realized it wasn't that bad she could go back.

Rawley grunted, thought the whole thing over, then laid it out bare.

"So you think that your daughter is the first girl born in your family since the sixteen-hundreds, and that she's the direct descendent of the stolen baby, and of that crawling thing?"

He always had a way of oversimplifying things to the point that they sounded ridiculous. That was exactly the effect he was striving for now. He didn't like the implications otherwise.

"Why her and not you then?" Terry asked. "You two share the same blood, the same genes."

"I don't know," he answered. "Try to think of it more like some recessive trait passed on through the generations. It's always been there and present but until Emily, it was dormant. Until Emily, that bunch of code was never expressed."

Rawley mulled it over more but still didn't like it. There were too many holes. The idea didn't quite hold water for him.

"Too much coincidence," he stated flatly. "I think we're all desperate to make sense of all this but there just isn't any sense to be made. What are the chances, if this is true, that you and your family would move back here?"

"Why *did* you move here, Nick?" Terry asked.

"I don't think it was chance at all," Nick said quietly. "I was just itching to get out of Palmdale after my first book sold, and it just so happens that right around that time was when we met a couple who had summered here off and on. That's how we first found out about Rockwell."

Rawley still shook his head.

"There's something else, too," he said. "Your little girl thought that she started this whole mess by playing with the Clem sisters, right? The whole blood on the symbols mumbo jumbo."

Nick nodded in ascent.

"Well, if that's the case, then how was it she saw the woman in the woods before all of that?"

This time Nick didn't have an answer. Rawley leaned back and shrugged, hoping like hell that he had dispelled the idea, or at least hurt it real bad.

It was Terry now who looked pale. She crossed her arms over her chest and closed her eyes for a moment.

"I know," she said. "Do you remember the first time we met?" she asked Nick.

"Yeah, in the park. We were having a picnic. It was our first day in town. We hadn't even started unpacking yet. Emily hurt herself playing and- you came over and cleaned up her wound."

A look of puzzlement crossed his face but Terry didn't give him a chance to ask any questions. Instead she looked at Rawley and continued.

"Emily tripped in that divot over by the War Memorial and fell. She cut her hand on it. I happened to be out in the park waiting for Jake to show up and I always carry a little can of Bactine with me, so I fixed her up."

"Shit," Rawley muttered.

"But the War Memorial?" Nick asked finally.

Rawley nodded.

"It's been here since the beginning," he said. "The town

didn't turn it into a memorial until the end of World War Two."

"Hey wait a minute," Terry said as she rushed back over to the book. "It's hard to tell for sure, but I think this map shows a chamber right under the memorial. Maybe there's some other clue there, maybe an answer. Even if there isn't, there's another path that I think goes out by Crosscreek on the Bedford Falls side."

"What good does that do us?" Rawley asked.

"Look here at the map. I can't really tell what the little drawing is but there are three of them, here, here, and here. This one looks like where we came in through the jail, so maybe this one is an entrance, too. Maybe we can get out past the downed trees."

"I didn't think the problem was ever getting out on foot," Nick said. "Couldn't we have just gone around the road block through the trees? We can't walk to Bedford Falls. We're just as much dead out there in the snow as we are in town."

"No," Rawley said. "I think she's right. I'm not saying I buy into all of this yet, but just in case, I think we should get Emily as far out of town as possible."

Using Nick's pen Terry drew a crude version of the map on her arm, Rawley picked up the slightly stirring Emily, and Nick did all he could to just keep moving with the lantern.

Together the four of them moved off at a crawl, heading for the underground chamber at the center of town.

9

Struggling for breath and blinded by the pain shooting up the length of his arm, Jake felt the first surge of adrenaline rush through his body. His mind shut off and switched over to a more instinctive and animal level not unlike Colin Green. This was something way beyond fight or flight now; it had become the last-ditch effort to survive.

Jake managed to bring his knee up, hitting Colin hard in the chest. The force knocked him backwards but still he maintained his death grip on Jake's broken arm. The pain of it being jerked away in Colin's grasp was unbearable, but instead of taking the fight out of him it only fueled his rage.

Images popped off in his head like strobe lights, showing him the faces of his friends, and Mother. As Colin lunged forward again, teeth gnashing and wild, Jake unleashed a cry that would've made the greatest warriors of his people cower down.

He pulled his shattered arm toward him, dragging Colin with it, then smashed his head down hard against his opponent's. There was a sharp crack of splitting bone but it was impossible to tell whose.

Colin released his grip and fell backwards, stunned. For a second his eyes began rolling back to show nothing but white, but then he was on the move again, unfazed.

In that brief moment of reprieve, Jake struggled to his feet but Colin was already barreling headfirst into his stomach before he could right himself all the way. His back smashed against the stone, then the two men were on the ground again grappling like animals.

This time it was Colin who swung his head down with all he had. He smashed into Jake's face, breaking his nose in a big explosion of blood. The sharp pain was all-encompassing. Bright flashes of white shot across his vision from the sides and suddenly nothing existed but the pain. Rivers of tears poured from his eyes.

Colin seized the moment and wrapped his cold steely fingers around Jake's throat. Throttling the very life out of him, he pulled up, then slammed Jake's head down repeatedly, each time his fingers squeezing tighter.

The bright flashes of white were gone now, replaced by a creeping blackness. Jake's head was getting light and the world was slipping away, becoming distant. His fingers clawed frantically at the ground as his brain began to starve for oxygen. Thoughts had begun to form again, but they came as goodbyes and regrets. Jake Blacktree was dying.

Things were fading so fast that he almost didn't realize what his fingers had grasped. His right hand opened and closed on it in spasms but still his brain had trouble understanding. It was the drill.

Even as he realized this, his fingers still opened and closed over it. Jake stared into the dark hate-filled eyes above him and tried to focus as more and more synapses stopped firing. Finally his fingers closed around the handle tightly. His arm felt like lead as he tried to move it, but it *did* lift. Almost as if it were a movie and not his own life, Jake watched as his hand and the drill connected with the side of Colin's skull. One of his dark eyes immediately turned red as blood rushed in just below the surface.

The drill bit was buried in the side of Colin Green's face. As his body slowly began to fall off of Jake it carried his hand and the drill with it. The fingers didn't release his throat, but they no longer squeezed either.

Jake was beyond the point of inhaling a giant lungful of air. Instead, his chest rose and fell rapidly as he swallowed tiny breaths, each only slightly larger than the last. The darkness began to clear from his vision little by little, but his thoughts were still empty.

It was ten full minutes before he was even able to turn his head. Colin's eyes still stared at him but now they were lifeless.

Jake finally let go of the drill and moved his fingers to his throat, prying off Colin's hands. Now he *did* take in a deep breath. Slowly he got back to his knees.

There wasn't a single part of him that didn't hurt. The pain was so total that it almost didn't seem to exist. There was no way to pinpoint any of it.

He reached down and pulled at the drill. The bit came out of

Colin's head with a wet sucking sound. Pressing it back into the rock he watched as it sprang to life once more but this time there were no sparks. Blood splattered and oozed from the hole as the bit spun away, slick, and lubricated by what had been in Colin's head. His hand and fingers began to tremble, no longer able to hold or work the drill. He was too weak.

All at once he let it go. The tool dropped to the ground, spinning its last. Jake leaned over and spat into the snow. A bright red spray of his own blood painted the ground. His nose had stopped gushing but his mouth was still filled with the thick metallic taste.

For the first time he realized that there were others coming for him now. He could hear their cries and howls moving closer, attracted by the fight. It was over. He had failed.

Looking over at the back pack next to him, Jake spoke softly. "Kamikaze, one ounce vodka, one ounce triple sec, one ounce lime."

This was his own voice, though, his own thoughts. There was no help from the great bartender in the sky. Slowly he placed the bag next to the stone, unzipped it, then began fishing his lighter out of his jeans. The bottom of the bag was damp from the snow, but the top half seemed dry enough.

Jake flicked open the lighter, sparked up a flame, then held it down against the bag. The synthetic fibers began to smolder and pop but soon enough the fire took hold. He watched the flames dance and grow brighter as they began to spread out.

There was a soft padding in the snow next to him. Jake's head whipped around but at first he didn't see it. Then, against the blanket of white, he caught the two black eyes regarding him silently. It was a rabbit, almost as white as the snow around it. The little animal turned, hopped a few steps away, then looked back again.

Without even thinking, Jake got on his knees and crawled toward it. The rabbit moved off a little farther, then stopped again, once more looking back. Now Jake was struggling to his feet and still moving forward. From too close behind him came several sharp hisses as fuses began to light.

The rabbit moved on.

CHAPTER THIRTEEN

"Take the next passage to the right," Terry said as she tried to read the drawing on her arm.

Ahead of her, Nick paused then swayed a little, unsteady. From behind she heard Rawley grunt and stumble.

The new tunnel was short. They had barely entered it before the walls began to spread out and the ceiling rose over their heads, forming a large circular chamber. Terry stopped and blinked rapidly as her head scanned the room.

She didn't know what she had expected to find there, but it hadn't been more bodies. The skeletons weren't stacked against the walls like they had been earlier. These had fallen apart and shed their skins in a mimicry of life. There were bodies resting together, some laid out side by side, others locked in an everlasting embrace. Small skeletons of children were nestled against the larger frames of adults. These had all been alive down there before death.

Nick stopped in front of her and turned back. The lantern light moved its glow across the bones, making the shadows that hid in them advance and retreat. Terry turned back to Rawley. But he wasn't there.

"*Emily,*" she said under her breath.

This time it was Terry who took off in the lead, Nick slumping his way along behind her and trying to keep pace. The two raced back the short distance to where she had heard Rawley stumble.

The big man was flat on his back, a trickle of blood running down his forehead. Emily sat across his chest, her arms raised high over her head and her hands clutching a large rock.

"Emily!" Nick yelled out, his voice echoing through the chamber.

The girl's head whipped around and her dark eyes regarded them with hate. The rock remained poised above her head, and a small thin smile began to spread across her lips. *She's going to do it!*

Terry never hesitated. She dove at her, springing forward with all the momentum she could muster. Her right shoulder connected with Emily's side and the two of them went flying off of the Sheriff. The stone dropped out of the air and hit the back of her head hard enough to slam her teeth together on the side of her tongue. Immediately she tasted the blood as it sprang out and ran down her throat.

Emily was up fast and on her before she could even roll to her back. The girl's delicate little fingers wrapped around her throat and began to squeeze. Terry began to choke and cough, a fine mist of red spraying from her mouth and onto the girl's face.

Nick was yelling something but he still seemed so far away. Her head was reeling from the blow and the panic setting in.

All at once she felt herself being pulled forward off the ground. Emily's hands remained tight around her neck, but the girl was being pulled back, dragging Terry with her.

Terry managed to get her own hands up, fingers desperately trying to pry off those around her throat. There was movement on her right and suddenly two giant hands pulled into frame. Emily's grip was broken and Terry went falling backwards, gagging for air. This time the massive hands grabbed her, stopping her descent just before her back smashed against the ground.

Rawley sat her up, then leapt to his feet with an ease she had never seen in him.

Ahead, the lantern lay discarded on the ground. Its soft

illumination showed Nick still dragging his daughter backwards as she twisted and flailed. Rawley was bounding away for them. Little drops of blood splattered from his forehead to the ground as he moved.

As Terry got up, the pain in the back of her head let loose a dull throb that she could feel all the way into her eyes. She felt a sudden rush of dizziness.

Using the wall for support, she hurried forward with an awkward gait. She didn't even realize that she'd been yelling until her teeth sank down on her swollen tongue, drawing more blood. Stopping to grab the light, she spat a thick puddle of scarlet onto the rocky floor.

The other three had stopped moving now. Nick was backed against the wall, Emily lashing out at him and almost free. Rawley closed the gap, pulled back his big thick arm, and swung. There was a soft, sickening thud as his fist connected with the girl's head. Her body went limp in Nick's arms.

For a second Nick just held her, his eyes were wide and unblinking. Then all at once he set her down and charged at Rawley.

"I'll fucking kill you!" he screamed.

Rawley moved once more with a swiftness that belied his bulk. He sidestepped the charge, grabbed Nick's arm and twisted it behind his back, dropping him to his knees.

Terry rushed to Emily, then over to the men.

"It's okay. She's okay," Terry tried to say. Each syllable made her throat ache. "He had to do it. Jesus, Nick, don't you see that he had to?"

Nick didn't say a word, but instead slumped and stopped resisting. Rawley let go of his arm then offered his hand.

"I'm sorry," he said, pulling the writer to his feet.

The three of them moved over to the unconscious Emily and struggled to lift her. Rawley hefted the girl in his arms again.

"I don't think we'll find anything here," he said. "We'd better keep going and make for that other exit."

"I'm not so sure we'll find one," Terry replied.

"I thought you said-" Nick began, but Terry cut him off.

"I know what I said, but take a look at these bodies. These people weren't killed. They died down here, trapped, and starving. Do you think that would've happened if there were other ways out?"

Nick began to speak but suddenly his words were lost, buried by a terrible thunder. Then the entire chamber shook all around them. Rocks detached themselves from the walls and ceiling and began to rain down in a cloud of dust.

"What's happening?" Terry tried to scream over the roar. The ceiling above them began to fissure, cracks spreading out like a web. A huge slab broke away and pounded onto the floor between Terry and Rawley.

She looked at him, her eyes wide with terror as he shoved Emily at her. She just barely managed to get a grip on the girl when she noticed Rawley's foot. His toes were wedged under the large piece of fallen ceiling.

"Run!" he yelled.

Terry looked away from his foot and back into his eyes as she shook her head.

"Goddamnit, I said *run!*"

More and more of the tunnel was falling down all around them now. Terry felt an arm wrap around her waist and begin pulling her away.

The last glimpse she caught of Rawley was fleeting. The world above peeked in through a hole in the ceiling, then the hole became giant as the passage collapsed. Rawley disappeared behind a wall of rubble.

Nick and Terry tried to run and balance Emily's weight between them. With every footfall the cascading rocks seemed to be catching up. Terry felt small pebbles bounce off her heels making her cry out in alarm.

They were coming to another junction ahead but she would

have to let go of Emily to check her hastily scrawled map.

"Which way?" Nick yelled.

"T-The left, I think."

As they rounded the corner Terry stole a glance back. Behind them, the tunnel was filling with rocks and snow. The grey swirling sky above looked down on what had once been the underground.

They scurried on just barely keeping ahead of the falling debris. Every time they stumbled, the cave-in seemed to grow a little closer.

Terry twisted her arm and craned her head, trying to catch a glimpse of the map as they ran. She didn't know how far they had gone or what lay ahead. Half-way between her wrist and elbow she could just make out the penmarks but now they were smudged with blood and dirt.

"Shit!" Nick cried out beside her.

Terry looked up. The passage ahead was blocked by a pile of boulders. They ran right up to it and set Emily down. Nick began clawing and digging frantically at the rocks but they were too large and heavy to move. Terry turned around slowly and stared as the world above raced to meet them in a shower of stone.

<h1 style="text-align:center">2</h1>

The force of the blast knocked Jake to the ground. He lost sight of the rabbit as the shockwave pushed through the air and lifted him off his feet. Pieces of rock whistled past him and pounded into the snow like meteors, each crater ringed, in pushed up, powdery white.

For a second there was an unnatural stillness, then the ground began to tremble.

Jake rolled over and shuffled backwards instinctively. His eyes raced to the War Memorial. The great wall was broken but still standing. Even as he watched, however, it began to crack further and collapse under its own weight.

Not fifty feet away he could make out the silhouettes of the group that had come after him, but now they weren't moving. They stood there, distracted and confused as the wall toppled over completely.

Beneath his body, Jake could still feel the earth shaking. Suddenly the shattered pieces of the monolith seemed to sink into the ground.

Several of the figures snapped back into action and took off racing for Jake. He could tell by their outraged cries that they were still changed. *It didn't work.*

Jake didn't try to flee. As the realization sunk in that their last hope had been wrong, he felt the rest of his energy slip away.

Leaning back on his good arm, he watched them come. Then in the blink of an eye they were gone, sinking into the earth like the wall. A long dark chasm opened in the ground, racing away on both sides from the memorial. He watched as one line became two, then three, and four, branching out and out like a web.

The buildings along Main Street began to tilt and crack. One would fall and then the next, going down like dominoes. Inhuman cries rang out in the distance as the ground swallowed up people and property alike.

Jake's whole body vibrated as tremors continued to course through the land. He eyed the ground in front of him warily, expecting it to open up and devour him any second. It remained solid though.

The quaking grew fainter and quieter as the fissures moved off toward the outskirts of town. Even through the onset of night and the thick, smoky air Jake could see the landscape had become something foreign and alien. Most of the buildings and trees were gone. It was almost as if Rockwell had never existed. Not a single home or business stood intact, the best preserved being mere shells of what they once were.

Getting carefully to his feet, he looked around with an equal part awe and sadness. *How did this happen?*

He moved forward slowly and cautiously toward the epicenter. The sky had grown dark and heavy with the cover of night, making the blackness below all the more impenetrable. Jake tested his footing, then knelt at the edge.

His eyes could just barely trace the outline of the largest unbroken section of wall as it angled down into the gloom like a ramp. Tears began to well up in the corners of his eyes, but it was all still so much to take in that he didn't know just what to cry for.

The wetness made his vision swim. Rocks and shadows seemed to crawl and move about in front of him. Jake closed his eyes and took a deep breath. He released the breath in a gasp as a hand reached out from below and clamped hard on his foot.

3

Terry and Nick were on either side of Emily, clutching the girl and each other as they readied themselves for death. Almost in unison they looked at each other and said, "I'm sorry."

As the avalanching walls and ceiling closed the remaining distance, a new sound mixed in with the pounding of falling rock. It was the splintering and cracking of timber. Not ten feet from them, a pile of trees and branches dropped down from above.

A final volley of stone hammered its way through the trees, sending off twigs and branches snapping in every direction. Terry cried out as a small limb smacked her shin.

Then everything stopped. Here and there a smaller piece of rock would dislodge itself from the wall, and the tree trunks groaned against each other as gravity tugged away, but the collapse was over. And they were still alive.

Terry tried to blink away the dust and grit that stung her eyes while her brain did its best to comprehend.

"How-" Nick said from beside her.

For a moment neither said another word.

"Do you think we can climb out?" Terry asked.

The fallen timber made a wall in front of them but it looked possible to scale.

"What about Emily?" Nick replied.

As if in answer the girl began to move. Their arms were still wrapped around her as she began to come around. Terry gasped and let go.

As Emily's eyes fluttered open she felt her heart begin to race.

"Daddy?"

The voice was quiet and unsure, barely a whisper. Nick's whole body began to shake as tears spilled from his eyes.

"Yeah, sweetie, I'm right here," he replied.

The three of them managed to climb out of the depths after what seemed like an eternity. Each collapsed to the ground, shaky and exhausted when they finally made it topside. The cold snow pressed into their backs, but it went unnoticed.

Terry looked into the darkened sky and watched as the towering trees on either side of them swayed and brushed their branches together. They had made it to the end of the tunnel out on Crosscreek.

The best that she could figure, the end of the cave coupled with the pile of trees from the blowdown had been what spared their lives. It was just enough to keep the shaft from falling in over their heads.

"What do we do now?" Nick asked from beside her.

"I don't know," she whispered. "I don't know."

They had managed the unthinkable and escaped with their lives, and yet they were still far from being in the clear. They would never make the walk all the way to Bedford Falls, not in the dark, and not without food.

Terry wanted so badly to just feel relieved, but the truth was they would probably still die out there long before anyone found them. Her mind went to thoughts of Jake then. *Jake, what happened to you?*

Curling into a ball, she began to cry at the hopelessness of it all. At first she tried to keep quiet for Emily's sake, but then even that didn't matter.

The little girl stirred next to her and Terry balled herself up even tighter, not wanting to be comforted, dreading the touch that she would have to shrug away.

"I see a light," Emily said. "There. Do you see it?"

Terry relaxed a bit but didn't move from the ground. Nick was sitting up now next to his daughter.

"Terry, she's right. It's moving this way," Nick added excitedly.

Getting to her knees and rubbing at her eyes, Terry looked on with the other two. There *was* a light. It bobbed and weaved in the distance, moving toward them from town. As it got closer it brought a faint hum along with it.

"I think I hear an engine," Nick said. "Is it a motorcycle maybe?"

Terry didn't reply. The road was just as impassible to a vehicle as it had been when the trees were stacked on top of it, the only difference being that it was a wide crack spanning from forest to forest that now blocked the way.

The light stopped a ways on the other side of the fissure. They could hear the unmistakable sound of the engine idling now. Then it growled to life, roaring out strained and loud. The light remained still, however. Suddenly there was a drawn-out squeal and it lurched forward.

"Jesus, they're crazy!" Nick said. "Come on, get off the road!"

The car barreled off the edge of the ravine, its back tires

spinning uselessly in the air as the vehicle flew forward. It hit the ground on the other side with a shower of sparks, then the rear tires began to whine and scream again as they fought and clawed for purchase.

Terry heard the driver gun the engine as the car began to slip backwards ever so slightly. Still the rubber squealed against rock and snow.

Finally they locked onto something just long enough to push the whole thing forward to safety. The car swerved and fishtailed as it suddenly went free, then skidded to a halt. The lone headlight cut a triumphant slice out of the darkness.

Terry's body began to shake so hard as the driver's door began to open that she dropped to her knees.

Jake Blacktree hauled his broken and battered body out of the car, also dropping to his knees. As Terry and Jake crawled toward each other, she never noticed Rawley come lumbering out of the passenger side.

"You're shaking," Jake said quietly as he wrapped an arm around her tightly.

She *was* shaking but the words barely registered. Just hearing him speak again was something magical. It was something she had never expected to hear again. Everything seemed to be trembling, not just her.

"It's the ground," Rawley's voice thundered in the darkness.

Terry pulled back, startled by his voice. She looked at the Sheriff, amazed and uncomprehending.

"We should go," he boomed again.

The five of them crammed into the car, their bodies protesting every bump and nudge. Nick got behind the wheel, Rawley hefted himself onto the front seat, and Terry, Jake and Emily squeezed into the back.

As the car sped off along Crosscreek toward Bedford Falls, they could hear the sounds of Rockwell disappearing and settling into the earth.

EPILOGUE

Nick set the phone back down on the cradle, then moved to the bed to sit down. It was the first time since the whole ordeal had ended that he found himself wishing for a smoke. He didn't just want one. He *needed* one. Taking a deep breath and running his hands through his hair, he brushed against the gauze still taped to his head. Under the delicate probing he could still feel the tender bruising beneath.

The last of the phone calls to family had been made. He had even managed to arrange the services for Rebecca without coming undone. Now, though, now it was all over. There was nothing left on his plate to distract him. There was nothing to focus on.

As the tears began to well up in his eyes, he instinctively looked around the hotel room for a pack of cigarettes even though he knew there weren't any. He had decided to quit. Living held more meaning for him now than he could have ever imagined, but it wasn't just living for himself. His daughter needed him, too. *God, I miss you, Becca.*

There was a quick knock on the door. Nick wiped the tears from his face and tried to compose himself before moving over to it.

Terry stood on the other side. Even with the black and blue marks and the bandages of her own, she looked radiant. There was a glow about her that shone out from the inside.

"Is everything okay?" she asked.

The words came out a little funny as she still struggled to

speak with a swollen tongue. Nick couldn't help but laugh.

"It's not funny," she said and mock punched him in the chest.

"I know, I'm sorry. Yeah, I think everything will be fine now," he said, stepping out.

Sitting in rocking chairs on the front porch of the Whitecrest Inn were Jake, Emily, and Rawley. Terry went over and reclaimed her seat on the porch swing next to Jake, while Nick settled into another chair.

Emily looked up at him with bright and jubilant eyes. The way she had bounced back still amazed him every time he saw her. You never would have guessed what she had just gone through by seeing such a carefree spirit. Emily turned her attention back to what she was doing. With a thick red marker she drew a picture on Jake's cast. The man's left arm was stretched across her rocker.

Glancing over at Rawley's foot, Nick saw that she had already left her mark there.

"You get everything taken care of?" Rawley asked.

Nick nodded.

"Have they found anyone yet?" Nick asked hesitantly.

Rawley had gone out earlier that morning with Bedford's town constable. The two of them had driven back to what had been Rockwell only days before.

"The rescue crews have been focused on finding anyone alive. They haven't even begun to deal with the others yet. So far it's just us. The town's nothing but a big hole in the ground now. No one's even been able to figure out how to tackle it yet. I'm thinking it might be best to get far away from here before they start bringing up the bodies," Rawley said.

Nobody replied. Their official story to the press and authorities had only recounted their narrow escape from natural disaster. Most of the national news had run with variations on the *Town Swallowed Whole* story, but the five of them had only given up the tip of the iceberg. They had never even hinted at the rest. *How could they?*

Nick knew that Rawley was right, though. Once the bodies started coming up there would be questions, and a lot of them. No one was prepared to handle that.

"Are we all going someplace together?" Emily asked.

Everyone stopped what they were doing and looked at the girl with her bright searching eyes, then slowly their gaze moved from face to face.

The five of them really had nothing left but each other. Their lives had been changed and altered so deeply that there was no one else they could truly share it with. Only the five of them could ever understand.

Jake began nodding slowly, then Terry and Rawley did the same. As Nick joined the others he felt a smile creep across his lips, and there was something else, too. He felt a warmth inside.

"I think maybe we are," he said to his daughter.

"Good," Emily said, then went back to coloring in the heart on Jake's arm.

As the afternoon light filtered through the trees it covered them in a golden glow. There they sat like wounded soldiers just off the front lines of battle. Together on that porch they had a future and a remembrance of the past.

Home wasn't a place they could ever go back to, but it *was* a place they could carry with them. And they would, from that day forward.

Made in the USA
San Bernardino, CA
08 July 2015